The Tiny Tempest

The Dragon Eaters

by Duke Warren Kittle

ISBN 978-0-9960046-0-2

Dedicated to my Uncle Jim and Aunt Lindy for their help in editing and sharing their experiences in writing. Also dedicated to my mother for believing in me.

Special thanks to my brother, Donovan, for the cover art.

Glossary

Akoa: A nation of bulls on the eastern coast of the continent of Velratha.

Aracheah: A subterranean race with the abdomen of an arachnid and a humanoid upper torso.

Braka: Several tribes of hyenas living in the woods west of Fenore across the mountains.

Cerra Sevatia (Cerra): The world in which the story takes place.

Fenore: A nation of lapines (rabbits, hares, etc.) and other smaller races of herbivore (squirrels, chipmunks, etc.) on the southeastern coast of the continent of Velratha.

Idassia: A nation occupying much of the eastern and central areas of the continent of Velratha. It is populated by many races, but dominated by tigers.

Kamadene: A race of lizards found on the island of Kesira east of the continent of Velratha.

Kerovnia: A city in the nation of Levansia and home of the Council of Stars. Due to its purpose, the population of Kerovnia includes many different races.

Khanifran: A race of lions living primarily in the Khanifran Desert in the southern regions of the continent of Velratha. However, the rulers of the Khanifran tribes are called Khans and resemble sphinxes, though their heads remain leonine.

Kylith: A nation of lesser felines, which was conquered by Idassia, in the central region of the continent of Velratha. Kylathians, the natives of Kylith, are the most widely spread race in the world.

Likonia: A colony of native Levansians who settled on the western continent.

Levansia: A nation populated by many races of the mustilidae family (weasels, minks, badgers, etc.). It stands on the western coast of the continent of Velratha.

Maldavia: A nation of dragons living on the western continent.

Madrigaarde: A nation on the western coast of the continent of Velratha consisting primarily of canines, lupines (wolves), and a high population of otters. Madrigaarde boasts the largest naval power in the world.

Mateah: A small nation on the northern border of Levansia predominantly populated by mice.

Velratha: The eastern continent divided into north and south.

Pronunciation Guide

All of the names in the story *The Dragon Eaters* are spelled as the characters themselves would spell them. But because of cultural differences which produce unique sounds for varied letter combinations, I have decided to include with this book a guide to the pronunciation of certain names as the characters would render them. A couple of cities/regions are included as well, and their pronunciation is sourced from either those who live there or the most widely used pronunciation.

Belthazuul: BELL-thuh-zool
Methystra: Meh-THIGH-struh
Malidath: MAL-ih-dath
Kaelus: KAY-lus
Alysryzara: Uh-LISS-rih-ZAR-uh
Shahdazhan: SHAW-duh-zawn
Exil'idya: Ex-ill-ID-ee-uh
Shalizan: SHALL-ih-zan
Idori Cephalin: Ih-DOR-ee SEH-fuh-lin
Idassia (Region): Ih-DAW-see-uh

MALDAVIA

Likonia .

SELIAN SEA

N

Velratha

Chapter 1

The spell had gone terribly wrong.

Tina stood in the middle of Master Hidrago's laboratory with her hands still perched over a piece of paper with a circle of runes drawn on it and her mouth agape. All that remained of the bottle, which had moments before sat in the center of that circle, were shards and glass dust. She slowly lowered her hands as what looked like waves of heat rising on a hot day faded from the front of her body. Had she not remembered her master's protective spell, she might have been injured.

But she still didn't know what had gone wrong. Carefully, Tina pinched the corner of the piece of paper and slid it out from under the remnants of the bottle, letting the glass dust and shards slide off onto the table. She blew on the piece of paper and shook it to throw off any stray glass dust. Holding it in both hands, she looked over the symbols she had drawn into it. Each one had been meticulously positioned and perfectly drawn, at least as far as she could tell.

Putting the piece of paper back down, Tina took a moment to collect herself and rubbed her hand against the side of her face. Her short claws rested in the brown fur on her cheek, and she idly wiggled her whiskers. She turned her eyes up from the table as if searching for a thought, and her breath caught in her throat.

The bright flash which had accompanied the instantaneous destruction of her attempted spell had also momentarily blinded her to the condition of her master's laboratory around her. All but a few of the shelves which had previously been attached to the wall had been shattered or had fallen to the floor, spilling precious spell reagents all over the ground. Bookshelves with priceless tomes had been knocked over, and many of the books had fallen into broken vials of both staining and acidic liquids. Some were covered by powders of various kinds from her master's toppled collection, many of which he had warned her should never be mixed.

When Tina saw two labels from a pair of broken vials lying next to each other, she could not help but release an alarmed 'eep!'

The mouse apprentice ran toward the stairs leading up to the door as she heard the telltale bubbling of the reaction she knew was on its way. Throwing the door shut behind herself, she squealed as she caught her tail in it. She yanked the door open and pulled her tail free before throwing the door shut again. Her tail stung from the painful slam, but she didn't have time to nurse it. She made a dead sprint for the front door of the house which stood over her master's alchemical laboratory and, as she threw the door open, ran head first into his chest.

The teenaged mouse woman practically bounced off the foot-and-a-half taller canine male. She landed hard on the floor, and her long, strawberry blond hair fell over her face. Pushing her hair out of the way, she recognized her master. "Master Hidrago!"

"Tina," the canine wizard ticked one eyebrow upward as he looked down at his apprentice, "what in Cerra's name has you in such a hurry?"

Tina's surprise over seeing her master was short-lived when she heard his question. "Master, run!"

"Run? What for?"

Tina didn't have time to explain. Calling upon her gift for magic, she collected together what looked like waves of heat between her hands. Throwing them outward, she unleashed a wave of pure magical force on her master and threw him twenty yards from the front of his house. The surprised canine let out a yelp as he landed on his back and bounced a few feet farther.

Tina jumped to her feet and sprinted away from the house moments before a fireball filled with every color in the spectrum erupted straight up through the house. The force of the blast threw Tina off her feet, and she rolled through the tall grass until coming to a stop next to a bush. The explosion had knocked the wind out of her, and she took a few moments to collect herself before getting up onto her knees.

There was little remaining of her master's cottage, and what was left was on fire.

Tina swallowed hard as the blood drained from her face. She had just destroyed not only her master's house but a collection of such irreplaceable spell reagents the likes of which could rarely be found in the world. She expected Master Hidrago to literally skin her hide.

The canine wizard looked as shocked as Tina had when her spell had gone wrong, though she could tell the depth of his in comparison to her own was far greater. She ducked her head down and pulled her knees up, wishing she could hide in the tall grass. Unfortunately, the explosion had blown all of it back.

A deep and furious growl poured from Master Hidrago's throat before he roared in anger. "Tina van Schtoffen!" He turned around and spotted Tina quickly.

As he marched toward her, Tina thought he looked angry enough to inflict upon her every terrible punishment in her imagining at once. When he grabbed the shoulder of her simple, grey apprentice's robe, she let out a loud squeak of fright. "I'm sorry, Master! It was an accident!"

Master Hidrago dragged Tina by her robe to the edge of the long grass and threw her to her knees in front of the burning cottage. Taking hold of one of her large, rounded ears, he forced her to look at the cottage. "That is not an accident, Tina van Schtoffen! That is failure on a catastrophic scale! What in Cerra's name were you trying to do!?"

Tina had her long incisors pressed firmly against her bottom lip and was doing everything she could to keep from biting through it. When her master let go of her ear, she dropped back to her knees and rubbed it with both hands. Tears were edging her eyes by then. "I-I'm sorry, Master! I was trying to create lightning dust."

"Lightning dust!?" He thrust his finger in her face. "You are but ten years an apprentice, and you were trying to create lightning dust!?"

Tina sniffed and nodded her head. "I th-thought I could do it, Master. I'm sorry. I'm so sorry."

Master Hidrago clapped his hand against the side of his head and growled angrily. "Tina van Schtoffen, the day your former master sent you to me to learn, I recognized that you possess a great talent." He glared at her. "But both you and your former master have a recklessness about you that seems emblazoned into your minds like a scar! This is not the first time you have been careless with magic at personal cost to me," he thrust his hand back toward the cottage, "but it is without question the highest cost I have had to pay for your foolishness!"

Tina whimpered as she looked down at the ground. She didn't know what she could do to make up for the damage she had done. Her family was poor, and she was no different. "I'm sorry, Master."

Master Hidrago growled. "No, Tina van Schtoffen. If you were sorry, you would have ceased your recklessness far before now." He lifted his hand and pointed his finger at her. "For this, you will learn what being sorry really means."

Tina felt her breath catch in her throat as she heard her master chanting. A string of runes flowed into the air from around his finger and leapt out toward her. She tried to push herself up, to run away from him, but she found herself unable to move. The string of runes wrapped around every inch of her body and disappeared beneath her grey robes. She felt her master's magic weaving into her more intensely than she had ever felt anything before.

When Master Hidrago lowered his hand, Tina could see nothing but grey clouding her vision. Her master's words then found her ears. Though his voice sounded strange, his words were clear in her mind, and they were full of venom.

"Go now, Tina van Schtoffen. You are no longer my apprentice. Go forth into the world and discover what fortune makes of you."

Chapter 2

Many years later…

The sea stretched on for an endless expanse off to the east. It seemed like such a long journey to cross the Selian Sea in order to reach the city of Likonia. But most of the trip lay behind the Madrigaardian trade ship christened Thorn's Side. A frigate, the Thorn's Side was not known so much for its carriage capacity as its speed in delivering its goods. For any other trade ship, the journey would have taken two months to complete. The Thorn's Side had made the run across the Selian Sea in a mere three weeks.

Tina was thankful for the ship's haste. She was thinking about the assignment given to her by the wizards' guild, the Council of Stars, while she watched the sunrise. One statement stood out in her mind. It had been given to her by the grand master of the House of Contemplative Stars, the wizards' guild's branch which dealt with prophets. 'Discover the truth upon which light is shed in the knowledge granted by those who are dead.' Another person might have been irritated by a cryptic hint, but Tina knew better of prophets. The flow of events appeared to them only in expansive equations. They could tell only as much as they could decipher.

The sound of boots thudding against the deck of the ship drew Tina's attention. Standing on the railing, she looked back over her shoulder at the Madrian Shepherd who approached. She recognized him by both his uniform and the dark and light patches in his fur. He was, after all, the only pure-blooded Madrian Shepherd on the ship.

"Wizard van Schtoffen," the first mate said, "we will be arriving in Likonia within the hour."

Tina nodded at him. Her voice was soft as she spoke, but the tone was substantial for one of her size. "Thank you, Allister. Please tell Captain Morgan I will be disembarking upon arrival."

The first mate bowed his head. "Aye, Lady. Would you like your traveling bag brought up from the cargo before we make landfall?"

Tina shook her head. "No. Thank you, Allister. I will retrieve it myself on the docks once it's been unloaded." She smiled. "It would be like looking for a pin in a stack of sewing needles if you went searching for it right now."

The Madrian Shepherd bowed his head once more. "As you wish, Wizard van Schtoffen." He cut her a proper salute, his hand straight as he touched his fingers to his temple.

Once the first mate had departed, Tina took one more look over the side of the ship. She drew in a deep breath and closed her eyes, then let it out slowly as she smelled the salty air of the sea. "Time to begin."

Tina leapt down from the railing and landed gracefully on her feet. She crouched down onto all fours and ran across the deck in more the manner one might expect of a feral long strider than a wizard. Her unique stature had caused Tina to adopt some unorthodox practices. One of those had been learning to run on her hands and feet rather than simply striding in a bipedal fashion.

The six inch tall wizard crossed the deck of the Thorn's Side swiftly and, upon reaching the door leading to the passenger quarters, slipped through the space between the door and the deck. When she emerged on the other side, she dusted off her purple, wizard's robe and looked around the relatively large hallway. Her eyes fell on the one doorway on the right wall which suited her size. Walking to it, she touched the gold-plated handle. It rested in the center of a circular doorway with long sun flares stretching from the handle to the outer edges of the stone door. The door looked as though it had been positioned between the cracks of the hall's wooden wall. She turned the handle and pulled the door open, then stepped inside.

Tina reached for the single, unlit torch sitting on the wall and pulled it free of its mantle. Upon her touch, the end of the torch ignited with dancing flames and brightened the stone hallway into which the wizard had just entered.

When Tina reached the end of the hallway, she placed the torch into a mantle next to the open archway, and the fire extinguished. The room beyond was made from the same cobbled stone but decorated with Tina's personal touch. She crossed through the silver light of a crescent moon which fell into the room through a single window. Though it was day outside of her little home, she enjoyed the sight of the night sky through her window.

Tina's gaze swept over the whole of the room as she checked to make sure she'd put everything back in its proper place. A book lay on the wooden table next to the head of her bed. She noted the presence of the book and walked to it, picking it up from the table and opening it to where a feather quill marked her spot. Removing the quill, Tina checked her writing, and then placed the quill back into the book with only the writing tip protruding from it. She turned to the crystal bookcase standing next to her bed and placed her hand on one of the shelves. When she pressed on it, the shelves slid down, and another row of books appeared on a new top shelf. Tina saw from where she'd taken the book and returned it to its proper spot.

With the book back where it belonged, she took another look around her room. It had taken her a very long time to achieve the spell which enabled her to create the small pocket dimension in which she'd built her portable quarters. For all the effort, practice, mistakes, and revisions, it had been well worth it.

After glancing at the bottle turned on its side in the fireplace, Tina walked over to it and knelt down. She gently tapped the glass with her fingers. The tiny embers flowing around inside the bottle grew brighter and gathered around the spot where she had touched. She had not fed them yet this morning. Turning back around, Tina faced her bed and extended her hand. One of the drawers under the bed opened, and a slip of parchment floated out of it and drifted to Tina's hand.

After closing the drawer, Tina picked up the bottle of everglow flames and set it on the mantle. She tore the slip of parchment into little pieces and removed the cork from the top of the bottle. The wizard was careful to make sure all the pieces fell into the bottle before she corked it again.

The embers within the bottle swished and swirled around the parchment, and it was swiftly incinerated. Newly fed, the embers grew into drifting flames which danced about inside the bottle happily.

Smiling at the reaction, Tina pulled the bottle down from the mantle and placed it back into the fireplace. With everything in its place in her room, Tina walked back to the archway leading out and reached for the torch on the mantle.

Before she touched it, she heard a soft clinking sound from within her room. Glancing back over her shoulder, she looked for the source of the sound. A knowing smile crossed her lips when nothing moved. She turned her head to look forward and then glanced back quickly to see her inkwell land on the fireplace mantle, tucking its long, grasshopper-like legs against its sides.

"Caught you." Tina adjusted her glasses and pointed back at the end table next to her bed. The inkwell rattled its base against the mantle on which it had settled, but resigned itself to returning to the end table. With another two hops, it was back where it belonged.

Tina wiggled her whiskers at the inkwell and then picked up the torch from the mantle. When it failed to ignite, she looked at the torch through her spectacles. A small, runic circle appeared in the center of the right lens. Through it, she could see the series of equations she had placed on the torch to give it its function.

Little sparks of light jumped off the torch as Tina used her gift to correct a fault which had appeared in the spell. She drew her hand away from the torch once the spell equations were corrected and blinked her eyes. After another brief examination, she determined that the spell was once again working properly.

She squeezed the torch, and it ignited, coming to life and casting firelight about the hallway. Tina was curious as to what had caused the faulty equation and looked at the mantle next to the door. The runic circle in her lens showed a deteriorated equation in the holding spell. It was a more complex function than the simple firelight spell on the torch and would take time to fix. She made a mental note to do so later, but with it being outside of her room proper, she knew it would not interfere with the room being moved.

Once Tina had replaced the torch in the mantle at the entry end of the hallway, she pushed the door open and stepped outside. Closing the door, Tina pressed her palm against the handle. She had turned it clockwise to open it. This time she turned it counterclockwise, and the handle detached. Both the doorway and the handle shrank in size until the door vanished altogether. The handle rested in Tina's hand, no larger than a pebble relative to her size. She lifted her star-shaped necklace and placed the door handle into the center of it so she could lock it into the socket.

The sound of footsteps drew Tina's attention once again. She looked down the hallway as she heard the rapid steps of the cabin boy. A black-furred, feline boy without a shirt, wearing old trousers a little too big for him, was running down the hallway from the door at the end. She stepped back out of his way when she saw him carrying an empty bucket as he headed for the deck. Tina mused to herself that, for his young age, the cabin boy, Thomas, was a good worker and tended to his duties diligently.

The mouse wizard had retaken her place on the railing of

the Thorn's Side to watch as the sailors and longshoremen of the ship got up and went about preparing the ship for docking. It had been a swifter process that morning than she had normally witnessed on the voyage across the Selian Sea. Preparations for docking and unloading cargo made for more work for the sailors than the everyday chores of maintaining and sailing a ship across sea. With the arrival being in the early morning on top of that, the day had to start earlier.

Tina had been preoccupied with observing the sailors when the barking of the first mate caught her attention. "Captain on deck!"

A grey-furred feline woman stepped out of the passenger quarters with her hand on the rapier at her hip. She was dressed in the same uniform as the first mate, marking her as a merchant marine, though her uniform was worn in a more casual fashion. In fact, Tina thought the eye patch the captain wore along with the red bandana hanging around her neck made her look more like a pirate.

"Is the port in sight yet, Allister?" Captain Morgan asked as she pulled her bandana up from around her neck and placed it on top of her head. She slipped her captain's hat on over it.

"Aye, Captain." The first mate cut a brisk salute. "The crow's nest called out half an hour ago."

"Thank you, Allister. I take it you've told the crew to start prepping the cargo?"

"Aye, Captain. All preparations for landing are being made."

Captain Morgan nodded and returned the salute. The first mate stepped away as the captain took a few moments to observe the deck and the sailors going about their work. She caught sight of Tina standing on the railing and flashed the Mateesh woman a toothy smile before approaching. "All set for your big investigation, Wizard?"

Tina wiggled her whiskers. "As prepared as the Council

11

of Stars can make me, Captain." She smiled. "You seem in good spirits this morning, Jessica."

Captain Morgan patted the railing next to Tina. "I'll always love the sea and my ship, Tina. But it's nice to set foot on dry soil once in awhile."

Tina giggled and then turned her head to look back over the railing. "Is there anything else you can tell me about Likonia we haven't already talked about on the voyage over, Jessica?"

"Actually, yes." Captain Morgan turned around and folded her arms as she leaned against the railing. "I remembered something last night after you'd gone to bed. I wanted to tell you, but I didn't want to disturb you."

"Oh?"

"It just so happens that you're not the first wizard to come to Likonia. I heard some talk among my men about visiting with the crew of another ship."

Tina lifted her eyebrow and reached up to adjust her glasses as she looked at the captain. "Visiting?"

"Gambling, more like," Captain Morgan replied. "They were talking about a trinket one of the sailors had won and how the sailor he'd won it from had said it was given to him by a wizard on ship. It turned out the sailor he'd won it from was aboard a trade ship called the Water Walker."

"An interesting tidbit, I admit," Tina replied, looking back at the water, "but what does it have to do with Likonia?"

Captain Morgan shrugged. "I saw the departure manifest in port before we left. Seems that the Water Walker was headed for Likonia."

"Have you been snooping around for something, Captain?" Tina peered over her spectacles at Captain Morgan.

The grey feline laughed. She shrugged her shoulders innocently. "I always check the departure manifest before leaving port. And besides, you know what they say about Kylathians."

"I thought you were born in Madrigaarde."

The captain smiled toothily at Tina. "I could have been born in the sky, and I'd still be born a Kylathian, Tina."

Tina smiled. "That you would. Just be careful. Curiosity killed the Kylathian, you know."

Captain Morgan simply laughed.

* * *

The Thorn's Side slowed as it drifted next to the pier. The sailors threw ropes over the side into the hands of waiting dock workers who helped pull the ship in. The dock workers pulled the arm of a large, wooden crane attached to the pier over the side of the ship so it hung above the deck. Calls were sent out, and the heavy ropes of the crane started moving. They turned wooden sprockets which lowered the thick rope down into the hold.

Captain Morgan called out for the gangplank to be lowered, and her sailors pushed the plank over the side of the ship to drop the end of it down onto the pier.

The pier foreman, a stocky badger with an open book in hand, called up to the deck. "You're early, Captain. We weren't expecting you until later this morning."

"We made good time," the captain called back down. "Helps when you have a wizard on board to give you the good wind."

The badger nodded and turned to walk back to a lectern attached to the pier. In the meantime, his workers started boarding the ship.

Tina turned to face the captain. "I marked the crate my things are in."

Captain Morgan nodded. "I'll see if we can get it unloaded first."

Tina shook her head. "There's no need to bother with that. I don't mind waiting a little while. I did want to ask how long you will be in port, though."

Captain Morgan curled her tail, and the thin appendage drifted back and forth behind her. "A few days, at least. We'll get unloaded and let the merchants do the trading. Probably take them a few days to haggle over prices, maybe a week at the most. Then we'll load up our cargo and head back."

Tina nodded. "I hope I'll be finished with my business here before you depart. I don't care for the idea of having to wait for another ship. Besides," she smiled, "good company makes for a swifter voyage, and I'd be happy to listen to your violin again on the way back."

Captain Morgan lifted the hat from her head and bowed regally to the wizard. "Always enjoy having a captive audience."

Tina giggled. "Until we meet again, Captain."

"Take care of yourself, Tina."

Tina leapt down from the railing on the side of the ship and landed on the deck. When the path was clear of dock workers and sailors carrying off smaller goods, Tina stepped onto the gangplank and scampered down it to the pier.

Once on the pier, Tina adjusted her glasses as she looked toward the city of Likonia beyond the port. She wasn't surprised to see it surrounded by a wall of logs driven into the ground with their tops carved sharp. It did seem a little odd for there to be two walls on the port side of the city, though. A single building stood tall enough to be visible over the wall, though the structure itself looked no taller than any of the other buildings. Tina guessed from the shape of the land where the city stood that it was on a hill. A tall hill stood on each side of the town with the wooden walls climbing the hills and rising over the crests.

Tina turned her attention to the dock workers and noted that most of them were badgers, weasels, or wolverines, all of which were native in Levansia. One or two of them had thinner frames with bright red fur and more sharply sloping muzzles. When Tina looked at the crane, she noticed one dock worker who stood out from the rest and was surprised when she recalled his species. "An Akoan...?"

Standing at the unloading area for the crane was a black-furred male Akoan who was seven-and-a-half feet tall and wore a load-bearing harness around his chest. The leather hide pants he wore matched the harness in color and ended at a pair of broad hooves. He looked to be the epitome of strength with muscles which flexed visibly as he reached for the crate being lowered by the crane. His muzzle was thick and rounded at the end. While most races of the world had some minor discolorations in their fur, he had none with fur as black as tar. The horns on his head sloped forward over his muzzle.

Tina was surprised to see an Akoan living in Likonia. He looked to her to be built for more than manual labor. In fact, he looked like a warrior, but he carried no weapons.

Realizing the Akoan was lowering the crate on which she had placed a minor arcane equation brought her out of her observation. The bull pulled the ropes from the crate and set it down onto the pier. He tugged ropes through the rings on his harness to wrap them around the box.

Tina made her way up to the pier where the Akoan was fixing the crate to his harness. Just as he was about to pick it up, she put her pinkies between her lips and blew a sharp whistle.

The Akoan stopped and lifted his head to look around for the source of the sound. When he spotted Tina standing on the pier, he stared at her for a long moment as if mystified by her presence. The Akoan shook his head with his large ears flopping. "I didn't drink that much last night."

Tina was perplexed for a moment until she realized the Akoan's meaning and smiled. She walked to the crate and climbed the side nimbly until she was standing on top. "I assure you, I am quite real." Tina adjusted the glasses on the bridge of her muzzle. "I have a few personal effects in this crate which I need to retrieve. I'll only be a moment."

The Akoan was momentarily stunned as the tiny mouse

woman spoke to him, and he watched, dumbfounded, as she climbed into the crate through a small hole in the wood. He was unsure if he should lift the crate with a tiny person inside. He considered that if he moved the box, the contents might shift and squash the little mouse. So he relaxed his posture and waited.

"Kravek!" The badger foreman stomped over to the black bull and whacked him on the back of his head. "You can pray to the pier on your own time! Get that crate up to the warehouse!"

Kravek grunted when he was struck, but more out of surprise rather than pain. "But Chief, there's someone in there."

"No 'butts' unless it's yours getting moved off my pier with that crate in tow, Kravek!" The badger grabbed one of Kravek's horns, tugging his head to the side. "Look, I don't care if you want to drink yourself into a stupor every night. But as long as you work this dock, you keep anything to do with beer off my pier! Now, get going!"

Tina climbed out of a hole in the side of the crate and quietly dropped to the ground with a small, lizard-hide rucksack over her shoulder. She looked up at Kravek and noted the presence of the foreman.

Kravek pulled the ropes on his harness tight again and muttered to the crate. "I've got to move you now. I'll be as careful as I can." He slowly rose, picking the hefty crate up and turning to carry it up the pier.

The badger foreman scratched the side of his head, then sighed. The sound of a loud thud came from the Thorn's Side, and the foreman stalked off, yelling at the dock workers to be more careful.

Tina smiled at the Akoan's consideration for her safety. She pulled the cords on her rucksack and tied them around her shoulders, securing them tightly. Kravek, as she'd heard the Akoan's name yelled, deserved at least an explanation.

Halfway up the pier, Tina caught sight of an unpleasant-looking wolverine, wearing a scowl and a suit of armor, walking toward the Thorn's Side. She noted the two guards following him were armed, and the gauntlets the wolverine wore had sharpened claws on their fingertips. The wolverine wasn't carrying any other kind of weapon, from which Tina could only infer that he preferred to use his hands in a fight rather than a blade or axe.

Once he had passed, taking no notice of Tina, she hurried up the pier to the warehouse. She reached the edge just in time to see where the Akoan was taking the crate.

Kravek loosened the straps on his harness so he could straighten up and stretch his back. Immediately afterward, he leaned down again and put his large ear to the top of the crate. "Are you all right in there?" He lightly rapped on the wood. "Say something if you can hear me."

When no answer came, the Akoan panicked. He grabbed a pry bar resting against the wall of the warehouse and raised it, ready to tear the lid off the crate. But he stopped when he heard a sharp whistle and turned his head.

Tina pulled her pinkies out of the sides of her muzzle and folded her arms across her stomach, smiling at the Akoan. "I was going to tell you I climbed out, but your foreman didn't look all that pleasant."

Kravek sighed in relief and put the pry bar down. "He's not bad. Just strict." The Akoan walked away from the crate and crouched down onto his haunches. He rested his arms on his thighs and leaned forward. His large hooves provided him with a stable base. "I was afraid you would get hurt while I was carrying you."

"You're very considerate, Kravek." Tina held her hand up toward the Akoan. "I heard the foreman yelling your name. I am Tina van Schtoffen of the Council of Stars."

Kravek looked at her hand and then at his own. It looked to him as though she was offering him a handshake, but how he could shake her hand vexed him. He decided to hold his hand out in the same posture regardless so she could at least shake a finger.

"Kravek Rivakian."

Tina turned her hand from the posture of a handshake to being open with her palm up. Kravek watched her for a moment and mimicked the gesture. With Kravek's hand open in front of her, Tina climbed onto it and stood up, pointing up. Kravek rose to a standing position with the mouse woman standing on his palm.

"You're very helpful, Kravek. Do you think you could show me the way to the home of Harkon Keldo?"

Kravek looked to the pier and pointed with his other hand toward the Thorn's Side. "They need me to help finish unloading the ship."

Tina smiled. "I'm sure that they would miss your muscle, but I'm also certain it's equally important to the governor that the emissary of the Council of Stars make herself known. Besides, that crate is the largest thing in the ship's cargo. I'm sure they will manage."

Kravek considered briefly before he settled back down onto his haunches. "All due respect, ma'am, I got a job to do. But if you want the governor, he won't be at his house right now." Kravek gently placed Tina back onto her feet on the ground and pointed toward the city. "Bunch of farmers came in from the homesteads last night. He'll probably be with them in the town hall. Middle of town, straight up the road from the pier."

Tina was growing to like the Akoan all the more for his commitment to his duties. "Thank you for all your help, Kravek Rivakian." She gave him one more smile, and then the wizard turned away and headed to the open gate facing the pier.

Chapter 3

If not for the Akoan's warning to Tina concerning the presence of the farmers in town, she might have been surprised by so many livestock striders and lesser thunder lizards in the streets. The pungent smell was enough to make Tina cover her nose.

The structures of the town were fairly rudimentary. All of them were made from wooden planks with a few years of weathering showing. There were only a few feet between buildings to make small alleyways, most of which were currently occupied by wandering striders. The alleys seemed like good places for the smaller lizards to avoid the larger thunder lizards. Even so, Tina caught sight of one shopkeeper using a broom to try to shoo a thunder lizard away. The thunder lizard had been trying to sharpen one of its horns on the corner of her shop.

When Tina reached a section of the dirt road through the middle of the town where the thunder lizards were so tightly packed that they blocked the road, she decided to make use of the tight grouping of the buildings. She walked to the corner of one house and made sure the cords of her rucksack were pulled tight. With nimble claws and practiced grace, she gripped the corner of the building and climbed. Her pace was rapid, and she reached the lip of the rooftop in less than a minute.

Tina hauled herself up onto the rooftop and crossed. She glanced down into the crowd of thunder lizards below. For all their size, the lesser thunder lizards were very docile, even friendly. But that wouldn't stop one from accidentally stepping on her.

When she reached the peak of the roof, Tina stopped to get a better look around the town from a higher vantage point. Just as it had appeared from the pier, the town was nestled between two hills with a log wall surrounding it. From the inside, she could see the reason the wall hadn't extended farther to the outside of the hills. On top of the hills on the inside of the outer wall stood a second, lower wall. The space between the two was easily one quarter the size of the town. Even from her elevated position, she couldn't see inside the walls, but could infer from previous designs she'd seen that it was a prudent design for protection of the townspeople should the city be overrun. From the safety of the two protected and elevated positions, invaders could be picked off by archers firing from both sides of the town. Neither wall could be attacked without harassment unless its twin had already been either breached or destroyed.

Diverting her attention from the battlements, Tina looked toward the center of town where Kravek had directed her to seek out the governor, Harkon Keldo. She saw an open town circle with roads leading off in the cardinal directions and one building larger by a single story than the others around it. Tina guessed it to be the town hall by the people standing outside, looking in through windows on its face, and standing in its open front doorway.

With the gap between rooftops being only a foot at most, Tina was able to make her way around the town circle by running from rooftop to rooftop and jumping the small gaps. Rather than entering the town hall and disrupting the meeting to introduce herself, she decided to climb through one of the windows on the second floor.

The room she entered was filled with empty chairs lined up in front of a lectern which stood at the head of the room. She thought it resembled a lecture hall back at the wizard guild in Kerovnia. At the front of the room, next to the lectern, she could see a closed door. The sound of voices coming from the first floor told her a meeting was already in progress. She crossed the lecture room and slipped through the space under the door, having to take off her rucksack in order to do so. Once she had retrieved it, Tina passed down the hallway outside the lecture room and descended a set of spiraling stairs.

She had only hopped down a few steps before she saw the stairway open up to the floor below. The room was filled with badgers and weasels dressed in simple clothing, and most of them were stained with soil. The smell of the earth in their clothing was almost as strong as the scent of the livestock outside, but not nearly as unpleasant. Tina deduced they were the farmers to whom the livestock belonged.

A few steps down, a badger was leaning against the railing of the stairs and watching a fox twenty feet away who was standing on an elevated platform at the front of the room. It looked like a stage, though the one speaking from it didn't have the garb of an actor. From the volume of the chatter coming from the crowd, it sounded to Tina as if they weren't too pleased with whatever had just been said.

Keldo held his hands up, speaking loudly, but calmly as he tried to get the attention of the room again. "My people, I beg your patience." It took a few moments, but the crowd finally became quiet. "As I have already told you, the last time I spoke with the Council of Stars, they assured me they would send a wizard to calm this situation with the dragons and these monsters who have encroached on both our territories and those of the dragons. I have already been informed that the ship he is to arrive on is in port, and Captain Cephalin will be bringing him here with all due haste. You may address the wizard with what questions you like, but please know that the sooner the wizard is able to do his work, the sooner this problem will be resolved."

One stocky badger at the front of the crowd stepped forward and spread his hands. "Governor, the last time you tried finding a solution to our problems with a wizard, it ended badly. What makes you think a solution with another wizard will be any better?"

Keldo lowered his hands and bowed his head. "I admit that I was at fault for the wizard's rash decision. And I also must admit I hired the wizard privately without the sanction of the Council of Stars. It was a decision I regret, but I tell you now, this change of heart from the High Theorist of the Council of Stars will most assuredly see an end to our trepidation."

Keldo tried to reassure the crowd with a smile. "We all know the skill of the magic users of the Council. Everyone here was born within a breath's reach of Kerovnia."

Tina wiggled her whiskers. She didn't like the manner of the governor's smile. It was a kind of smile that hid deceptively sharp teeth.

One woman near the back of the crowd called out. "How are we supposed to know we can trust this wizard? The High Theorist condemned the building of this town and intervened when even the king wanted to send us aid!"

Governor Keldo folded his hands into the sleeves of his robe and bowed his head. "I have assurances from the High Theorist and from the king. This situation will be sorted out in good order. Even if you do not trust the word of the High Theorist, surely you will trust the promise of the king."

Tina wiggled her whiskers again. Though the reassurance had certainly calmed the crowd, she was not aware of any promise made by the king of Levansia. But Keldo was apparently using a political device in order to silence further objection. Any objection raised against the king's promise could be interpreted as treason. The fact Keldo was lying told Tina, should any further question arise, Keldo would probably use that device to stifle it.

The stocky badger at the front of the crowd spoke up. "Governor, if the wizard is able to deal with these monsters, what happens next? We can go back to our homesteads and return to our work. But what about the Maldavians?"

The governor nodded to the badger. "An appropriate question, Lazur. We have had our conflicts with the Maldavians in the past, but the Council of Stars has a good relationship with the dragons. I will see to it personally that the wizard speaks with the Maldavians on our behalf."

Before another question could be raised, a commanding voice came from the doorway. "Clear a path!" Heads turned at the sound of the voice, and Tina noted it had come from the wolverine she had seen on the pier only a short while ago. His order apparently carried some weight as the farmers stepped aside, having to squeeze more tightly against the walls.

Captain Cephalin's guards followed behind as he approached the stage on which the governor stood. The captain stepped up onto the platform and moved next to the governor, speaking quietly enough to keep his words from the farmers, but not quietly enough to evade Tina's hearing. "The captain of the Thorn's Side said the wizard left her ship just before I arrived, but I have not seen him about."

"Nor are you likely to at this rate." Tina muttered to herself. She made note of the stocky badger who had been challenging Governor Keldo during the meeting. His muzzle was a little broader than usual, and his gaze was keen and discerning. She marked his face into her memory, and then she rose to climb back up the stairs.

"Captain Cephalin!" A call came from the front of the building as a female mink shouldered her way through the crowd. The farmers finally cleared room for her once they recognized she was also one of the guards.

The wolverine looked out from the stage. "What is it, Lieutenant Copaire?"

"Sir, there's been another report from one of the scouts that a Maldavian is wandering in the woods."

"An emissary?" The governor stepped forward.

"No, sir. The scout reported that it was wounded. It has an Albatross with it."

Captain Cephalin folded his arms. "Is that all?"

The mink looked surprised at the captain's lack of concern. "Sir, it's injured."

Tina's ears straightened up and faced the mink as she listened intently. She was aware the colony had trouble with the Maldavians before the arrival of these Dragon Eaters. It surprised her that this Lieutenant Copaire looked concerned with the Maldavian's well-being.

When the captain didn't respond, the mink hesitated before she spoke again. "Sir, a wounded Maldavian will attract the Dragon Eaters, even in daylight…"

Tina listened to the reason the mink had given, but her face, her demeanor, and her uncomfortable posture suggested she had just given an answer the wolverine would accept. But it looked to Tina as though the mink was showing genuine concern.

The wolverine grunted. "If those monsters find it, they'll put it out of its and our misery. Tell the scouts to stay well clear of the area and return to your post."

Lieutenant Copaire looked disappointed in the decision, but cut her brisk salute. "Aye, Captain." She turned away and left the room.

Tina adjusted her glasses. She'd seen enough for the time being. She climbed back up the stairs and returned to the second floor. The captain and governor may not have cared about a wounded Maldavian, but it was certainly a concern for Tina.

Once she was back to the second floor of the town hall, Tina climbed out onto the roof again and ran to the edge. She caught the mink at the edge of her vision and took a moment to observe the buildings next to the town hall. The direction in which the mink was going was covered well enough by the buildings. Tina would be able to follow on the rooftops. And so she did.

The mink was not difficult to follow as she wove her way through groups of livestock in the street. Tina noted that the lieutenant was taking a straight course back to the western gate of the city. The gate was closed as opposed to the eastern gate through which Tina had entered. She came to a stop on the building nearest the wooden wall and watched as the mink climbed the stairs leading back up to the platform which ran the length of the wall. Lieutenant Copaire called down to the other side, relaying Captain Cephalin's orders. Tina could not see the scout, but her ears were sharp enough to hear the sound of the scout's voice.

"Understood, Lieutenant. What about Lazur Thulfa's farmstead? It's just on the edge of his field."

"Captain Cephalin's orders stand, Corporal. Carry them out." The lieutenant cut her salute, and then walked away from the gate.

Tina seated herself on the rooftop and rested her chin in her hands. She remembered the governor calling the stocky badger by the name of Lazur. She could only hope he was the same one. But Tina also wondered how willing this Lazur would be to help her, especially since he seemed to be more concerned about the people.

The Council of Stars hadn't exactly been Likonia's greatest advocate. But Tina wanted to meet with the wounded Maldavian, and she would need to assess the character of the badger soon enough. She pushed herself up from the rooftop and made her way back to the town hall. She hoped that if the meeting had adjourned, she might still be able to catch Lazur Thulfa before he was gone.

Tina was able to make it back to the town hall within a matter of a few minutes. By the time she returned, the farmers who had been gathered within the town hall were dispersing. Perched on top of the front awning, Tina was able to spot the stocky badger easily since he was one of the last to leave. Tina touched the armlet she wore which was shaped like two arms clasping a circle-cut sapphire, and the gem glowed dimly.

Just as Lazur walked out from under the awning, Tina leapt down and landed on top of his head. The circle cut sapphire

25

flashed once as it absorbed the momentum of Tina's fall, both preventing injury to herself and keeping Lazur from feeling her land. The spell then faded, and Tina lay flat in the hair on top of the badger's head to avoid detection. The mouse woman then cupped her hands over her mouth and quietly spoke into Lazur's ear.

"Excuse me."

Lazur stopped and turned, looking around for who could have addressed him. When he saw none of the other farmers looking at him, he reached up and scratched his ear.

"I don't mean to alarm you, but you will not see me if you look for me." Tina continued to speak quietly. "I need to speak with you in private."

Lazur wrinkled his forehead. He looked down, then up at the roof, but saw no one there. "Who…?"

"You will not see a wizard who does not wish to be seen, sir. Please, walk somewhere private so we may speak."

The badger grunted. He walked around the corner of the town hall and came to a stop once he was standing next to a small wagon where a pair of lesser thunder lizards was munching on hay. He spoke with a grudging tone. "This private enough?"

Tina leapt down from the top of Lazur's head and landed gracefully on a corner of the wagon. She folded her arms and turned to face Lazur, clearing her throat to get his attention.

Lazur looked at the corner of the wagon and blinked. He leaned down and rested on his haunches to look at Tina at her eye level. "What in Ulfengir's name…?"

Tina pushed her glasses up on the bridge of her nose. "I apologize for the method of my greeting, but at the moment, I think it necessary."

"Necessary to lead me into a private place for a conversation with someone no taller than the length of my foot? What is it you want with me, wizard?" The tone with which Lazur spoke the word wizard made it sound as if it tasted bitter in his mouth.

"First of all, I should introduce myself. My name is Tina

van Schtoffen." Tina bowed her head in greeting.

Lazur snorted. "Lazur Thulfa. And I haven't got a lot of patience for wizards, Tina van Schtoffen, so get to the point."

"As you wish." Tina folded her arms across her stomach. "I need your help. You heard Lieutenant Copaire's report in the town hall a few minutes ago, I take it?"

"Eavesdropping on a town meeting isn't the best way to ingratiate yourself with the locals, wizard. But what of it?"

"I have come to understand that the sighting of a Maldavian was made near your farm. I would like you to take me there so I may speak with the dragon and its Albatross."

Lazur lifted one eyebrow and scrutinized Tina. "Would you? Can you give me a reason to oblige you, wizard?"

Tina wrinkled her muzzle, her whiskers wiggling. "I am the wizard sent here by the Council of Stars, as you have probably already guessed."

"Then why don't you introduce yourself to the governor? I'm sure he'd be willing to offer you any help you need, as long as it serves him."

Tina shook her head. "I will make myself known to the governor in time. But thus far, his character has not impressed me as one of trustworthiness."

"Only the man with one finger can lay blame without also accusing himself." Lazur pointed at Tina with one finger, showing that three of his other fingers were pointed back at himself. "You won't find a lot of friends in this town, wizard. The Council of Stars left everyone in Likonia to bleach in the sun while we starved through winters and droughts."

Tina adjusted her glasses. "Yes, I am aware of High Theorist Mythran's decision years ago. But I should also tell you the Council of Stars has sent me here to help this town."

Lazur snorted again. "I don't mean to discount anyone for their size, Tina van Schtoffen, but do you know anything about the monsters we're dealing with?"

"Very little. But they are who I am here to learn about and sort out. And I would appreciate your help in doing so by taking me to your farmstead."

Lazur rubbed the tuft of fur on the end of his chin. "Why should I trust you, wizard? How do I know that the Council of Stars hasn't actually sent you here to drive us from this land so you can give it back to the Maldavians?" Tina looked at Lazur in a confused manner, and Lazur shook his head. "Don't think me dumb just because I work with my hands, Tina van Schtoffen. I don't think there's anyone in Likonia who doesn't know why your High Theorist stopped the king from helping this colony." He pointed at her again. "The wizard's guild and the dragons have been trading goods for years."

Tina crossed her arms at the small of her back. "It is true that the Council of Stars sided with the Maldavians years ago, Lazur. But do you really think you're trusting the right person in Harkon Keldo? After all, he is the one who led your people here, and he is also the one lying to you even now."

Lazur half-smiled. "He lies about a lot of things, wizard. What lie are you referring to?"

"The one he spoke of in which the king promises help outside of the High Theorist's decisions concerning this town. He will not go against Levansian law, and I guarantee you Harkon Keldo in particular does not have his ear."

"I expected as much." The badger straightened up. "Still doesn't tell me why I should trust you more than him. At least his aims, whatever they are, have kept this town alive."

Tina adjusted her glasses. The badger was a little more shrewd than she had given him credit for, she had to admit. "Then perhaps I should tell you the real reason the High Theorist stopped the king from intervening on this town's behalf. He wasn't just concerned about the Maldavians controlling this territory. Did you know that your town is within a hundred miles of the Maldavian Monolith?"

"Maldavian Monolith, huh?" He folded his arms. "And what exactly is a Maldavian Monolith? Some dragon holy site?"

"The Maldavian Monolith is far more than a holy site for them." Tina brushed her fingers across her brow. "I'm sorry. I could explain it to you as many times as you have the patience for, but it's unlikely that someone without an education in magic will truly grasp its significance."

Lazur wrinkled his nose. "There's an old saying that if you can't explain something simply, you don't know it well enough."

The corners of Tina's mouth curled up slowly. "A fair point. Very well. The Maldavian Monolith is a spire of stone surrounded on all sides by mountains containing the dens of hundreds of dragons. To them, the monolith is the resting place of Shahdazhan, the Dragon King. The dragons are magic incarnate, and the monolith acts as a focus and central hub for the flow of magic in this part of the world." Tina pushed her glasses up on the bridge of her muzzle. "That is why the High Theorist of the council did not want Harkon Keldo and your people to settle here. Your presence threatens both the Maldavians and the monolith."

Lazur unfolded his arms. "A threat to the monolith? If that's true, instead of barring the king's help, why didn't the High Theorist try to find an alternative? Why not come and speak with us or help us relocate?"

Tina observed Lazur briefly as she studied his expression and the tone of his voice. His demeanor was genuinely flabbergasted. "It would seem that Governor Keldo has been keeping you and your people more blind than you know. The High Theorist, Sythus Mythran, negotiated with the governor repeatedly, but he would not agree to move this colony farther north or south."

The stocky badger sighed. "That is news. There must be something here Harkon wants."

"You seem to know him very well."

Lazur gestured toward the town hall. "I've known him for a long time." The badger folded his arms again. "You've put some

29

trust in me, so I'll offer you the same courtesy. If you want to see this Maldavian near my farm, I'll take you there."

Tina smiled. "I greatly appreciate your help, Lazur. Once we are near, I should be able to find the dragon myself."

Lazur knelt down and put himself back at eye level with Tina. "I have to ask. I know the Mateesh people are short, but you really seem to have gotten it to excess. Why are you so small?"

Tina was used to such a question, and so answered it without hesitation. "I was cursed by a wizard when I was still an apprentice."

"I would have thought something like that would make you hate magic."

Tina shook her head. "I hated the man, not his means."

Lazur snorted and straightened up again. "I see. Well, I am going to need a little time to get ready to go. Someone's going to have to look after my livestock, and I need to get a few things for the road. It's a three hour walk on foot."

Tina didn't like the idea of delays, but some could not be helped. "Time is a concern. If there is a stable in town, we—"

Lazur held his hand up to stop her. "What you see in the street is what we have for animals. Most of the long striders were either killed by the monsters or are reserved for the small cavalry group who came with Captain Cephalin."

Tina took a moment to consider. "I see. In that case, I will arrange our transportation. In the meantime, while you see to your animals, can you recommend a place for me to stay in town?"

Lazur looked Tina over. "Hole in the wall?" He chuckled before pointing over his shoulder. "Small inn at the edge of town called the Stumble Drum. It's mostly for visiting sailors. It's hard to miss. There's a wide canvas stretched across the front of the second floor."

Tina curled her tail around her legs. "Thank you, Lazur. I will meet you at the western gate when you are ready to leave."

Chapter 4

Tina stood in front of a two-story building which looked all the larger from her diminutive height. As early as it was in the morning, she could detect the lingering smell of eggs, meat, and freshly baked bread coming from the building with a canvas stretched across the front of the second floor. The Stumble Drum looked in better repair than Tina had expected since Lazur had told her it was meant to house sailors. Having been able to observe Captain Morgan's crew and the crews of other ships in her travels, she knew them to be a spirited bunch. Tina thought spirited was a kind word. They were usually rowdy in port, at best.

The Stumble Drum had seen a little wear, but the shutters on the front windows were still intact and, at the moment, closed. Tina would have expected for the Stumble Drum to leave its window shutters open to spread the smell of breakfast to beckon hungry patrons. But the presence of long striders and thunder lizards all over the town made her think the owners of the Stumble Drum probably didn't want their establishment trampled by hungry lizards. Even the front doors were shut tightly. Fortunately for Tina, that wouldn't prevent her entry.

Slipping under the doorway, Tina dusted off her robes and looked over them. Her clothes were already getting soiled from walking around the town and crawling through windows and doorways and on rooftops. She made a mental note to put on a change of clothes as soon as she had space to place her room.

The interior of the Stumble Drum had within it a much stronger version of the scent she had detected outside. The smell was coming from a small collection of sailors and dock workers. Tina recognized many of them as Captain Morgan's crew. It looked as though they'd already finished unloading the ship and were making use of the opportune arrival time. Tina wondered if she might see the captain in the inn, but as she scanned the room, she detected no sign of the grey-furred Kylathian. Tina put the thought out of her mind. While she enjoyed the captain's company, she didn't have time to waste searching for her.

At the far end of the dining room, Tina saw a counter behind which stood a male mink who was wiping down the countertop. He had just picked up a plate and, once he had wiped down the counter, turned to carry it through an open doorway to an adjoining room behind the counter. Tina thought to approach him when a large foot plopped down in front of her. The mouse wizard staggered back a step to catch herself. She looked up at the woman to whom the foot was attached and was mildly surprised to see that she wasn't a native Levansian.

The woman had a narrow, pointed muzzle with a teardrop shaped tail, grey fur, and long ears poking up through the black hair on her head. Tina recognized her as one of the Fenorian people from the southeastern region of the Velrathan continent, the same continent the Levansians and her own Mateesh people called home. The Fenorian Triumvirate was simply on the other side of the continent.

The Fenorian rabbit was wearing an apron over a simple, cloth dress. From the conversation Tina could hear between the rabbit woman and a group of sailors from the Thorn's Side at a nearby table, Tina realized she was a server.

Tina waited until the woman had finished her exchange with the sailors to put her fingers into the sides of her muzzle. She gave a sharp whistle. The Fenorian woman's ear visibly twitched at the sound and swiveled down toward Tina. The woman's head was soon to follow as she looked down at the mouse woman and blinked. She closed her eyes and rubbed her forearm across them, then looked down at Tina again. The woman turned her head back to the sailors at the table. "D'you see her?"

The sailor, whom Tina recognized, nodded at the rabbit. "She came with us. Better be careful how you talk to her. She's a wizard." The sailor set his hands level and shook them, imitating the casting of a spell.

"Oh! Well, that explains a little, I guess." The rabbit woman settled down onto her knees on the floor and rested her hands on her thighs. "Hello, ma'am. Welcome to the Stumble Drum. What can I do for you?"

"My name is Tina van Schtoffen, and I'd like to rent a room here." Tina adjusted her glasses on the bridge of her nose. "To whom do I need speak?"

The rabbit woman put one hand on the ground and pointed toward the counter with the other. "You'll need to talk to Mr. Kilba, ma'am." She looked down at Tina again. "But I think all of our rooms are rented out right now, Ms. van Schtoffen."

Tina smiled at the rabbit. "I think I'll be able to arrange something. Thank you for your help." She bowed and then walked past the rabbit woman, heading for the bar.

Upon reaching it, she used her short claws to climb one side and seated herself on top to wait for the mink to return. He was back behind the counter in short order, and Tina considered briefly how she could most easily get his attention. She pulled off the rucksack tied to her shoulders. After untying the cords on it, she reached inside to remove a small pouch which jingled when she lifted it. Closing the rucksack and setting it down beside her, Tina pulled out two coins. She kept them between her fingers until the mink had moved within earshot. She then tossed the two coins into the air.

Released from Tina's fingers, the coins suddenly expanded a hundred times in mass and landed on the countertop with a distinctive clatter. As Tina had expected, the sound caught the mink's attention. When he saw Tina at the end of the counter, he looked startled. Walking to her, the mink leaned down. "Can I, uh… help you, miss?"

"You are Mr. Kilba, are you not?"

The mink nodded his head. "He, I be. What can I do for you?"

"I'd like to rent a room here for the next few days."

The mink straightened up and interlaced his fingers while tapping his thumbs together. "Well, I'd like to rent you a room, miss, but a ship just came in today. I won't have a room proper until tomorrow at the earliest. I do apologize, ma'am."

"Oh, I don't need an ordinary room. Just a small space in a lightly traveled area." Tina pointed to the other side of the counter which stood next to a set of stairs leading to the second story. The counter extended under the stairway all the way to the wall, but there wasn't enough room for a seat in front of it. "In fact, that space would be ideal."

The mink looked to where Tina had pointed and rubbed the back of his neck. "I'm… not sure, miss. It'd be awful noisy, and you wouldn't have much privacy."

"Privacy, I can manage. What do you charge for a room per day?"

The mink looked down at the coins sitting on the table and tapped the edge of one. "These are yours, miss?"

Tina nodded.

"Not to be impolite, but... how on Cerra did you carry them?"

"Well, I am a wizard, so you may infer what you like from that."

The mink's ears stood up, and he looked surprised. "Oh, uh, I can't charge you for a room, miss." He looked suddenly quite frightened of the mouse woman. "Y-you use whatever space you think you need!"

Tina wiggled her whiskers and considered the mink's reaction. She rose to her feet and walked in the direction of the area she had previously pointed out. "While I appreciate the offer, keep the coins I have left as payment for the space. I am still using your building, after all."

Tina stepped into the space where the counter crossed under the stairway. She took a few moments to briefly examine the wall. There were spaces between the boards which would do for her purposes. Tina pinched the small, golden knob in the center of her socketed necklace and twisted it to pull it free. The knob grew in size until it fit her palm. She then placed it between the spaces of the boards.

The doorknob shimmered, and the wood around it warped outward to form a perfect circle. A stone doorway formed in the new space. Long marks depicting sun flashes pushed outward until they reached the edges. Tina turned the golden handle, and it clicked. She opened the door and disappeared inside, letting it swing shut behind her.

Once inside the familiar space of her pocket quarters, Tina picked the torch up from the stand on the wall. It ignited of its own accord, illuminating the grey, cobblestone hallway. She walked the short hallway and saw the flickering lights of the room ahead still dancing about. When she reached the end of the hallway, Tina placed the torch into its rack on the wall, and the flame from the torch winked out.

Crossing to her bed, Tina seated herself and opened a drawer under it. Inside the drawer were a single pan and a small bottle which contained a fluid with a soft, pale blue glow to it. Picking up both implements, she closed the drawer.

Tina rose from the bed and walked to the window which still depicted a starry sky with a crescent moon filling it. She set the pan down on the window ledge and rested the bottle next to it. The starry sky was a beautiful sight, but it wouldn't serve her purposes for the time being. Her eyes closed. She could practically feel the starlight on her skin.

Tina slipped into a place where the rest of the world knew nothing of her, and she needed not think of anything else. After the encounters with various characters in the town, she wanted a few moments to let her head clear. It was peaceful. It was serene. And she wished for it not to end.

After the brief pause, Tina looked at the stones lining the edge of the window. There were symbols carved into each of them with runes representing particular structures with which Tina was familiar. She touched specific runes until she had made contact with a combination of three. Then she rested her hands on an imperceptible barrier between herself and the scene beyond the window. The three runes appeared as the scene disappeared. She manipulated them, adjusting for geometric synchronization. The three runes slid into each other and formed a new rune with characteristics of all of its originating symbols. The barrier glowed briefly, and Tina blinked.

In the moment of blinking, the scene beyond the window had turned to that of a large city as seen from a bird's eye view. The city stretched out for miles with stone pathways crossing it at symmetrical intersections. They exactly divided the parts of the city into eight sections spread out over an inner and an outer circle with each possessing four divisions. Every structure looked finely crafted and made from various materials ranging from wood to stone to thatched huts. Around the entirety of the city stood a monolithic wall, the edge of it only a few yards away from any of the interior buildings. The wall looked as if made from a single piece for its entire length with no cracks or grooves to suggest it had been physically constructed.

Standing at the center of the city was a compound made from grey stone. Even though the compound stood in the middle of the city, it appeared self-contained; a second wall surrounded it with only one door cut out on the southern face.

Tina knew the compound well with its almost monastic design. It was the home of the Council of Stars. The structure, though surrounded by a circular wall, was an octagon with a tower standing taller than the wall at each of the eight corners. At the center of the octagon were five separate towers arranged into a square with a single tower in the middle. These towers were considerably larger than those at the eight points of the octagon.

Tina recalled that each tower represented one of the schools of magic taught by the Council of Stars; the southern tower contained the House of Observant Ritual, the northern tower contained the House of Prodigious Means, the eastern tower contained the House of The Vexing Eye, the western tower contained the House of Contemplative Stars, and the center tower contained the House of Demonstrative Theory.

Tina turned her eyes toward the sky, wanting to assess the time of day by the sun, but clouds covered it. There was even a little rain falling on the city. She pushed her glasses up on the bridge of her muzzle and picked up the bottle of glowing fluid. She loosened the cords on her rucksack and placed it onto the bed.

After taking a small, wooden box from the rucksack, Tina withdrew a piece of parchment and rested it on the window sill next to the pan. She then removed a painter's brush and a short knife from the box and set the box on the bed next to her rucksack.

Tina put the piece of parchment into the pan and used the short knife to cut out a paper doll with a torso, head, arms, and legs, all of which were squared off at the edges. Setting the rest of the parchment aside, Tina pulled the cork out of the bottle and dipped her brush in it. After wiping off excess fluid in the mouth of the bottle, Tina used the brush to paint two symbols on the paper doll. The two symbols represented the senses she required for the paper doll – light and sound.

Satisfied with the work, Tina removed the paper doll from the pan. She held it forward and let the paper doll touch the barrier between the scene which lay before her and herself. The paper doll sank into the barrier and drifted freely on the other side, unaffected by the rain.

Tina closed her eyes and let the image of the drifting parchment be all she could see in her mind. As it floated through the air, she focused on the organic variable of her personal equation and modified it. Once again calling her gift forth, Tina imagined one of the legs of the paper doll curling in to form a small spiral. It shaped itself into a humanoid leg. Tina thought about its toes wiggling, and they did so. Her thoughts shifted to the head of the doll, and it curled inward as well to form a sphere.

After repeating the process for the limbs and body of the doll, the image in her mind became a feminine figure, but featureless aside from being curled strips of parchment. Tina then imagined the paper being sheathed by the rune she had drawn onto it representing light. The rune expanded and warped light around the doll. Within a few moments, she could see herself formed from the paper doll. The piece of parchment on the other side of the barrier landed in one of the windows of the central tower of the compound beyond the window.

Tina opened her eyes and blinked several times as they adjusted to the light. She paused to observe her surroundings. She realized she was standing on the ledge of a window of the large room which served as an antechamber to the High Theorist's study. A Kylathian and a Khanifran stood on each side of a large, wooden door at the far end of the room. A long, narrow carpet made from grey cloth extended from the door and stopped just shy of the window where it diverted to one side and ran down a set of stairs. Tina realized the room seemed to be to scale for someone standing at a height of five feet. She had manifested herself through the doll at a size relative to her surroundings since the last frame of mind she'd been in was that of her own pocket quarters.

Windows lined the long, rectangular room, but Tina had appeared through the paper doll at the far end. She reached up to adjust the glasses sitting on her muzzle, but her hand swept through them, and Tina remembered she hadn't drawn a rune onto the paper doll for touch. It was just as well. If she had given the doll the ability to touch, the rain would have driven it straight to the ground.

Tina slipped away from the window sill, and her feet touched the floor and carried her toward the doorway. Though she could not feel the ground beneath her feet and knew that it did not actually support her, she was also aware the paper doll's illusion moved by a manifestation of her will. So it mimicked the common movement of walking as she crossed the room.

The Kylathian male met Tina's eyes and nodded his head in recognition of her for both who she was and her status as a wizard. He then nodded at the Khanifran woman. The Khanifran woman was covered by a layer of golden fur and had a squared, blunt muzzle and a long, thin tail with a tuft of fur on the end of it. She stood at just over six feet in height. She wasn't terribly tall for a Khanifran female. Her armor was that of a desert wanderer with toughened leather covering her chest and hips, but little else. She wore simple cloth garments to cover the rest of her body, but Tina knew that to be a courtesy for others around Kerovnia. The Khanifrans never wore very much because their fur was more than sufficient for the southern desert in which they usually dwelt. She pushed the door to the High Theorist's study open for Tina. Tina nodded thankfully at the Khanifran woman and passed through.

The study on the other side of the door looked like a library with book shelves standing on each side of the entrance. Three layers of long shelves lined sides of the room and faced in toward the grey carpet leading to a heavy wooden desk at the center. With several hundred books standing on the shelves, Tina recalled their value. She had her own, small library back in her room, but outside of the Council of Stars, books were a true rarity. The only reason the Council of Stars had as many as it did was a result of the writing of students, teachers, and visiting spell-casters. Outside of the Council of Stars, one was lucky to find more than one book in any of the smaller cities. Even in larger cities, most writing was done on scrolls and individual parchments.

Beyond the bookshelves, Tina could see a few personal

items of the High Theorist which decorated the room. A large, glass sphere stood in a polished wooden stand. The sphere was filled by several glimmering lights which circled inside it. They swirled around slowly and changed colors in slow patterns. It was the sort of thing into which, Tina imagined, someone wanting to contemplate on deeper thoughts might stare.

Across from the sphere hung a tapestry depicting the landscape around a volcano. In spite of the volcano's presence and the black rock that covered it, trees grew in patches low at the foot of the mountain. Below them grew a veritable forest of vegetation with thunder lizards and striders roaming across it. Tina observed as the threads of the tapestry shifted of their own accord as if weaving the movements of the animals.

Behind the wooden desk was another level of floor with paths leading up to it. On the raised level stood the High Theorist, Sythus Mythran.

A pair of large, feathery wings protruded through holes in the back of the High Theorist's robes. While the wings had a base golden color, the primary feathers were white. The royal blue robes he wore had golden trim lining the edges. A thin, leonine tail protruded from the bottom of his robes and swayed back and forth while Sythus looked out through the window. While he did not hold his staff, it stood next to him like a lamp stand. The staff slowly rotated which turned the crystal at the tip which was surrounded by four carved, feathery wings. The wood of the staff was cut into a spiral which ran all the way from the base of the staff until it spanned outward right before it met the wings.

Tina walked up in front of the High Theorist's desk and folded her arms. "Let the stars guide you."

The High Theorist responded immediately as if he'd been waiting for the phrase. "Though the soil defy you. Welcome, Lady van Schtoffen."

"Thank you, master."

The High Theorist turned from the window and gave Tina

a welcoming smile. "The last time you visited my study, you were only this tall." He leaned down and put his hand six inches off the ground. "My, how you've grown."

Tina giggled. When the High Theorist straightened again, he rested one hand on his staff. A Khanifran male, the High Theorist had a leonine face with a blunt, slightly squared muzzle and a degree of muscle inborn to the Khanifran race. In spite of being just under seven feet tall, he was actually thin for his kind.

"I hope your trip across the Selian Sea was an uneventful one."

"It was, master. As you requested, I have come to report my arrival and give an initial assessment of the situation."

The High Theorist nodded. "Proceed."

Tina crossed her arms at the small of her back. "I feel the first thing I should report is that I am not the first wizard to come to Likonia."

One of the High Theorist's eyebrows ticked upward. "Intriguing. Have you met this other wizard?"

"No, master. If a wizard is here, he is staying out of sight. But I listened to a town meeting shortly after my arrival, and there was talk of another wizard who had tried to solve the problem in Likonia before the Council of Stars was ever notified."

"Do you know what problem in particular this other wizard was trying to solve?"

Tina shook her head. "No, but from the context of the exchange and the impression made upon me by one of the farmers, it was not to solve the problem of the Dragon Eaters. I admit to some surprise they trusted a wizard in the first place. Many of them don't have a very good impression of us."

Sythus sighed. "I'm afraid that cannot be helped."

Tina knew that statement for the truth in it. "I have seen, but not yet introduced myself to, the governor and the captain of the guard in Likonia. Neither of them leaves a good impression on me."

"The captain of the guard stands out in your mind?" The High Theorist walked to one side and descended the ramp leading to the lower level.

"He does. One of his guards called him Captain Cephalin."

The High Theorist stopped and looked directly at Tina. "Idori Cephalin?"

Tina shook her head. "I did not hear his first name, master."

The High Theorist rubbed the sides of his chin with his thumb and forefinger as he thought. "A Levansian with a nasty temperament, even for the Capathian breed. He carries no weapon but a pair of metal gloves sharpened into claws. And from the way he looks at you, it's as if he's biting you."

"He has not seen me yet, but he was ill-tempered and the gauntlets you described, he was wearing." Tina recognized the term Capathian in reference to the wolverine breed of native Levansians.

"I recommend you be careful of that man, Tina. He was a terror while among the king's soldiers. The Massacre of Empusa is laid upon his shoulders, and it is the reason he was discharged from the king's service." The High Theorist reached the bottom of the ramp and approached Tina. "If he is the captain of the guard in Likonia, Harkon Keldo is either more reckless than I had feared or has chosen to ride a wicked wind."

"My lord, if this Capathian is responsible for the Massacre of Empusa, why was he not executed?"

Sythus shook his head. "No living witnesses, even among his own men who had accompanied him into Empusa."

"My lord, if there were no witnesses, how could he be responsible?"

"That is why he could not be executed. One of our prophets was allowed to view his memories of the event. She was nearly killed by blind rage and, when she awoke a week later, could not remember anything of what she had seen."

Tina shuddered. She did not like the implication of such a thing. A prophet being blinded by pure rage from a single person was akin to saying a mountain fell because a rock was thrown at it. "I will be very wary of him, master."

The High Theorist nodded. "Back to the matter of the wizard. What have you heard of him?"

"Nothing aside from the fact that he was in Likonia some time before my arrival and appears to be there no longer." Tina reached up to adjust her glasses, but her finger passed through them again. She had to remind herself again that she had not painted the rune for touch onto the paper doll. "According to the captain of the Thorn's Side, there was a wizard aboard another ship, the Water Walker, who traveled to Likonia a few months ago. Whether it was the same one, I don't yet know."

"And you trust the source of this information?" The High Theorist questioned off-handedly.

"I do. The captain of the Thorn's Side is an old friend. I do not believe she would have any reason to deceive me."

The High Theorist spread his wings as he seated himself behind his desk. "Is there anything else you wish to tell me of your initial impression?"

"Just one more thing, my lord. Aside from the Likonians' distrust of wizards, they aren't fond of the Maldavians either." Tina stepped in front of the desk. "There is a wounded Maldavian near one of the farms, and the guard captain and the farmers don't seem to be very concerned about it."

The High Theorist's eyebrow ticked upward. "Do not take this the wrong way, Lady van Schtoffen, but you do not seem all that alarmed yourself. A wounded Maldavian should take priority over your report to me."

"I am waiting on the farmer who owns the farm near where the wounded Maldavian was last sighted. Without his help navigating the countryside, it might take days trying to track down a wounded dragon who might not want to be found."

The High Theorist nodded. "I see. Your report thus far will suffice, then. See to the Maldavian and then continue your investigation. May the stars guide you."

Tina curtsied with practiced grace and rested her hand on her chest. "Though the soil defy you." She then closed her eyes.

When the Mateesh wizard's eyes opened again, she blinked several times at the scene in front of her. The window displayed a starry sky centered around a crescent moon. She looked down at the pan in front of the window and saw the remnants of the small paper doll sitting in the circular pan she'd laid in front of the open window. Tina picked up the pan and emptied the torn pieces of paper into her hand.

When she turned to walk past the bed, Tina felt a moment of vertigo and quickly sat down. She took a deep breath and let it out slowly. Having only been connected with two of her senses for the duration of her visit with the High Theorist, it was disorienting to have all five of them kick back so suddenly. But it was not a feeling with which she was unfamiliar. Tina waited a few moments to get her bearings and then rose from the bed. She walked over to the bottle in the fireplace where the dancing flames that illuminated the room resided.

After Tina let the dancing flames devour the remains of the paper doll, she walked back to the window to put her tools away. Once her rucksack was repacked, and the pan and bottle stowed under the bed, Tina pulled her rucksack onto her back and tied the cords around her shoulders. It was time to meet back up with Lazur Thulfa.

Chapter 5

Tina sat on the ground outside of the western gate of the city with her legs folded in tailor style. She looked up at the sky and watched the few white clouds drifting across the great blue expanse. The western side of the city was completely open and not much more than flat grasslands. She could see over the entire area with little difficulty. A wide path led out of the western gate with unlit torch stands lining it on each side. The air was still cool in the mid-morning with late spring not yet having summoned the warmth of summer.

Tina could hear the footsteps of soldiers patrolling the wall above her, but with her diminutive size, it was easy to overlook the Mateesh wizard so close to the wall. The sound of the gates to the city being opened reached her ears, and Tina turned to see who was coming out. When she saw the badger Lazur Thulfa stepping through the gates, she pushed up to her feet.

Lazur was already looking around at his feet when Tina came into view. He placed a wide, cone-shaped straw hat on his head just as Tina reached him. She leapt onto his leg and climbed up quickly. The badger was startled for a moment, but refrained from making any sounds of alarm.

Tina seated herself on the badger's shoulder, hidden from view by the straw hat. She adjusted her glasses on the bridge of her muzzle. "I take it you were able to make arrangements?"

Lazur snorted. "Wouldn't be here if I hadn't."

Tina wrinkled her muzzle. "Take us to the edge of the woods, and I will get you transportation faster than feet."

Lazur eyed the wizard on his shoulder briefly. After the

gates had shut behind him, he started off on the path leading to the edge of the woods. "You wizards like to throw around magic a lot, don't you?"

"On the contrary." Tina laid her tail across her lap and rested her hands on top of it. "Magic is a tool. We make our best attempts to use it as little as possible and only out of necessity when another solution cannot be found. And since time is of the essence, I have reached the conclusion that magic will be necessary to get us to that Maldavian as swiftly as possible."

Lazur shook his head. "Most folks seem to get by without it. What makes it a necessity for wizards and the like?"

"Most folks," Tina imitated, "don't have to deal with the same problems as wizards."

"Like problems created by other wizards?" Lazur cocked his head, glancing at Tina on his shoulder.

"That is one capacity for the use of magic, yes." Tina's whiskers twitched. "Speaking of which, I have come to understand there was another wizard here before me, one not attached to the Council of Stars."

Lazur nodded, turning his eyes back to the road as they approached the edge of the woods. "Was. He's dead. Killed by the Dragon Eaters."

Tina wrinkled her muzzle. She had hoped to have a chance to speak with the wizard somehow. But it was much harder to communicate with a dead one. Though, for another wizard, it was not impossible. "How did it happen?"

Lazur shook his head. "He was trying to capture those monsters when they attacked him, and they ate him. Pretty clear-cut."

"When a wizard is involved, there is usually very little which is clear-cut." Tina climbed down from Lazur's shoulder once the badger stopped next to the trees. "Now, to find a clear spot off the trodden path."

"Plenty of them back there." Lazur gestured back over his

shoulder at the grassy area through which they'd just passed.

"I can't be seen from this distance in Likonia. Would you like to give the guards the impression that you are a wizard yourself when they see you standing next to the result of my spell?" Tina folded her arms and looked up at Lazur.

"In Cerra's name, no." The badger walked a few paces deeper into the woods to be sure he was out of sight.

Tina gave a small smile and then looked around. She saw a patch of dirt beyond some of the underbrush. "There. That might do." She made her way off the path and ducked under a small clump of bushes.

When she emerged on the other side, Tina saw a shallow impression in the ground about as deep as she was tall. There were several patches of mashed grass and a flower that had been pressed into the ground. She looked around the large impression. The edges of it were uneven, but it would do for her purposes.

Lazur rounded the bush which Tina had passed under and came to a sudden stop. "Uh, wizard."

"Tina." Tina replied.

"Tina, do you see what you're standing in?"

Tina looked down at her feet. "...Dirt?"

Lazur crouched down and beckoned to Tina. "More than that. Come here for a moment."

Tina looked at Lazur curiously, but acquiesced. She walked back to the edge of the impression, and when Lazur lowered his hand for her, she stepped onto it. When Lazur stood, he held her back from the impression so she could get a better look at it.

The impression was almost six feet long and three feet wide. The back side of it was rounded with a smaller, circular impression six inches wide behind it. Three long gouges jutted from the front of the impression, each one about four feet long with a fourth one only three feet long.

It was a footprint.

Tina was startled by the size of it. She'd seen footprints

from greater thunder lizards. This one was bigger than most. "Is that," she questioned with a brief pause, "from the Dragon Eaters?"

"I wouldn't be surprised. They were out here last night, looking baleful and hungry."

"Your town needs a bigger wall." Tina cleared her throat and then jumped down from Lazur's hand. She landed in the soft dirt at the edges of the footprint and climbed back into it. Something caught her eye, and Tina looked at what was next to the footprint. There were rocks and the scorched remnants of kindling vines wrapped around parts of them. All were blackened from fire as was the grass around it. She pointed at it. "Do you know what caused that?"

Lazur looked at the scorched rocks. "I do. The guards used a trebuchet to heave a flaming rock at one of the monsters out here. The blasted thing caught it and crushed it like a berry. Didn't even seem to feel it."

Tina felt a cold chill run up her spine as she inferred three things from Lazur's comment. The first was that the creatures hadn't felt pain from a flaming boulder heaved by a trebuchet. The second was that it had the strength to crush said boulder with what the badger regarded as little effort. The third was the one which worried her the most; the creature had recognized the threat and taken steps to prevent it, which implied problem solving intelligence.

However, while problem solving intelligence was a worry, Tina considered that detail momentarily. If the creatures were intelligent, then it was possible they could be reasoned with.

Tina came out of her momentary contemplation and looked back at the footprint. "Made by the Dragon Eaters or not, it will still serve my purposes." She pushed her glasses up on the bridge of her nose and untied the cords of her rucksack. Removing it from her shoulders, the mouse wizard set the rucksack down and pulled it open. She removed from it a rolled up leather kit which she spread out on the ground.

Tina plucked from it a small, metal wand the size of a needle for the average Cerran. She inspected the two runes drawn into the base of the wand. Picking up a small, glass bottle, she removed it from the kit and pulled the cork out. Walking down into the indentation, she used the metal wand to trace lines into the ground. The lines looked jumbled at first, but she continued tracing them.

Collectively, they began to form an image. By the time she was finished, Tina had traced out a rudimentary creature with six thin legs, each leg ending in a four-toed foot. The toes were spread apart like the foot of an avian, though they lacked talons. Walking to the back end of the dirt drawing, she drew a long, whipcord-like tail covered by scales.

She traced a line from the tail leading to the front of the drawing's body to create its back. Stopping at the middle of the back, Tina drew on a simple saddle and then continued to the drawing's head. She sketched a short snout covered by wide scales and ending in a pair of pointed, boney lips resembling an avian's beak. She next added a pair of round eyes. Tina completed the drawing with a few other needed details including a pair of long, pointed ears and a bridle on the creature's head.

Once finished, Tina walked around the drawing and tapped the silvery powder inside the bottle into the lines she had drawn. The silver powder glimmered inside the lines as it touched the soil. And once Tina had finished pouring the powder, she corked the bottle again and put it and the metal wand back into the kit from which she'd taken them. She rolled the kit up and put it back into the rucksack.

Tina put the rucksack back on her shoulders and walked to the front of the drawing. She held her hands out in front of her and chanted her personal mantra to help maintain her focus. The process of summoning required a greater degree of concentration than most other spells.

Tina multiplied the organic variable inside her personal equation, taking the excess magic produced from it and gathering it between her hands. She formed a sphere with the fingers on one hand and swept the other hand out over the drawing which was several times larger than she. With each sweep, wisps drifted off the sphere of pure magical energy in her hand and poured over the drawing like a fine mist. The mist faded into the silvery catalyst which floated up from the soil. Each sweep of her hand caused more of the magical energy to pour through the catalyst and made the silver dust drift into the air for an instant with each sweep.

Once she had applied sufficient magical energy, Tina allowed the remainder of her summoned magic to return to her body. She pushed both hands forward, and her fingers formed a pair of cones facing the intricate drawing. The silver dust filling the lines rose and carried with it bits of soil. The soil spiraled in the air in a long cylinder which lay on its side. Commanded by Tina's will, the cylinder formed a long body with the bits of dirt becoming suspended in the air. Some of them drifted downward from the formed body, and Tina cupped one hand to collect the falling dust in an inverted cone beneath the forming creature.

The dust in the inverted cone rose and connected to the creature's body and formed three pairs of legs. The creature's feet touched the ground, and it held itself up on its own. More of the soil rose from the ground to create the creature's long tail just as its head started forming. Once its mouth was complete, the creature let out a quiet groan.

Tina clapped her hands together sharply, and dust burst away from its body. The dust drifted to the ground to reveal her creation. Its body was a deep, earthen brown with green scales on its shoulders, along its snout, covering its back, and extending down the top of its tail. The saddle formed was brown like the rest of its body, but softened into leather.

Tina lowered her hands and drew in a deep breath before

she shivered. The expenditure of magic to animate a creature with a spark of her own life force left Tina feeling drained. She sank to the ground and crossed her legs with her hands on her knees. The creature blinked a few times, its eyes rotating to take in its surroundings. Upon seeing Tina, it leaned down and gently bumped her cheek with the side of its snout. Tina smiled weakly and rubbed the side of the creature's muzzle.

Lazur whistled lowly at the animation of the creature. "Magic or not, that's impressive. Is that thing really alive?"

Tina looked up at the creature's eyes. It gently bumped her with its snout. "It has a spark of life. But not a strong one. The best way to say it is that it shares my spirit."

"That sounds a little dangerous."

Tina nodded. "It is taxing. Fragmenting one's spirit in any way tends to be like that. But this is a creature I created sometime ago before the banning of long term animation within the Council of Stars."

Lazur stepped forward and tentatively rested his hand on the creature's back. He lightly rubbed its scales. "But they let you continue to use animation?"

Tina rose to her feet, and the creature dipped its head down to lift Tina up on its snout. It tilted its head back and let Tina slide down between its shoulder blades. "Once a spirit is fragmented, mending it can be more dangerous. The Council of Stars did not make the law retroactive."

"But you just created this creature now, didn't you?"

Tina shook her head. "The ritual for creating life is far more complicated, time-consuming, and requires several reagents I do not possess. This creature, I merely summoned from a spell I had already enacted some time ago."

Lazur looked down at the creature, lightly bumping its scaly side with his knuckle. "Your spirit resides in it. Does that mean you feel what it does?"

Tina shook her head. "It's as conscious as I am, but it is

contained within its own vessel. We are not linked that way."

The badger grunted. "Not entirely sure what you mean by that, but I think I get the idea."

Tina gestured toward the saddle. "We're losing time. Please, climb on."

Lazur scrutinized the creature briefly, then threw his leg over it. The creature shifted with his weight, then settled. The badger picked up the reins attached to the bridle and wrapped them around his hands. "You train it to respond like a strider?"

Tina smiled. "There's no need. Just hang on." She turned around to face the creature's head. "I will get her moving. Just guide her where we need to go." When Lazur nodded, Tina put her hand on the creature's back. She thought of the act of running.

In an instant, it responded and started forward smoothly. Lazur pulled the reins to one side, the creature following his lead. He turned it back to the road, and by the time they had reached it, the creature was practically sprinting.

Lazur kept a tight grip on the reins. "It rides much more smoothly than a strider."

Tina smiled. "She." Her head tilted down, and she closed her eyes. "The magic I have been using today has left me a little drained." She rested her back against the front of the saddle. "As little as you may think of magic, it is a stress on even a gifted spell-caster's body and mind. You may think that wizards throw magic around, but to do so without regard for the power we wield is reckless, dangerous, and to the careless magic user, deadly."

"Then why do it?" Lazur looked down at her.

"For most, it is a choice to seek some greater goal." Tina opened her eyes. "I try to help people with my gift. But even if my aims were entirely hedonistic, I no longer have a choice, if I want to survive."

"Because of your curse." Lazur stated in understanding. "You seem pretty knowledgeable about magic. Haven't you found a way to cure it?"

"Oh, I found the cure a long time ago. But the wizard who cursed me did his work well. The curse spread to my spirit before I found the cure. Were I to undo his spell, it would kill me." Tina softly sighed. "I have been using a great deal of magic today. I would like to rest."

Lazur wrinkled his muzzle. "Putting more trust in me, are you?"

Tina tilted her head up to look at him. "Trust can only be bought with trust." She smiled weakly and lowered her head. "There is one more thing I would like to ask before I rest, though."

Lazur nodded. "Go ahead."

"It's about the wizard who was here before me. You've told me he was killed by the Dragon Eaters. How did he come to be in Likonia at all?"

"The governor recruited him, far as I know. Nobody really trusted him, but it didn't have anything to do with him being a wizard." Lazur adjusted the reins and turned the riding beast as they came to a bend which, once rounded, brought them out of the woods to start the climb up a hill. "It was because he was an Idassian."

Tina's eyes opened. "The governor trusted an Idassian wizard to capture the Dragon Eaters?"

Lazur shook his head. "Not exactly. The wizard came before the Dragon Eaters even appeared. He was supposed to be dealing with the Maldavians. Then the Dragon Eaters showed up and attacked the Maldavians. After the wizard was killed trying to capture them, they started raiding our crops and attacking farmers."

Tina flicked one of her rounded ears. A wizard from Idassia wasn't unheard of, but many of them tended to have one thing in common. "Did you ever see this wizard yourself, Lazur?"

Lazur nodded. "I did."

"Did he wear a deep purple traveling cloak with maroon, feathery wings sewn into the sides and a hood with a pointed tip like the beak of a bird?"

The stocky badger looked down at Tina. "Yeah. That's a pretty accurate description. Does it mean something?"

"It can. That cloak means he is part of a cult in Idassia." Tina sighed as she rubbed her forehead. She thought back on the words given to her by the prophet in the Council of Stars. 'Discover the truth upon which light is shed in the knowledge granted by those who are dead.' The Cult of the Red Phoenix used magic relating to life and death. Such a wizard may not be beyond Tina's reach.

Chapter 6

Tina had been able to rest for almost an hour while leaning against the saddle. She had let her mind drift into a meditative
state, but her eyes remained open. She had been conscious of her
surroundings as they traveled. After passing over the hill beyond
the edge of the woods, mountains came into view on the horizon,
and those mountains had remained in view as they crossed into
tilled terrain.

Farmland stretched out in all directions with simple, wood-
en houses dotting the landscape. Most of the farms were relatively
small, but there were many of them. The land was mostly flat,
and there were several tributaries running around and through
the larger farms. Tina and Lazur had turned north after passing
two smaller farms. Their path skirted the edge of one larger farm
upon which a bigger house stood. It looked as if it could house
three or four families by itself.

After they passed the larger farm, they came to a dip in
the landscape where a river ran between two farms. One of those
farms had a small house and a field only large enough to support
a single family. The second farm was considerably larger, but the
fields of the two farms were so close together that they could have
been regarded as one.

"We're getting close. This beast of yours moves very quickly." Lazur clicked the reins.

The creature snorted, bucking Lazur in the saddle once
and glaring back at him.

The corners of Tina's mouth curled upward. "She doesn't
like that. The bridle is just to help you keep your grip and guide

her." Tina lifted her head, blinking her eyes a few times as her mind came out of the meditative state between dreams and the waking world. "This doesn't seem like a journey that would have taken three hours on foot."

Lazur chuckled. "Like I said, your beast moves swiftly. The uphill hikes can feel almost abusive."

"She was made from the soil. It gives her strength and keeps her refreshed." Tina pushed her glasses up on the bridge of her muzzle. "These two farms are very close."

"They are. Their owners are as well." Lazur inclined his head toward the larger of the two farms, pointing out the house at the head of the field to which it belonged. "That's mine. The other one belongs to Garina Stelliker."

Tina noted the tone of the stocky badger's voice softening in the slightest manner when he spoke of the owner of the smaller farm. She decided, despite her natural curiosity, not to question the reason. Instead, Tina lifted one hand and curled her fingers as if holding a sphere in her hand. When she spread them, a small, golden orb appeared and expanded outward until it was approximately the size of Tina's head. Within it, the landscape appeared along with several semi-transparent, waving lines which traveled through both the land and air.

Lazur observed the orb. "Thought you were tired from using magic."

"The Abascus Compass does not require a wizard's gift in order to be used. Only the knowledge of how to look into it." Tina pressed her fingers into the golden sphere and closed her digits. The view within the compass spread to cover a larger area. At the center of the compass, Tina could see a pair of figures with several runes flowing around them. She knew the figures to be Lazur, herself, and her animated mount.

Lazur could see them in the expanded view as well. "What are those?"

Tina pointed to the three figures. "These depict the three

of us. The runes tell a few minor details about each of us. Living, breathing, moving, awake. Details which help to define the kinds of entities we are according to cross-referenced categories."

Lazur grunted. "And those two bright, flashing red ones?"

Tina adjusted her glasses on the bridge of her muzzle. Her ears stood up, and she rested her hand on the riding mount's back. She thought of the direction in which she wanted to go, and the creature quickly turned, deviating from the road. "I told you I would be able to find the Maldavian once we were nearby. Those bright, flashing red runes denote a loose grip on a spirit."

"What's that mean?"

"It means the Maldavian is dying." Tina thought with urgency, and the riding lizard let out a keen. It lurched forward and hastened its pace as it headed toward the edge of the woods on the far side of Lazur's farm.

Lazur gripped the riding lizard's reins firmly and locked his legs around its middle. He let his hips bounce with the animal's movements. "What's the other one beside it?"

"A Maldavian Albatross. They are servants created by the Maldavians and bound to their life force." Tina closed her fingers. She memorized where the Maldavian was relative to their own position so she could use her hands to maintain her balance. "If a Maldavian dies, so does its Albatross."

"Bad luck. Why would the Maldavians make servants who die when they do?"

"Think of a Maldavian Albatross being like Shasta." She patted the riding lizard's back. "A fraction of a Maldavian's spirit is invested in his Albatross. If I were to die, so would Shasta. So it is the same for an Albatross."

"Are you going to save them?"

Tina hesitated to reply. The runes she'd seen around the Maldavian had been grim. Saving the Maldavian and its Albatross would take a great feat of magic. "…If it is within my power."

Shasta broke into the woods which trampled the underbrush. Lazur ducked under the branches with a practiced grace which made Tina think he had spent a good deal of time riding. It was a thought she pushed to the back of her mind. The Maldavian was more important.

As they rounded a large boulder, Shasta came to a sudden stop. Beyond the boulder lay a clearing unnaturally created. Several trees were felled, and if Shasta's trampling of underbrush were increased in magnitude, it could be compared to the path of destruction which lay ahead of them.

Tina touched the side of her glasses, and a small, runic circle appeared in her right lens. Looking through it, she could see that the equations running through the trees had not been modified through use of magic as far as she could tell. They'd been trampled. "The dragon must have caused that." She looked at Shasta, thinking that the riding lizard should follow the path.

Shasta responded to the thoughts directed at her and turned to follow along the path's edge. It stretched for almost a hundred yards, but a sudden sound brought Shasta to a halt. It was the ringing of metal.

Lazur looked up suddenly. "Move!"

Shasta didn't respond to his command, but Lazur acted quickly. He dived off one side of the riding lizard and shoved her legs out from under her. Shasta fell with Lazur's weight just as a halberd slammed into the ground right where Shasta had been standing. A red-skinned figure landed next to the halberd and ripped it out of the ground, raising it to strike again.

Tina tumbled off Shasta, but caught herself on the ground. Lazur had swept Shasta's legs in a way that kept his own from being caught under the beast. Provided the freedom to move, Lazur pushed up with his hands and threw himself back to avoid the halberd as it slammed down into the ground just above Shasta's back, peeling scales from the saddle.

Shasta swiped with her legs, trying to scratch at the red-skinned figure holding the halberd. The figure leapt back, taking the halberd with it and brandishing the weapon with menace.

Tina rose quickly, observing who had attacked them. It was a woman with red, leathery skin. Tina thought it looked like the hide of a dragon bare of scales. The pair of black horns on her head curled backward like a ram's with its tips jutting slightly outward and forward. The woman's face was relatively flat with a triangular nose and long, wild, blonde hair. The hair looked ruffled and messy as if the woman had just awakened. The woman was baring her teeth, six of which were fangs. The four fangs on her upper mandible were in the place canines usually would have been. The two fangs on the lower mandible fit up between them which denoted a vicious, locking bite.

Her feet were flat with the heels touching the ground, which was an unusual feature on a world dominated by creatures with digitrade feet. Most Cerrans had feet with raised ankles and longer, broader toes. Her thick, reptilian tail had a bladed spade on the end which could be used for striking. The woman also had a pair of feathery, white wings protruding from her back, both of which were raised and fanned in a warning fashion. The spread wings made the woman appear much larger than she was in reality.

On her body was metal armor fashioned for both protection and flexibility. The armor was finely made with flowing grooves which made it look like lava frozen in the metallic depiction.

Recognizing the woman as a Maldavian Albatross, Tina threw her hands up and cried out loudly in the Maldavians' native tongue. *"Dragon daughter, we do not come to fight!"*

The Maldavian Albatross looked surprised to hear her native tongue spoken. Her stance did not become any less threatening, but she held from delivering a further blow and replied, *"You are not Maldavian. Who are you to speak our tongue?"*

Tina walked forward, keeping her hands up in plain view. *"My name is Tina van Schtoffen. I am an emissary of the Council of*

Stars."

The Albatross lowered her halberd, and her wings folded. "*Your name is known to my master.*" She stepped forward, letting one hand leave her halberd as she went to her knees. "*Please, Wizard. You must help my master.*" Her tone was suddenly much more pleading.

"*I will do what I can.*" Tina climbed up onto Shasta's side and knelt down. She rested her hands on the riding lizard's scales. It didn't take long for her to feel that Shasta was startled but unharmed.

Lazur was on his feet and had taken a defensive stance. He relaxed a little when Tina and the Albatross spoke in a foreign tongue. "What's going on, Tina?"

Tina looked at Lazur. She realized he hadn't understood the Maldavian tongue. "This is the Maldavian's Albatross. She probably thought us a threat moving toward her master. Please see to Shasta. I am going with the Albatross." Tina looked up at the Albatross and spoke Maldavian again. "*Please lend me your hand.*"

The Albatross lowered the hand she had taken off her halberd, and Tina climbed onto it. "*I am Angelica, Wizard, Albatross of Master Shalizan.*"

Tina acknowledged the greeting with a bow of her head. "*Thank you, Angelica. Please, take me to your master.*"

Angelica nodded and rose with her wings fanned. With a powerful flap and a leap, she landed on a thick branch above. Using it to jump higher, she flapped her wings again and was above the trees in an instant.

Tina held on firmly as the Albatross took her over the path of destruction she and Lazur had seen from the ground. It was a trail which led back into the woods for hundreds of yards. It came to an end in the middle of the woods. Tina adjusted her glasses as she looked at its termination.

Lying against a felled tree was a Maldavian dragon of great

size. His wings were loosely sprawled over the ground on one side with gouges torn out of the nearer of the two. The dragon's body was covered by red scales which matched the color of Angelica's leathery skin. His body was powerful with a long, thick tail ending in a spade. While Angelica's was elegant and sharp, his was thick and muscular. The dragon's tail spade also had several layers which lay separated with twin blades on the upper and lower sides of the spade. One of the horns on the dragon's head had a jagged edge. Tina could tell it had been broken in the middle by comparing it to the horn on the opposite side of his head. It swept back, dipping in the center before coming to a sharp point on the end.

With the dragon lying on his side, she could see several claw marks across the upper part of his hind legs, chest, and a long tear across his middle. One of his arms was clutching the wound on his stomach. The other arm looked unusable, twisted and broken in several places. Tina had to put her hand over her mouth at the sight of the wounds, even from afar. They looked mortal.

As the Albatross landed next to the dragon, she ran to his head. Kneeling down, Angelica put Tina on the ground and then quickly moved to touch the dragon's brow. *"Master, a wizard is here to help you."*

The dragon's eyes opened, and he looked up at Angelica. When the dragon spoke, his voice was deep and commanding, despite his grievous wounds. *"Angelica."*

The Albatross shushed him. *"Please, master, save your strength."* She stroked the dragon's brow. Even with the vicious looking halberd in her hand, the Albatross had a comforting expression as she cooed to the dragon. *"Everything will be all right."*

The dragon laughed weakly and closed his eyes. *"Everything will be all right. But that does not mean I shall live, Angelica."*

Angelica looked pained at the dragon's statement, fighting to keep the corners of her mouth from curling downward. She looked to Tina, on the verge of tears. Her voice was weak and pleading. *"Please... help him."*

Tina looked at the wounds on the dragon's chest. She started walking to his underside, but the dragon blocked her with his arm.

"*Your intentions may be honorable, Wizard. But you cannot help me. And trying to do so would claim your power and your life.*" He put his arm down again.

Tina looked at the wounds again. From afar, they had been sickening. Up close, they murdered hope. She looked up at Angelica. "*I am sorry. But your master is right, Angelica. It would take divine intervention to heal your master's wounds.*"

Angelica clenched her teeth, her fangs tightly pressed against each other. "*No... master, please.*"

The dragon rumbled to Angelica comfortingly. "*Be still, dragon daughter.*" He opened his eyes and looked down at Tina. "*You are known to the Maldavians, Theorist. Why have you come, Tina van Schtoffen, to the site of my grave?*"

Tina walked around the dragon's head so he could rest it and still have her in his field of vision. "*I wished to aid you, if it were possible. But I came to this place because I am bound to discover what may be done about the monsters the Likonians call the Eaters of Dragons.*"

The dragon closed his eyes and snorted in derision. "*Eaters of Dragons. What fools these interlopers are.*" He opened his eyes and looked at Tina again. "*These Eaters of Dragons are more than that, Tina van Schtoffen. These creatures are devourers of magic.*"

Tina stepped forward and sat down. "*I know your wounds are great, Dragon Shalizan, but I need to learn of these Eaters of Magic.*"

"*Though it cost me my last breath,*" the dragon replied, "*I would tell you of them. But for what purpose do you take this offered knowledge?*"

Tina glanced back toward the woods when she heard movement. She saw Lazur leading Shasta and waved to him.

When he looked at her, she gestured for him to stay back and then turned back to the dragon. *"Dragon Shalizan, I have come to Likonia to investigate the origin of these Eaters of Magic. They threaten your All-Father. They threaten the Likonians. They threaten your kind."*

The dragon weakly chuckled. *"I will grant you knowledge if you will grant me a last request, Wizard. I've not the strength to cast a Ritual of Preservation on my Albatross. I ask that you do so once I have given you the knowledge you seek."*

Tina wiggled her whiskers. It took only a moment to consider. She had not the time to hesitate. *"It is agreed, Dragon Shalizan. I will cast a Ritual of Preservation on your Albatross, though I fear I cannot buy her a great deal of time."*

Angelica whimpered and dropped her halberd. She put her hand on top of her master's head. *"Please, master. Do not send me from your side. I would walk into the arms of Shahdazhan with you."*

"So you shall in time, dragon daughter. But I wish you to walk this world awhile longer." The dragon looked at Tina. *"What do you wish to know of the Eaters of Magic, Wizard?"*

Tina asked the most pressing question she could think of first. *"What do these monsters want here, Dragon Shalizan?"*

"They follow only what drives them, Wizard. They crave magic. They need it. In order to survive, they would devour all of Cerra if it kept them alive." The dragon made a sound like a cough combined with clearing his throat. *"It is not unreasonable for them to wish to continue their existence."*

"Where do they come from?"

"Magic they crave. From magic, they were born. Beyond that, I know only that they appeared from the east and have driven my people back to the Ring of Fire."

"Do you have any knowledge of how they may be overcome?"

The dragon grunted in pain. *"Had I, I would have used it to keep them from performing my evisceration. I know not how they may be slain. Magic will not bind them. Fire will not burn them. The strength of dragons cannot overcome them. They possess protection from every measure we Maldavians may summon. They are as colossal as we, but mindlessly driven."* The dragon looked down at Tina. *"A giant may not overcome a giant, but the giant who steps on a thorn may tumble down the mountain. Though we cannot touch them, perhaps you may find their weakness."*

Tina questioned that notion but withheld comment. She had another question to ask. *"How many of these Dragon Eaters are there?"*

"We have seen only three. Always the same three. A red-scaled male and two females, one with scales like moss and another with scales the color of the sun." The dragon closed his eyes, craning his neck. *"I fear my time has grown too short, Wizard. I ask you to cast the Ritual of Preservation on my Angelica."*

Tina wanted to ask more questions, but she would not risk denying the dragon's last request through inaction. She turned to look at Angelica. *"Are you willing to fulfill your master's last wish, Angelica?"*

Angelica had tears openly streaming down her cheeks by that time. She closed her eyes and hugged her master's head more tightly. Though she did not hold long, it was obvious she was reluctant to let go. *"I will."*

Tina looked back down at the dragon. *"Then I will perform the ritual now."*

The dragon looked up at the Albatross. *"I am too weak to aid you. Help the wizard to weave the spiral, Angelica."*

"I will, master."

The dragon closed his eyes as Angelica rose. Though Tina knew the Albatross's heart was breaking, she saw the mantle of control fall over the woman's face. Her eyes had become calm in spite of the tears, and the frown on her face had been replaced by an emotionless expression. Angelica drew the halberd from the ground and looked down at Tina. *"When you are ready."*

Tina nodded solemnly. While it was against her nature to aid someone in the grips of an emotional decision, time had been too short, and her promise had been the price to which she had agreed. *"Carve the spiral."* Tina looked at the dragon's head. *"I will require a drop of your blood, Dragon Shalizan."*

"I had expected as much." The dragon rolled his head to turn his face toward Tina. *"I will not have you suffer the sight of my wounds."* The dragon's jaw tightened, and a quiet crunch came from his mouth. He turned his head to show a drop of his blood on one of his second molars.

Tina withdrew a small, glass globe from the rucksack on her back. Twisting it, she pulled the top half off and held up the bottom half. The dragon jerked his head, and the drop of lava-colored blood fell from his tooth. Tina caught it in the glass orb, letting her hand sink to prevent any splash. She replaced the top half of the orb and twisted it shut. Her eyes returned to the dragon Shalizan. *"It is very likely that the performance of this ritual using your blood will claim what life you have left, Dragon Shalizan. Is there anything else you would have me do for you?"*

The dragon laid his head back down and closed his eyes. *"There is a dragon named Methystra in Maldavia, protected within the Ring of Fire. Once I have perished, I would wish for you to return to her and tell her my last thoughts were of her."*

Tina knew of the dragon Methystra. She nodded. *"She will know of your final thoughts, Dragon Shalizan."*

"You are compassionate, Wizard van Schtoffen. In the words of your Council of Stars, may the stars guide you."

"Though the soil defy you," Tina replied. She bowed her head to Shalizan. *"In the words of the Maldavians, the All-Father grant you grace, Dragon Shalizan."*

"Goodbye, Tina van Schtoffen." The dragon's body relaxed. His chest still slowly rose and fell, but she knew he would not rise again.

Tina lowered her head respectfully and turned away. By

the time she and the dragon had shared his last words, Angelica had completed the spiral required for the casting of the Ritual of Preservation. Tina inspected it, wanting to be sure that every detail was correct, lest she run the risk of something going wrong.

Using her halberd, Angelica had carved a rune into the open ground. The rune represented breath. Individual lines had been carved from the sides of the rune which led out in the four cardinal directions, though they curved around the other sides of the rune in a spiraling pattern. At specific spots on the spiraling lines significant to only a spell-caster, four more runes had been drawn.

Tina crossed each one, carefully stepping over the lines. The runes were drawn with practiced grace. Little more could be expected from the servant of a race of beings so thoroughly entwined with magic as the Maldavians.

Once her inspection was completed, Tina set the orb of Shalizan's blood down on the rune in the center of the spiral. She removed another from her rucksack and held it up toward Angelica. *"Your turn."*

Angelica looked down at the bottom half of the glass sphere. She knelt down as she lowered the tip of her halberd. She pricked her finger and squeezed a single drop of blood into the glass sphere. The Albatross's blood was similar to that of Shalizan's but in a deeper red hue.

Tina closed the glass sphere and walked to one side of the rune in the center of the spiral. She placed the two spheres down on the sides of the rune, one sphere on the northern side and the other on the western side. She then walked to the eastern side of the sphere and retrieved her metal wand. Using it, Tina traced a glyph into the ground, the symbol representing thought. On the southern face of the central rune, she inscribed one more rune which represented speech.

With the final runes drawn, Tina walked out of the spiral and seated herself in lotus position. She put the metal wand back into her rolled up kit. Pausing briefly to take a breath, Tina gathered her thoughts. The extensive lengths to which she had been using her gift for magic that day were starting to wear on her, even with the time she'd been allowed to meditate on the way to Lazur's farm.

Tina began multiplying the organic variable within her personal equation. Her eyes half opened, and she focused on the four runes drawn on the branches of the spiral. She placed a small portion of the result from her organic variable into each of the four runes, and magic wove a path back through the spiraling lines until it reached the two small, glass orbs. The glass orbs shook as Tina's magic reached them, and the orbs suddenly burst open. The blood within them seemed as though it had multiplied a thousand times as it followed the trail of Tina's magic back to the four glyphs drawn on the branches of the spiral. The blood filled the lines of the central rune for breath, flooded into the rune for speech, and then poured into that of thought.

"*The spiral is prepared.*" Tina turned her half-lidded gaze to Angelica. "*Place yourself within it.*"

Angelica looked back at the dragon Shalizan with her halberd still grasped in hand. The dragon seemed to sense it, and his head turned to gaze back at her. The two of them shared a long look before Angelica turned her head away and crossed into the center of the spiral.

Tina spoke calmly, but loudly. "*Ageless wonders of stars beyond number, heed my word and do not encumber. Delay you the cold hands of unfeeling death, render to this one a final breath. One thought, one word, one breath do we ask, enough for this one to fulfill a final task.*"

The four runes on the branches of the spiral glowed brightly with silver light which spread from the runes to flow through the branches of the spiral. Once they reached the three center runes, Angelica gasped as she was bathed in the silver glow.

Tina spoke again with her gaze focused on Angelica. "*Your*

word."

Angelica closed her eyes and released her breath in a quiet word. *"Who."*

Tina watched as the rune representing speech changed shape into the single word. She spoke again. *"Your thought."*

Angelica replied quietly. *"My master, Shalizan."*

Tina watched as the rune representing thought changed shape into the dragon's name. She spoke a final time in the casting of the spell. *"Bound you are to the conditions of this extension. Until the time comes, you will be held in detention. When you awake, and heed these words well, you will be afforded only the offerings of this spell. One thought, one word, one breath once returned. These gifts, use wisely. No more may be earned."*

Tina sucked in a deep breath and rose to her feet. The muscles of her body flexed, and she extended her hands. Drawing them together, she grasped the threads of magic woven into the branches of the spiral. The light coming from the runes on each of them grew more intense and bright, and silver lines rose out of the ground. The carved lines disappeared as each silver line of magical energy rose into the air.

They lashed around Angelica and inscribed her body with the runes each one held. Angelica closed her eyes as the glow of magic became blindingly bright. Tina's hands continued to weave in the air as the bright glow swirled around Angelica like light being sucked into a dark star. In a sudden flash, a spire of light ascended into the sky. The brightness blotted out the light of the sun, its glow so intense that Lazur and Shasta turned away.

The world was dark for an instant following the flash. The darkness faded in the light of the sun, and Tina fell to her knees, her hands resting in the dirt. She panted heavily. Her heart pounded in her chest, and she felt a few moments of panic as if she'd pushed herself too far. Tina could feel that her grip on her mind was starting to slip. She wanted to scream, but she clenched her jaw tightly shut, and her incisors pressed hard against her bottom lip. She thought she might bite clear through it.

After a few moments, Tina's breathing slowed, and she began to calm down. The pace of her breathing became more steady, and the pounding of her heart lessened. The feeling of panic slipped from her mind. The organic variable of her personal equation slowly stabilized. She felt herself coming back under control.

Shalizan let out a quiet groan, and his head fell to the ground with a dull impact. Tina looked to where the spiral had been drawn. It was gone. All that remained was a small, lava-colored crystal the size of Tina's palm and a pair of empty, glass spheres. The spell was complete.

Lazur turned back to survey the scene once the light had faded. He rested his hand on the back of Shasta's head, and the riding lizard turned to face Tina again. Lazur spoke quietly. "What in Ulfengir's name was that?"

Tina rose from the ground and collected her shawl in the crooks of her elbows. She walked to the crystal lying on the ground and picked it up. Opening her rolled up leather kit, she slid the crystal into a small pouch and closed it. She replied with a single word. "Dramatic." Tina wobbled on her feet before her legs gave out from under her, and she landed on her rear. "Oof."

Lazur grunted. He walked to Tina with Shasta following next to him. The riding lizard picked Tina up in her beak and lifted her carefully to place her onto the riding lizard's back. The stocky badger looked down at Tina. "You look like a ghost, wizard."

"I do not think I was far from becoming one." Tina sagged against the front of the saddle. "I need rest. Much more than meditation."

Lazur nodded. "I'll take you to my farm."

The sound of a distant roar suddenly echoed through the forest. Tina tiredly lifted her head. "That... is not a Maldavian."

Lazur climbed onto Shasta's back. "It's the Dragon Eaters.

On second thought, my farm may not be safe."

Tina lowered her head. "The Maldavians call the Dragon Eaters 'Eaters of Magic'. The spell probably attracted them. We need... to go."

Lazur nodded and looked down at Shasta as he took up her reins. "When you're ready."

Tina turned her thoughts to Shasta. She rested her hands on the lizard's back. The lizard sensed Tina's thoughts to return to Likonia with all possible haste. Shasta turned and ran with a hurried pace. Tina rested back against the saddle. "Thank you, Lazur."

The stocky badger looked down at Tina. "For what?"

"Protecting Shasta from the Albatross's halberd. The Maldavians... bless the weapons of their Albatrosses to purge magic." Tina closed her eyes. "Shasta would have been killed... and I would not have been able to bring her back."

Lazur grunted. "Was more habit than anything. You're welcome, either way."

Chapter 7

Tina awakened. Her eyes opened slowly. Her sleep had been dreamless. However long it had been in reality, it felt as though only an instant had passed in her mind. Though her body felt refreshed, she still felt mentally worn out. It would not do.

Rising from the bed, she realized she was still wearing her robes. She pulled them off, knowing that after all the crawling and trudging around in the dirt she had done they were filthy. She let them hang from the footboard of the bed. Seeing how dirty her robes were made her think she probably needed a bath as well. She tried to recall the events leading up to going to bed to figure out why she hadn't taken care of either of those things before sleeping. But her head hurt when she tried to concentrate.

Tina crossed her legs into lotus position on the bed and closed her eyes. She took in a deep breath and slowly let it out. For awhile, she needed to think of absolutely nothing. The tuft of fur on the end of her tail flopped slowly back and forth with the calm beat of a metronome. Her mind remained dark as she breathed with a steady, slow pace. She let her grip slip away freely to abandon higher thoughts so her mind could do what it needed to recover.

Time became imperceptible as she drifted into the hypnopompic space between the waking world and dreams.

* * *

"The Jirai Wyrm has only one natural predator in the world." *An old, grey-furred Kylathian male let his eyes scan across his small*

71

procession of students.

Tina had been introduced to the older feline by her former master. He'd left her in parting with the words, "Master Gri'end is the foremost mind with knowledge of the creatures roaming this world, Tina. Note him well."

Tina had at first wondered why she needed to learn about the various creatures of the world of Cerra Sevatia. But in the time she'd spent in Master Gri'end's tutelage, she had come to learn many valuable lessons from the various beasts of which he'd spoken.

"Culthis Majori is a creature with a cone-shaped head, a long, snake-like body, and a pair of glaive-bearing arms protruding from its body approximately a foot below its head. It has a particular skill which has come to protect it from the Jirai Wyrm's hunting method."

One of the other students raised his hand. "Master, what's a Jirai Wyrm?"

Master Gri'end scrutinized the student for a moment, then his eyebrows lifted. "Ah, yes. Nordis, isn't it? You were sick for our lesson on the Jirai Wyrm last session. Can anyone tell Nordis about the Jirai Wyrm?"

Another student raised her hand. "The Jirai Wyrm can grow to ten meters in length with a two meter girth. It tunnels underground and hunts its prey by digging holes for them to fall into. Then it swallows them whole and burrows deeper into the ground to let its food digest."

"Very good, Tessa." Master Gri'end ticked a finger in the air. "But Culthis Majori, or in terms of the layperson, the glaive snake, detects these Jirai Wyrms by feeling their movement through the soil. When it finds a Jirai Wyrm's trap, it uses its glaives to collapse the hole. The Jirai Wyrm then comes and eats the glaive snake." Master Gri'end tapped the side of his muzzle. "Once capturing its potential prey, it takes its meal down into the ground."

"Inside the Jirai Wyrm, the glaive snake coats itself in a layer of mucus which protects it from the Jirai Wyrm's stomach acids.

It will then proceed to use its glaives to tear the Jirai Wyrm apart from the inside out." Master Gri'end chuckled. "Always a lesson to remember; be careful of what you eat. With the Jirai Wyrm slain, the glaive snake has enough food to feed it for a month."

* * *

Tina opened her eyes and blinked several times. She didn't know how long she'd been meditating, but the effect of it had been significant and immediately noticeable. She thought clearly, and her memory of the previous day was returning to her. After casting the Ritual of Preservation, she had asked Lazur to bring her back to the Stumble Drum so she could rest. Tina had entered into her pocket quarters and collapsed in bed without the energy to even undress.

Having met with the Maldavian and discovered more about the Dragon Eaters, she decided it was time to introduce herself to the governor. But first, she wanted to wash up and clean her robes.

Tina threw her legs over the side of the bed and opened one of the drawers to pull out a simple, grey cloth slip. Pulling it on over her head, she collected her robe and removed her armlets, necklace, and ring. She picked up her belt as well and stowed all of her personal jewelry in the drawer from which she'd taken the slip.

Looking down at her necklace, Tina retrieved it from the drawer. She noted the empty socket which usually held the door handle for her quarters. Recalling the crystal produced by the Ritual of Preservation, she retrieved her leather spell kit and opened it. She removed the precious, lava-colored crystal. She wanted to keep it safe. There wasn't a need to take it outside her quarters while she bathed, but afterward, she would want it close.

Tina put the crystal against the necklace and closed both hands around them. It took a little concentration and a touch of her magic, but when she opened her hands again, the crystal was fitted into the necklace as if they'd been crafted for each other. She set the necklace back into the drawer and closed it.

After grabbing her rucksack, Tina walked out of her pocket quarters and onto the counter of the Stumble Drum. She took a moment to observe who might be up, also wanting to know the time of day. The light of the stars and moon came through the windows, and the only patrons inside the Stumble Drum consisted of one passed out weasel in a far corner and the familiar black bull whom Tina had met at the docks. The bull was drinking from a mug at the far end of the counter and didn't seem to notice Tina. A badger woman was roaming the tavern with a mop as she cleaned the floor while the rabbit woman Tina had met was putting chairs on the tables upside down.

The mink who had been behind the counter that morning emerged from the door leading to the kitchen. He was carrying a tall, broad pan which he set on the counter. He deposited a couple of mugs and wooden plates and bowls from the counter into the pan and carried them back through the door.

Tina crossed the counter with her robes over her arm and perched at the edge in wait for the mink. When he emerged again, she called to him. "Mr. Kilba."

The mink lifted his head and looked around for who might have called him. Tina had to call for him again before he was able to focus on her tiny figure. He set the pan down on the counter next to her and wiped his hands. "Ah, Wizard. I hope you're feeling better. Lazur was concerned about you." The mink scratched the back of his neck. "Wouldn't have thought he'd give any kind of care about a wizard."

Tina pulled her glasses from the bridge of her muzzle to fold them up. "None of the people here are too fond of wizards, it seems."

The mink seemed confused for a moment, but then nodded his head. "Oh, yes, well, there isn't much favor for wizards

74

in Likonia because of the High Theorist's decision, but Lazur has more reason to dislike wizards than the rest of us."

Tina wrinkled her muzzle. "What do you mean?"

Mr. Kilba hesitated. "Ah. Well, maybe it's something he'd be the one to ask about. But, I digress." The mink clasped his hands. "Was there something you wanted, Wizard?"

Tina wiggled her whiskers. "There is, in fact. I wonder if you wouldn't mind selling me one of your wash bowls. I need something to take a bath in." Tina set her glasses on her robes. "I'd ask to borrow one, but I don't believe your patrons would thank you for washing dishes in a bowl someone had bathed in."

"Ah, that's probably right." The mink scratched his chin. "But since you've paid for a room here, it's kind of included in the cost." He shrugged. "I don't think we'll miss one wash bowl."

"I see." Tina gave a friendly smile to the mink. "It's appreciated, Mr. Kilba."

"Not at all. Ah, where would you like it set up?"

Tina pointed toward the stairs. "Just set it next to my door, if you would, with a cloth so I can cover it for some privacy."

The mink nodded his head. "Have it for you in a moment, Wizard." He turned and walked back into the kitchen.

Tina watched him leave and was about to walk back to the stairs when she remembered the bull sitting at the far end of the counter. She recalled that his name was Kravek. The fact he was drinking at this late hour gave some credence to his foreman's frustration over his "praying to the pier," even if he hadn't been correct about the situation at the time. It struck her as odd. Her exchange with Kravek hadn't left her with the impression of him being a heavy drinker. He had been pleasant, friendly, and helpful. Yet, she saw him drinking very heavily from his mug.

The mink returned with the bowl and placed it under the stairs with a cloth over top. He turned to Tina and wiped his hands. "Anything else I can get for you, Wizard?"

Tina shook her head. "No thank you, Mr. Kilba. Your

hospitality is greatly appreciated. Though, if you could answer a question, I would appreciate it."

The mink nodded. "Of course."

Tina gestured toward Kravek. "Is he always here this late?"

Mr. Kilba looked at Kravek and nodded. "Yes, Wizard. He has a room here, actually. Drinks a lot, but never causes any trouble."

Tina thought to ask more about the black bull, but she was beginning to feel nosy, and it occurred to her that it might be rude to be asking about him particularly when he was only a few yards away. Having taken on the role as an investigator, being nosy had become a habit. But inquiries of a personal nature didn't fall under the job of an investigator. She gave the mink a smile. "Thank you, Mr. Kilba. That's all I need."

The mink nodded, retrieved his pan, and returned to collecting dishes and mugs from the counter and nearby tables.

Tina thought to go speak with Kravek and thank him for his treatment of her that morning on the docks. But she wasn't exactly dressed for casual conversation, needed a bath, and needed to wash her clothes. She walked back to the bowl of water and disappeared under the cloth laid over top of it. Once undressed, Tina climbed into the bowl of water. She noted that Mr. Kilba had only put in enough water to reach halfway up her shins while she stood. It was just right.

Tina pulled the cloth over top of the bowl, covering it up again and concealing her from the rest of the tavern. She had just started washing herself when she heard the door to the Stumble Drum swing open. The sound of heavy, armored footsteps entered the dining area. Tina kept one ear turned back toward the door to listen, but otherwise continued to wash. The armored boots approached the bar, and Tina heard Mr. Kilba's voice. The name he spoke made Tina pause.

"Captain Cephalin," Tina noted the hint of anxiety in the mink's voice as he spoke, "what brings you to the Stumble Drum at this late hour?"

"I have been informed," the wolverine began, "the wizard from the Council of Stars is staying here."

Tina wrinkled her nose. Only a few people from Likonia knew she was at the Stumble Drum. From the look of it, the rabbit woman, the badger woman, and Mr. Kilba had a busy evening. She imagined only one other person would have told Captain Cephalin of her whereabouts. After the conversation she'd had with Lazur, it surprised her that he would have told the wolverine. On the other hand, she didn't know a great deal about Lazur, and as Mr. Kilba had said, he had more reason than other Likonians to distrust wizards.

"Ah, yes. She's staying here, but with all due respect, I don't think this is the hour to be disturbing her, Captain."

Tina heard a thud from one of the armored boots and felt an impact on the bar. She pushed the cloth from one side of the bowl so she could see what had caused it. The captain of the guard was holding the mink's shirt and had him all but pulled across the counter, the claws of his metal gauntlet tearing the fabric.

"With all due respect to your patrons, Kilba," Captain Cephalin's words dripped with malice, "I could not care less about the hour. She was supposed to report to the governor upon her arrival. It is long past the time the ship carrying her arrived. So I will disturb her regardless of the hour if I have to snap your key ring from your belt and wake every patron in this inn searching rooms for her."

The mink looked terrified that the wolverine would make good on his promise and beat Kilba to a pulp beforehand without a moment's hesitation. From the look of the wolverine, he'd probably do it again afterward just for good measure. Tina decided she should intervene, regardless of her state of dress.

Before she could, Tina saw the black bull stand at the end of the bar. The sound of his hooves on the floorboards of the dining area was as distinctive as the wolverine's boots had been.

Kravek gripped the wolverine's wrist, pushing his fingers against spots where only chain mail covered rather than plates. The wolverine's fingers slackened as he was forced to release the mink.

"Not a need for that, sir." Kravek ushered the wolverine's arm back from the mink and let go of his wrist.

Captain Cephalin turned and glowered at the black bull. "Are you looking for another night in the stocks for public drunkenness, Akoan?"

"No, sir. But the wizard is preoccupied."

Tina blinked. She didn't think Kravek had taken notice of her speaking with Kilba, let alone to have heard what she had asked. In spite of the clarity with which he spoke, Tina could see slack in the bull's stance common to someone who was inebriated.

Captain Cephalin sneered. "You know, Akoan, you're about due for another stint in the stocks." The wolverine punched the metal gauntlet against his palm, the resulting sound a metallic clank. "Another charge of public drunkenness and impeding a guard in his duties are plenty justification."

Kravek stared at the wolverine dully for a moment. He didn't look ready to react to anything, let alone to be able to put up a fight. Once more, Tina felt it was time to intervene. But what happened next startled her.

The wolverine swung at the apparently drunk bull, but Kravek moved with the ease of a trained soldier. He turned his shoulders so the punch glanced one side of his chest while he slapped the wolverine's armored shoulder with a massive hand. Even his bare fist left the metal ringing. It threw the captain of the guard off balance, forcing him to overextend. Kravek gripped the slapped shoulder and with a yank, slammed the wolverine into a quickly rising knee.

The resounding clang from the wolverine's breastplate almost hurt Tina's ears. Kravek tossed the wolverine backward, sending him stumbling. Cephalin looked down at his breastplate and noted the dent in the front left by the powerful bull's knee. He looked up at Kravek with a smirk.

"Assaulting a guard. You'll be in the stocks for a month, Akoan." The wolverine, armed with the knowledge that Kravek wasn't as drunk as he appeared, opened his fists to reveal the metal claws. He didn't seem intimidated by the bull's ability to dent his armor.

Just as he was about to lunge for Kravek, Tina pulled herself out of the bowl and quickly yanked the cloth from the top of it to cover herself. She then clapped her hand around her throat and loudly cried out. "That's enough!"

The wolverine paused at the sudden shout and looked back over his shoulder. He blinked at the sight of Tina. And blinked again. "What in Cerra's name...?" In spite of his perplexed state, he still looked ready to deliver a rake of his claws to the black bull.

"Captain Idori Cephalin," Tina spoke, holding the cloth wrapped around her as she walked across the bar, "this is far more than is necessary for keeping the peace. I am Theorist Tina van Schtoffen, Wizard of the Council of Stars."

The wolverine finally lowered his hand. He turned around to look at Tina with his back facing Kravek. "You were supposed to report to the governor on arrival, Wizard van Schtoffen. Is there a reason you did not?"

"I was supposed to report to your governor at my convenience, Captain. Or has your governor decided to start making up my orders from the High Theorist just as he's making up promises from the king?" Tina stopped several feet away from the wolverine. "I was in the middle of taking a bath. Out of courtesy to me, Mr. Kilba informed you it was not a good time to disturb me."

The wolverine lifted his hand and pointed a metal claw at Tina. "Courtesy would have led you to the governor when you arrived here."

"Judgment led me not to introduce myself when I found him. I am not obliged to your governor, nor you in any way. Your governor asked for a wizard to investigate this situation, and unless Harkon Keldo is as forgetful as he is a liar, this investigation is to be conducted with his help, not his permission or guidance." Tina reached up to adjust her glasses but realized she wasn't wearing them and just rubbed the bridge of her muzzle. "Once I finished bathing, I was prepared to leave for the governor's home to inform him of my arrival, nothing more or less."

The wolverine sneered at Tina, but held his tongue in check. He turned his head for an instant, noted Kravek's position behind him, and abruptly stabbed his elbow upward. The black bull's head pitched back suddenly when the armor-clad elbow slammed right into the space between Kravek's chin and throat. The bull fell to the ground with a heavy crash. Sprawled out on his back, Kravek's head lulled to one side.

Captain Cephalin smirked. He looked back down at Tina. "See that you do. I have to take this disturber of the peace to the stocks."

Tina glared at the wolverine. "That was not necessary."

The wolverine shrugged. "But it was lawful." He tapped the dent in his breastplate with a metal claw and then looked at Kilba. "On second thought, send for a couple of guards to retrieve this lummox." He then turned to look down at Tina on the counter top. "Get dressed, wizard. I will escort you to the governor's house."

Tina wasn't happy with Kravek being arrested for interceding on her behalf. As she headed for her door under the stairs, she resolved to do something about it.

Chapter 8

"Come in."

Captain Cephalin pushed the door open in front of Tina and gestured with his gauntlet-clad hand for her to enter. She stepped inside with the expectation that the captain would follow her, but a voice from the high-back chair settled in front of the fireplace changed that notion.

"Thank you for coming, Theorist. Please, have a seat." Governor Keldo's orange tail gestured to the other high-back chair across from him. "Captain, please wait outside."

Captain Cephalin looked down at Tina, wrinkled his muzzle, then turned and closed the door behind him.

Tina walked to the chair to which she had been directed and climbed its corner nimbly. Seating herself in tailor style, she bowed her head to the governor. "I apologize for the late hour and for not coming to see you sooner, Governor."

Keldo straightened up in his chair and put his hands down on the armrests. He looked startled by Tina's appearance. But he leaned back in his chair a moment later and steepled his fingers together in front of him. "I admit to some surprise at your appearance, Theorist," he smiled at her, "but I also think you must be an extremely talented wizard for High Theorist Mythran to send you to deal with this situation. May I offer you anything before we get down to business?"

Tina shook her head. "I appreciate the offer, Governor, but I think it would be best to get straight to the material." When the governor nodded, Tina adjusted her glasses. "My name is Tina van Schtoffen, Governor. I am an investigative theorist working for the Council of Stars, and I have come, in accordance with the request you made of the High Theorist, to find out what I can about these Dragon Eaters and recommend to the High Theorist a procedural course to resolve the situation they have caused here in Likonia. It would be in the best interest of all if I could find a resolution which would suit the people of Likonia as well as the Maldavians."

Keldo nodded. "I agree. Though the Maldavians have been somewhat adversarial to our presence, perhaps this common enemy would help everyone to see things from a more objective perspective."

Tina folded her hands into her lap. "Perhaps. But my job right now concerns only the Dragon Eaters." She removed her glasses from the bridge of her muzzle and used the edge of her robe to clean them. "It has come to my attention that there was a wizard in Likonia before me. Were you aware of this?"

Keldo bowed his head. "I was. It was an unfortunate matter and one of my own doing." He straightened to lean back in the chair. "I enlisted the wizard before the Dragon Eaters appeared for several reasons, most of which had to do with agriculture and advice concerning the Maldavians. Since the Council of Stars had gone so far as to prevent aid from the king, I believed I would need to seek out a wizard not attached to the council."

Tina slid her glasses back onto the bridge of her muzzle. "Why did you believe you needed a wizard at all?"

"At first, I did not." Keldo sat up in his chair and rested one hand on his knees while he gestured at Tina with the other. "The wizard approached me when he heard I was recruiting retired guards and ex-military for protection in Likonia. We spoke awhile, and after having a conversation with him, I believed him trustworthy even though he was an Idassian."

"Idassian wizards are as welcome as any other in Levansia," Tina replied, "but because of Idassia's adversarial relationship with Madrigaarde, Levansia's closest ally, they tend to be educated by another more dangerous entity in their homeland rather than come to us. Were you aware of that, Governor?"

"I am and was at the time. Being aware of the political climate involves more than just knowing who's trying to stab who in the back." The governor chuckled. He leaned back again and steepled his fingers with his hands resting on his stomach. "But I was desperate for help. And while I was aware he was attached to the cult in Idassia, he seemed reasonable and helpful enough. So I hired him."

Tina wiggled her whiskers. The governor was being a little more forthcoming than she had expected. When she'd heard Lazur's description of the wizard's attire, she suspected he was part of the cult. But the governor had known all along. Putting that thought into the back of her mind for the moment, she proceeded. "Would you be willing to tell me a little of the wizard's activities here in Likonia after his arrival?"

The governor frowned. "I would, Lady van Schtoffen, but I'm afraid that the wizard's activities in town were fairly limited. He spent most of his time working in a wizard's tower some distance north of the town. I'm not aware of what he was doing there, but I do know he was able to augment our crop growth, and he was glad to lend the assistance of his assistants to farms which needed extra hands."

Tina's eyebrows rose, and her ears swiveled toward the governor. "Assistants?"

Keldo nodded. "Yes. A pair of Kamadene women came with the wizard when he arrived on the Water Walker. They were both very kind and helpful but also very quiet. Unfortunately, I have not seen them since the wizard was killed by the Dragon Eaters."

Tina's ears twitched as a thought occurred to her. "You mentioned a wizard's tower, but I saw no tower to the north when I arrived in the city."

"Yes, I could not see a tower to the north either," Keldo

spread his hands, "but that is where he said he was when I inquired. I just assumed it must have been set up in the caves along the cliff farther north. It's only a few hours walk to get to them, but they face away from the harbor." He inclined his head to the north. "If you wish to verify the tower's existence, I would appreciate it as well. Should it be in the caves, you can find a path down the cliff side which leads to the largest one on the northern side of the cliffs."

Tina nodded. "I would like to take a look, at least." Tina laid her tail across her lap and curled the tuft of fur on the end of it against the back of her hands. "If I may, Governor, there's another matter I'd like to address."

"Anything, Wizard."

"The Akoan, Kravek Rivakian, was arrested earlier tonight." When Keldo simply nodded his head, Tina became curious. "This doesn't surprise you?"

"It does not," he replied. "Unfortunately, the Akoan has been known to cause a disturbance now and again. As I understand it from Mr. Kilba, the Akoan likes to drink a fair bit."

"If it's a common problem," Tina wrinkled her muzzle, "why do you allow it to continue?"

The governor sighed. "There are many things I need to consider when upholding the law here in Likonia, Lady van Schtoffen. One of those considerations includes the fact that the Akoan has been invaluable to our docks. He is incredibly strong and able to move crates and large items by himself and without the aid of a crane." He tapped his fingers together and then folded his hands into his lap. "His size also makes it difficult to stop him from doing much. He's been arrested a handful of times for drunkenness, and on one or two occasions, for damaging a guard's armor."

"You seem to know his activities well."

Keldo nodded. "He does stand out. And his activities have warranted my personal attention." He waved his hand dismissively. "One way or another, he doesn't cause enough trouble to warrant banishment or prolonged incarceration. And when he hasn't been drinking, he is quite amiable. Even when he dented a few breastplates, he put in the labor at the blacksmith's to repair them."

Tina thought that sounded a bit more like the Kravek she'd met on the docks. She shook her head. It had occurred to her to suggest a course of action, but it wasn't her place to tell the governor how to handle his law enforcement. "I see."

Keldo leaned forward. "Why do you bring it up, if I may ask?"

"I wanted to ask if he could be released from his punishment."

The governor's eyebrows shot up. "I'm afraid that would be counterproductive. And as there are no ships arriving in the next few days, and the Thorn's Side has been unloaded, his muscle will not be needed at the docks." He rubbed his chin. "I just hope he will take to it this time."

Tina rubbed her incisors against her bottom lip in thought. "Governor, if this method of punishment has not worked before, do you really believe it will work this time?"

Keldo shrugged. "Some nails take more strokes of the hammer to drive into place."

"Perhaps," Tina replied as she adjusted her glasses, "but there is an old saying that doing something again and again and expecting different results is insanity." She held her hand up. "I don't mean to be insulting, so please don't think I mean to imply such." Her hand returned to her lap. "But if I may, I'd like to have Kravek released." She cleared her throat. "Partly because I think I may be able to offer an alternative, and partly because I believe I am somewhat to blame for his misconduct tonight."

The governor raised one eyebrow in curiosity. "How so?"

Tina rested her elbows on her thighs and leaned forward. "Kravek stepped forward to intervene on my behalf because Captain Cephalin was being a little too enthusiastic with Mr. Kilba in trying to find me at the Stumble Drum. Had I stepped forward more quickly, the entire incident might have been avoided."

Keldo turned to look at the fire burning in the fireplace. "Perhaps. If you would like to claim responsibility for his actions, though," he looked back at Tina, "you will also need to claim responsibility for him in the days following."

She nodded. "I understand. And, if you agree, I'd like to offer Kravek the job of accompanying me as a guide while I'm here."

"I can understand the desire, but I would prefer it if a guard accompanied you." He glanced over his shoulder toward the front door. "Though I could understand if you didn't want Captain Cephalin."

"Actually," Tina rose to her feet, "if it's possible, I'd like Lieutenant Copaire to accompany me."

Governor Keldo looked surprised. "You know of the Lieutenant?"

"I saw her earlier in the day in town and watched her briefly." Tina swept her tail behind her. "She left a good impression."

"You're quite the watcher, Lady van Schtoffen, a trait which is likely helpful in your duties as an investigator." He tapped his fingers together, but his answer came more swiftly than Tina expected. "Very well. Kravek and Lieutenant Copaire will accompany you while you are here."

Tina hesitated for a moment over how quickly the governor had agreed, but nodded. "Thank you, Governor. I hope, with your help, to settle this matter of the Dragon Eaters swiftly."

The governor smiled. It was that same smile Tina had seen when he was talking to the townspeople, and it made her tail twitch uncomfortably. "As do I, Lady van Schtoffen. As do I."

* * *

Captain Cephalin pulled the key out of the lock holding the stocks around Kravek's wrists and ankles. He pushed the stocks open and glanced at Tina. "I'll inform Lieutenant Copaire of her new duties." Without giving Tina time to reply, he turned and walked toward the front gate.

Tina watched the wolverine depart, then looked up at Kravek as he rose from the stocks. "Feeling all right?"

Kravek rubbed his wrists. "I've been in the stocks before. I'll be all right." He took a step and stumbled against the side of the stocks, fumbling his attempt to grab for them to keep himself standing. "Oof."

Tina adjusted her glasses. "I suppose that answers that question."

Kravek pulled himself up with a hand on the stock and set his feet. He took in a deep breath and then blew it out. "Hoo. Nothing like ale to soften a guy's hooves."

Tina folded her arms across her stomach. "Are you going to be all right to walk?"

Kravek took a moment to get his bearings. Removing his hand from the stocks, he settled down onto his haunches and balanced on his hooves. "I'm all right. Just disoriented after being bent over in the stocks for awhile." He gestured to Tina. "But why?"

"Why did I get them to release you?" Tina walked to Kravek's hand and jumped up to take a hold of one of his thick fingers. Pulling herself up, she climbed into his palm. "For a few reasons, one of which is feeling a little responsible for you getting in trouble this evening." She waved a hand in front of her nose at the smell of alcohol still lingering in the bull's fur. "Though I've been told you wind up in the stocks more often than most."

Kravek sighed. "It happens. Don't feel responsible, though." He stood up and placed Tina onto his shoulder. "I'm the one who dented Cephalin's armor."

"I suppose. But I also came because I'd like to offer you

a job." Tina folded her legs beneath her and seated herself on Kravek's shoulder. "Do you have any plans for the next day or two?"

Kravek scratched the side of his chin. "Nothing worth the time." His hand moved under it to rub the sore spot where he'd been elbowed. "There's no work at the dock right now. What kind of work are you offering?" He let his hand fall back to his side as he glanced at Tina on his shoulder.

"In effect, to be my legs for a bit." Tina smiled and wiggled her whiskers. "I need to leave the city and head north tomorrow. If you don't mind doing my walking for me, I'll pay you for your time."

Kravek swept the tuft of fur on the end of his tail around and slapped it against his side. "You want me to get something for you up north?"

Tina shook her head. "Oh, no. I'll be accompanying you. I'd just be riding on your shoulder, much like I am now." She smiled up at him.

"So... you just want me to walk?" He tilted his head and looked down at her.

"That's about the size of it." She pushed her glasses up along the bridge of her muzzle. "I need to go to a cave north of town. Lieutenant Copaire will be accompanying us as well."

Kravek folded his arms. "Are you going to Dragon's Mouth?"

Tina wrinkled her muzzle. "I'm not familiar with that name."

Kravek pointed to the north with his thumb. "A group of caves on the cliffs facing the sea."

Tina nodded. "That sounds like the caves the governor described."

"I know how to get there. And since I'm free," Kravek grabbed one of his horns and turned his head to one side until a pop came from his neck. He sighed in relief, "I'll take you there.

As far as pay goes, if we're going to be gone long, something to eat for lunch will do."

Tina smiled. "I think I can manage that. In the meantime, you should get some rest for the walk. Would you mind taking me back to the Stumble Drum?"

Kravek shook his head. "Course not. I'm staying there myself." He turned and walked down the road leading back to the Stumble Drum.

While Kravek walked, Tina thought. It was strange to her that Kravek was proving to be as helpful as he was and yet maintained a reputation for being a heavy drinker among the guards as well as his employer. She wondered over the reason or if there even was one. "Kravek, I have to ask. Why is it you have garnered the reputation of a heavy drinker?"

Kravek flicked one of his large, floppy ears. There were long moments of silence before he finally answered, and the Akoan looked uncomfortable doing so. "I drink a lot when there's no work."

"Have you always been a heavy drinker?"

"No."

When Kravek offered no further explanation, Tina took a moment to examine his expression. His jaw was set tight, and the muscles were flexing. His eyes were turned intently forward on the road ahead, and his expression was dark. Tina decided not to press the matter. Whether he was a heavy drinker was a personal issue, and she didn't want to pry.

As Kravek and Tina approached the front of the Stumble Drum, the last of the lights on the inside of the inn were being put out. The badger woman Tina had seen mopping the floor of the dining area was throwing out her mop water before she disappeared through the front doors. Tina was surprised when Kravek stopped before the doors.

"I don't know if you have any notion to care, Tina, but I have been drinking because it helps me." Kravek looked at the mouse wizard on his shoulder. "There are things I came to this place to forget."

Tina wiggled her whiskers. "I can understand wanting to leave things behind, Kravek. But don't you think there might be a better way to do it?"

"I function and I work. For now, that is enough." Kravek pushed on the door to let himself into the Stumble Drum.

"Wait a moment, Kravek." Tina took hold of one of Kravek's ears and pulled herself up to the top of his head. She seated herself, leaning forward onto her hands so that she could look down over his brow. "Where do you plan to go from here? Are you staying in Likonia for the duration?"

Kravek looked up at Tina perched over his brow. "It's comfortable enough."

Tina waited for further comment, but none came. "So that's it, then?"

Kravek sighed. "There isn't much else for me, Tina." He lifted his hand to rub a spot on top of his head next to Tina. "I just... don't know what else to do. I want to do more. But... I feel like I just need time."

Tina ran her fingers through Kravek's hair in a comforting manner. She felt as though she wanted to rub his shoulders, but she hardly had the reach. Instead, she scratched the spot where Kravek was rubbing. "I know the feeling, Kravek. I don't mean to be prying. You just seem like a good man to me." Tina leaned over so she could scratch the back of one of Kravek's large ears. "I knew another good man who got lost in his sorrows and drank himself into the grave."

Kravek took a step back from the door and tilted his head a little to raise the ear Tina scratched. "If I go to my grave, it won't be surrounded by a sea of ale." He closed his eyes. "Thanks. That feels good."

Tina giggled. "You're very welcome. You know Kravek, for being drunk, you don't seem to be all that impaired."

"Impaired?" Kravek stepped toward the door again, but his hoof caught the edge of one of the floorboards on the porch. He tried to bring his hands up to catch himself, but before he could stop, the black bull's horns slammed right into the door and imbedded themselves deeply.

Tina snapped forward sharply, but managed to grab Kravek's ear. The force of his trip swung her out wildly, and she just missed hitting the door. She clung tightly to Kravek's ear as she dangled in the air next to his muzzle.

Kravek tried to pull his head back, but his horns were too deeply buried in the wood. He looked at Tina hanging beside his head. "Tarsus, that was close. Are you all right?"

"Close!?" Tina opened her eyes and looked at the door just inches away. "Any closer and I'd be a lot thinner!"

"Sorry." Kravek tried to jerk his head back again, but the wood simply wouldn't give. "Uh… I think I'm stuck."

Tina climbed up Kravek's ear and onto one of his horns. The angle at which his head was tilted made it difficult to walk down safely, but she managed to scoot herself to where the door and Kravek's horns met. She adjusted her glasses on the bridge of her nose, glad they hadn't completely fallen off. "You're jammed in pretty deep, Kravek."

"Well, I am big. A lot of weight behind me when I fall." He put his hands on the wall and started to pull back.

Tina could hear the wood creaking. She waved her hands at him. "Wait, wait. If you pull out now, you're going to break something. Just give me a minute." The wizard turned back to face the door so she could examine the wood again.

Kravek stopped pulling. "Can't you just magic me out or something?"

"Magic is not a cure-all, Kravek. I can use a spell to get you out, but I might cause more damage to the door or your horns in the process." She made her way back up along his horn and climbed into his hair. "You know, Kravek, I think you're stuck here for the rest of your life."

Kravek cocked one eyebrow. "You're kidding."

"Well, at least until someone opens the door." She held one hand up and drew a finger across it. "Maybe they'll cut your head off." Tina giggled.

Kravek rolled his eyes. "I'd rather just make them a new door."

Tina smiled. "I'll have you out in a second." The runic circle appeared in Tina's right lens as she examined the door. If she was going to get Kravek out, she could either compress the cracks and have them force Kravek's horns out or widen them and risk the cracks growing into a split. Since the second solution meant Kravek could keep his horns, she decided to widen them. "All right, try pulling back while I do this."

Tina lifted her hands in front of her and crossed her wrists. She focused on the disturbed equations around the cracks in the door and drew on her gift. Casting it into those equations, she slowly increased the size of the cracks while Kravek pulled back. In a few seconds, she heard the whining groan of the wood before Kravek's head pulled free.

But the bull's balance was not as sound as Tina would have liked, and she lost her focus as Kravek stumbled backward and landed flat on his back. Tina flipped in the air a few times before landing on his chest flat on her back as well.

"Oof." Kravek mumbled as he rubbed his head. "Maybe I should lay off the ale."

Tina sat up and carefully searched for her glasses. "Truly an epiphany, Kravek."

He chortled as she ran her fingers through the fur on his chest. "Trying to make me laugh?"

Tina thumped his chest with her fist. "Hold still, Kravek. I dropped my glasses." He stopped laughing and let out a slow sigh, holding his breath. With Kravek's chest still, Tina felt her fingers brush against her glasses and picked them up. She put them back on her muzzle. "Found them."

Kravek started breathing again. "I'm sorry, Tina."

Tina walked up Kravek's chest and prodded the underside of his chin. "We'll live. Head inside. I'm going to fix the door."

He tilted his head to look down at her. "Want some help?"

Tina curled the corner of her mouth. "Thanks, but I think you just need to lie down. I want to fix the door, not finish the job of breaking it."

Kravek waited for Tina to climb off him and sat up. He sighed before pushing himself to his feet. Tina thought she saw an odd hint of sadness in Kravek's eyes before he pulled the door open and went inside.

Chapter 9

While Tina closed the holes which Kravek had left in the door of the Stumble Drum, she couldn't help but let her thoughts drift to the Akoan. He seemed like a kind enough man, but with his strength and size, he could be a real danger if he wished to be. Her thoughts turned to how easily Kravek had put a dent into a metal breastplate with his bare hands and the help of a knee.

"He's a good man." A low, feminine voice came from the end of the porch in front of the Stumble Drum.

Tina lowered her hands and looked for the source of the voice. Standing at the end of the porch was the badger woman who had been cleaning the floor and had just thrown out her mop water. Tina turned her attention back to the door. "He's a good man. There have been a lot of broken hearts preceded by that phrase."

"I'd bet I've seen more of those than you have," the badger woman replied. She walked around the porch to the steps with a burning lantern in hand and seated herself. Producing a short, cob pipe from her apron, the badger stuffed it and then removed the cover from the lantern.

After lighting a small stick with the lantern flame, she lit her pipe. "But he really is. He's just fallen on hard times. Any of the Akoans who are left would be just as wounded, don't you think?"

Tina's ears stood up. She lowered her hands and turned her head to look at the badger. "...left?"

The badger woman pulled the pipe from her lip and narrowed her eyes at Tina. "So you don't know. I would have thought a wizard of all people would be aware." The badger slapped her knee. "Here Ol' Willa Hodgis knows something a wizard doesn't." Willa grinned, putting the end of her pipe between her teeth.

Tina rolled her eyes. She walked to the edge of the porch and seated herself with her arms folded across her middle. The smell of tobacco from the woman's pipe urged Tina to stay on the far end of the steps. "What do you mean 'left'?"

Willa's smug expression turned serious, and she shifted her pipe to the corner of her mouth. "Idassia attacked the Akoan hill country a year ago. The Braka turned on the Akoans." Willa pulled her pipe from her mouth and blew the smoke into the air away from Tina. "And he's all I've seen left of his people. The news of it spread as far as Levansia. I'm a little surprised you didn't hear about it."

Tina felt the warmth drain from her body. She had known Akoans over the course of her life. The thought that all of them were suddenly gone was something hard to believe. "That can't be. The Akoans were a race of warriors. Even Idassia could not overcome the Akoans on their own."

Willa put her pipe back into her mouth. "A proud race of warriors, Wizard. They would have fought to the last." She pulled the pipe from her mouth again, using it to gesture back toward the Stumble Drum. "Almost, it seems."

"How can you be so certain of this?"

"You've seen that Kravek drinks. One night, when he was drinking very hard, he spoke of his troubles to me." She folded her arms across her stomach. "Can you imagine what it would be like to lose everyone you ever knew? And not just to lose them for awhile. To lose them forever."

Tina looked away from Willa. The wizard rubbed her arms as she felt a familiar pain rising in her chest. Tina was silent for long moments before she spoke again. "I see. But to think of the things Kravek could do if he ever became angry does frighten me a little. For all my gifts as a wizard, I am more fragile than

95

most people in this world for obvious reasons."

"And as much of a brute as Kravek appears, he is more fragile than he might look." Willa pulled her pipe from her mouth to blow another plume of smoke into the air. "And with good reason."

Tina knew that Willa was right about Kravek. Even though he looked like a brute, he hadn't shown any aggression toward her at all, and the loss of one's... everything could leave anyone with wounds easily reopened. Tina rose from her seat. "Thank you, Willa. I think I'm going to go back to my room now."

Willa nodded her head and tapped out her pipe. "Take care of yourself, Wizard."

As Tina entered, she had expected to find the tavern area empty, but she saw Kravek standing at the foot of the stairs with his back to the door. His hand rested on the column next to the stairway, and his head was turned down with his eyes fixed on the base of the stairs.

Before Tina could approach him, she heard him speak. "Tina. I'm sorry."

Tina stopped. She took a moment to consider before speaking again. "Kravek, Willa told me about your people."

Kravek snorted, but he didn't seem upset at the news. "Willa means well. But don't pity me, Wizard. Pity my people. I have pitied myself enough."

Tina felt a wave of empathy for the Akoan. She wanted to offer words of comfort, but she knew they would not help. "Kravek, I know what you must be feeling right now. I—"

"No, Wizard. If you did, you would let this go."

Tina paused at Kravek's words. Knowing he was still inebriated, Tina thought he was probably right. "You're right. I'm sorry I brought it up."

Kravek sighed and started up the stairs. "I'll be ready in the morning."

Tina watched Kravek until he disappeared at the top of

the stairs, and she closed her eyes with a sigh. She walked to the corner of the counter and, using her short, sharp claws, climbed up so she could head for her door under the stairs.

Before she reached it, a familiar voice came from the far end of the bar. "Oh, Wizard!"

Tina turned around. She saw the waitress who had been there when she first came into the Stumble Drum. Tina hadn't even noticed the rabbit woman while she had been talking to Kravek. "Yes, uh…?" Tina hesitated. "I'm sorry. I never got your name."

The rabbit stopped next to Tina and seated herself on a stool with her hands in her lap. "It's Beth, ma'am."

"Nice to meet you, Beth. Please, call me Tina." She walked to the edge of the counter. "Did you need something?"

"Well, two things, Miss Tina. Lazur wanted me to tell you he needs to talk to you when you get a chance." Beth's long ears swiveled forward.

Tina wrinkled her muzzle. She wasn't entirely certain she wanted to talk to Lazur, but if he had any helpful information, she couldn't afford to ignore him. "I'll make a note of it. And the other thing?"

Beth looked both hesitant and a little anxious. "If it's not too personal, how did you become a wizard, ma'am?"

The question made Tina curious. "It's not too personal, but what makes you want to know?"

Beth squeezed her hands together in her lap. "I was just wondering how a person becomes a wizard."

Tina slid her glasses off the bridge of her muzzle and used the edge of her robe to clean them. "Are you wondering if you could be a wizard, Beth?"

"Oh! Oh no, ma'am."

"Then why do you ask?" Tina put her glasses back on.

"Well…" Beth wiggled her toes, and then curled them. "I was just wondering if someone I know could become a wizard."

Tina smiled in a friendly manner. "Truth be told, Beth, becoming a wizard takes a lot of dedication, time, and training. But before any of that, a potential wizard has to be born with the gift for magic. People without the gift can learn to use magic, but they have to be much more careful and would never be able to use magic with the same potency as a wizard born with the gift."

Beth tilted her head and looked at Tina in confusion. "Potency?"

"They wouldn't be as powerful as a wizard with the gift." Tina seated herself on the edge of the counter. "I became a wizard when another wizard noticed I had the gift and offered to train me."

Beth leaned forward. "How can you tell if someone has the gift?"

"It usually takes another wizard to recognize it." Tina cleared her throat. "Beth, what is this about? You seem nervous."

Beth straightened up again. "Well, you see ma'am, I was just wondering if… well, if my son could become a wizard."

Tina folded her hands together and rested her chin on them. "If he has the gift, it's a possibility. Does he want to become one?"

Beth lifted her hands and held them up in front of herself. "Oh no, ma'am. He doesn't know anything about magic."

Tina remained silent as she looked at Beth and simply waited for the rabbit to continue.

Beth finally did. "Ma'am, I'm happy with my lot in life. Aside from the idea the Dragon Eaters might someday decide to change their diet to rabbit, I live a good life. My family doesn't have nice things, but I have a roof over my head, eighteen sisters and brothers who love me, and a good job."

"Eight… teen." Tina boggled at the number in reference to siblings. She shook the thought from her mind. The important part was that she understood where Beth was going at last. "But for your son, you want something more."

Beth smiled, though Tina thought she looked a little sad. "Aiden's father was a wizard, ma'am. He wasn't from Levansia, but I'm certain he'd been trained. Aiden doesn't have what I did as a little girl. I had a large family to grow up with, but Aiden is among a lot of other children he doesn't seem to get along with very well. He spends most of his time in his room playing by himself. I try to get him to make friends, but he just hasn't taken to it."

"It sounds to me like you just need to get him out of the house. Becoming a wizard is no small matter." She laid her tail across her lap and rested her hands on it. "Why ask about him becoming a wizard anyway? Does he do unusual things like make chairs and tables levitate?"

Beth looked at Tina curiously. "Levi... what?"

"Float."

Beth shook her head. "No, ma'am. I just wondered if he might have gotten the gift from his father." She rested her hands on the counter's edge and slid off the stool to her knees so she could look up at Tina. "Would you be able to tell if he has the gift, Miss Tina?"

The request wasn't one unfamiliar to Tina. After all, she had come to understand in her life that being a wizard could seem very glamorous and a goal to which many might want to aspire. Tina leaned out to push up on the underside of Beth's chin, urging her to get up. Beth apparently got the message because she rose and retook her seat on the stool.

"Beth, if you want me to, if you really want to know if your son could be a wizard, I will at least meet with him for you. But," she tapped the bridge of her glasses to push them up on her muzzle, "I have three things to ask you first, and four if the answer to all of them is yes. The gift for magic is uncommonly rare. If I determine Aiden is not a wizard, will you trust my word on it?"

Beth tilted her head but nodded. "Of course, ma'am."

"If I determine that he is a wizard, but not trainable, will you trust my word on that as well?"

Beth nodded again. "Yes, ma'am."

Tina set her hands into her lap with one on top of the other. "Will you keep it a secret that I am examining your son?"

Beth looked confused, but once more nodded. "Yes, ma'am."

Tina finally came to the last question and the one she knew would probably be hardest for Beth to answer 'yes.' She asked quietly and spoke compassionately. "Would you be able to live with the possibility that you would never see him again?"

Beth paused. She curled her toes and fingers in anxiety and rubbed her incisors against her bottom lip. "Is... is it likely?"

Tina nodded. It was a painful realization for a mother, but Tina wanted Beth to be certain. "Very."

Beth lowered her head. She stared at the floor for long moments in consideration. Her eyes closed as she answered, and Tina could hear a hint of sadness in Beth's tone. "I... think so."

"Beth," Tina waited for Beth to open her eyes and look at her again, "you have to be sure. The path to becoming a wizard requires focus and many years of study. You could be long dead before he completes his training."

Beth lowered her gaze again. There was another long pause before she spoke. "If it means a better life for him," she looked at Tina once more, "then... yes."

Tina rose from the counter and walked to Beth's side. She put her arm around as much of Beth's as she could to squeeze it comfortingly. "Then I will examine him. But Beth, please don't get your hopes up. As I said before, the gift for wizardry is uncommonly rare. Just because his father was a wizard doesn't mean he has the gift for it." Tina ruffled her own hair. "Both of my parents have brown hair and fur. But I was born with brown fur and strawberry blonde hair, thanks to my father's parents. Some traits are there, but just don't show up in every child."

Beth looked down at Tina holding her arm. She smiled in spite of herself. "I understand, ma'am." She leaned down and touched the end of her nose to the top of Tina's head. "You're very kind to do this for a stranger, ma'am."

Tina patted Beth's cheek. "As little as I've seen of you, Beth, you're gentle, humble, and kind, and you love your son. All of these things are admirable." She stepped away from Beth and folded her arms across her stomach. "I'm happy to do what I can. Now, if you'll excuse me, I need to rest and prepare for tomorrow. Once I have sorted out this matter with the Dragon Eaters, I will see your son."

Beth smiled appreciatively and rose from her seat to bow at the waist to Tina. "Thank you, ma'am. Please sleep well, and I wish you the best of luck!"

When Beth turned away, Tina watched her leave. She really did admire Beth. In all of the thoughts of danger from the Dragon Eaters and living in a town far from her native lands, Beth had a smile to show. Tina turned around and continued on her way to her door. She rubbed her mouth with her hand and widened her eyes for a moment in amazement. "Eighteen. Goodness."

Chapter 10

The sound of Kravek's hooves descending the stairs was as distinct as an Akoan's presence among the Likonian town folk. Tina had already risen and was waiting for Kravek under the stairs, which made it all the easier to hear him descend. She closed the small tome from which she'd been reading and tucked it into the rucksack tied around her shoulders. Coming out from under the stairs, she whistled to get Kravek's attention.

Kravek turned his head when he heard the whistle and approached the bar counter. Tina wondered if Kravek had any other clothes with him aside from his lizard hide pants and that load-bearing harness which didn't cover anything of his upper torso. At least the pants looked as though they'd been cleaned.

Kravek stopped in front of the counter and rested his hand on it next to Tina with his palm turned up. Tina adjusted her glasses as she looked up at him but didn't climb onto his hand.

Kravek looked at her curiously. He then realized why she might be hesitating and lifted his hand from the bar and took a step back. Picking up one leg, he balanced on one hoof. "Don't worry. I won't be breaking any more doors for awhile."

Tina giggled and rose to her feet. "I'm glad to hear it. Also, good morning, Kravek. I hope you had a good night's sleep."

Kravek nodded. "I'm satisfied with it." He set his hoof down and put his hand next to Tina. When she hopped into it, he lifted her up to his shoulder and let her jump off. Standing on his shoulder, Tina could see Kravek had a backpack attached to his load-bearing harness. Kravek raised one of his large ears and held it over Tina. "Where to?"

"The front gate. Lieutenant Copaire sent word earlier this morning she would be waiting for us there." Tina seated herself and folded her hands in her lap.

Kravek nodded. "Well, best not keep her waiting." He started to turn, but Tina tugged his ear.

"Hold on, Kravek. You haven't eaten breakfast yet, and there's the matter of your pay." She pointed under the stairs where a cloth bag rested. "I decided to cover two stones in one bound."

Kravek chuckled. He picked up the cloth bag and removed his backpack. He checked the contents of the cloth bag first and rubbed the end of his nose. "I'll wait on breakfast. My eyes and my stomach don't agree right now." He closed the bag and put it into his backpack. "But thank you."

Tina shrugged her shoulders. "Not many people work just for a meal, Kravek."

"Don't they?" He glanced at her on his shoulder with both eyebrows raised as he put his backpack on his load-bearing harness.

"Good point." She took hold of one of his ears and climbed up to the top of his head. Rearranging his mane a little, Tina made herself comfortable as she sat down in the soft hair facing backward on Kravek's head. She pointed toward the door behind Kravek whose back faced the front of the building. "Forward!"

Kravek chuckled as he headed out.

After leaving the Stumble Drum, the walk to the front gate had been short. Lieutenant Copaire was already waiting outside with a long strider standing next to her. Tina took a moment to observe the beast. It had long arms and long legs with which to stride. A layer of turquoise scales covered its body with light blue striations resembling an Idassian tiger's stripes which ran all the way down its thick tail. While it had sharp teeth and claws, the beast looked amiable as the mink ran her fingers through the short, sharp-looking hairs on the back of its head.

Tina rose on top of Kravek's head and bowed as the bull

came to a stop a few feet away from her. "Good morning, Lieu-tenant."

The mink turned away from her strider with her bushy, copper-colored tail sweeping behind her. Tina noted the cloth ties on the lieutenant's tail which held the otherwise free-flowing, bushy fur in check. She cut a brisk salute, apparently unfazed by Tina's appearance. "Lieutenant Luna Copaire. I understand we're heading north."

Tina nodded. "That's right, Lieutenant. I will call you Luna if you have no objections."

The mink looked surprised but pleased. "I would be honored."

Tina smiled appreciatively, then glanced down at Kravek. "I can summon a mount for you."

Kravek started to shake his head but caught himself when he remembered Tina was there. He glanced up toward her. "No need. I can keep up with a long strider."

Tina tilted her head for a moment. Remembering the hill country of Akoa, she thought to herself that she shouldn't be surprised an Akoan would be able to keep pace with a strider. She seated herself. "Very well." Tina returned her gaze to Luna. "You know the way to this place called Dragon's Mouth?"

Luna nodded and swept up onto her long strider's back, taking its reins in hand. "Little Bit is ready."

Tina wiggled her whiskers, unaware of what Luna meant. She hesitated for a moment and wondered if Luna was making some kind of joke over Tina's diminutive stature. "Little Bit?"

Luna nodded and patted her long strider's neck. "Even after a long ride, she always seems able to go a little bit farther."

Tina giggled. "That's cute." She cleared her throat and pointed north. "Well then, if all are ready, let us proceed."

* * *

The ride north had been quiet as Luna's long strider led the way to the Dragon's Mouth caves. Conversation was limited while Kravek was controlling his breathing to keep pace with Little Bit. Tina had thought to strike up a conversation with Luna, but the mink had been keeping a fair lead as she showed them the way. The wizard decided to relegate herself to holding on to Kravek's mane while she let her mind wander.

The trip was shorter than Tina expected. Governor Keldo had told her it was a few hours on foot. Apparently, the governor hadn't taken into account Kravek's speed while keeping pace with a long strider. The landscape was rising after forty minutes, and both Kravek and the long strider had to slow down to make up for the resistance of the terrain. When they finally settled into a steady walking pace, Luna had slowed her strider so she could walk it next to Kravek.

"I'm impressed, Akoan." Luna turned her head to look at Kravek. Tina noted that on Luna's strider, the mink was eye level with the black bull. "There aren't many who can keep pace with any strider for so long."

Kravek was breathing more heavily than Luna, but was gradually slowing down as their pace changed to a walk. "I was a warrior before I came here."

Tina adjusted her glasses and straightened up on Kravek's head. It had been a bumpy ride, but they were making good time. She removed her rucksack from her back and put it down in Kravek's mane. After pulling it open, she produced a small vial with pink fluid in it. Tina pressed on the stopper and shook the vial for a few seconds before opening it.

The pleasant smell of vanilla and brown sugar flowed into the air around them. Kravek blinked as he detected the smell in the air. It was a refreshing scent. "What is that?"

Luna sniffed at the air as well and seemed confused by it. "Is someone cooking something?" Even Luna's long strider apparently picked up the scent as it sniffed at the air and rumbled with delight.

Tina giggled as she held the vial out with the stopper released. "It's just an herbal mixture."

"It's... refreshing." Kravek looked toward the top of his head. "Magic?"

"A little, but mostly alchemy. The Council of Stars has a handful of wizards who dabble in chemical mixtures."

Luna gave Tina a questioning look, "Chem... what?"

Tina replaced the stopper and put the vial away. "To put it plainly, alchemy is the study of turning one thing into another through a means which most often doesn't require magic." She gestured toward Luna. "In some ways, it's like baking. You take flour, yeast, a little water, and a pinch of sugar or drop of honey, go through the process of mixing the right ingredients at the right times, let it rise, cook, all of that, and the product is bread. Alchemy is much the same. The process is different for whatever you want to make, but you probably get the idea, yes?"

"I think so," Luna replied, "but how can baking make what you had in that vial?"

"There's a lot to explain to understand alchemy entirely," Tina pulled her glasses off and started cleaning them with the hem of her robe, "but that particular mixture comes from the idendra flower, a tiny amount of vanilla extract, a sugar called kurovadia which isn't much more than sugar and molasses, and a little magic on the vial itself to help spread the scent." She replaced her glasses on the bridge of her muzzle and smiled. "It's meant to help refresh the mind a little."

"It worked," Kravek commented. He pointed ahead toward a sharper rise in the terrain. "We're almost there."

As Luna, Kravek, and Tina approached the rise of the cliffs, they could all hear the sound of the waves crashing against the rocks. The scent from Tina's vial was replaced by the smell of salty seawater. It was a smell that had been everywhere on-board the Thorn's Side.

"That is the top of the cliffs." Luna pointed to a hill crest which, from their point of view, had nothing behind it but sky.

"Governor Keldo said there's a path leading down to the Dragon's Mouth caves." Tina leaned over the edge of Kravek's brow to look for a dip in the terrain where a path might start.

Kravek walked toward the crest of the hill. Once he reached the top of it, he lifted his hand to the top of his head and held it in front of Tina with his palm turned up. When she stepped out onto his hand, he went to a knee and set her down on the ground. Leaning out over the edge of the cliff, Kravek pointed down to the waters below. "The entrance to the caves should be right there."

Tina leaned over the edge of the cliff and looked down. She could feel the moment of vertigo accompanying the illusionary feeling of falling over the side one gets when looking down from a great height. "It's a long way down. But I don't see any kind of entrance." She looked up at Kravek. "Are you sure that's the spot?"

Kravek nodded and pointed to an outcropping of rocks sticking out of the cliff face near the bottom. "It's called Dragon's Mouth for a reason. Those rocks there that look like teeth are at the top of the cave."

"The Maldavians tell a story about Dragon's Mouth." Luna dismounted from her strider and let her bushy, bound tail sweep behind her as she turned to face Kravek and Tina at the edge of the cliff. "Its name is practically literal." She opened one of her long strider's saddlebags and pulled out a tightly packed backpack and slung it onto her shoulders.

"Wait." Tina sat back on her heels and looked at Luna. "This isn't the Maw of Kaelus, is it?"

Luna blinked in surprise at Tina, and her ears swiveled forward to focus on the mouse wizard. "Maw of Kaelus?"

Tina nodded. "The Maldavians tell a story of two dragons named Kaelus and Malidath. Both of them were bound in the earth at the edge of the sea for killing the dragon king's consort,

Alysryzara."

Luna folded her arms. "You know the story."

Tina nodded. "I've visited Maldavia before. As the story goes, Kaelus and Malidath were the sons of Shahdazhan and both born of Alysryzara, his prime consort. They were sun dragons, just like their father. But they turned against him in an attempt to overthrow him as the rulers of Maldavia. Shahdazhan battled with them for days before Kaelus was able to capture Alysryzara. He threatened her in order to trade her life for Shahdazhan's compliance. Not believing Kaelus would kill his own mother, Shahdazhan refused to stand down. He was correct about Kaelus who stayed his jaws. But Malidath wouldn't back down."

"Malidath tried to use Shahdazhan's distraction to strike a killing blow, but Alysryzara protected the dragon king." Tina folded her hands in her lap. "She was stricken instead. The wound was a mortal one. When Alysryzara died from it, Shahdazhan was enraged, as were the rest of Alysryzara's children. Kaelus and Malidath were eventually captured and stripped of their power as dragons. Instead of executing his own sons, Shahdazhan turned Kaelus and Malidath to stone and imprisoned them in the earth at the edge of the sea."

"How do you know this is Kaelus?" Luna walked up next to Tina and knelt down.

"Well, if the story is true, and I believe it is, the Maw of Malidath is always submerged so he would forever suffer a drowning undeath. Because Kaelus would not slay his mother, Shahdazhan left Kaelus's mouth exposed to the air so he can breathe."

Luna folded her hands in her lap. "You know the story better than I do. But that still sounds pitiless of Shahdazhan."

Tina adjusted her glasses. "Though he didn't kill her, Kaelus was held responsible along with Malidath for Alysryzara's death. Shahdazhan, having lost both of his eldest sons and his most beloved consort, eventually returned his body to the sun and bound his spirit into the Monolith of Maldav, the first dragon."

"That's a tragic story." Kravek rumbled.

"Not every story has a happy ending." Tina looked up at Kravek. "But the Maldavians still revere Shahdazhan as their king, even though he no longer roams the world."

"Does it make a difference if this is the Maw of Kaelus?" Luna's bushy tail bobbed behind her.

"Maybe not, but it could be significant if the wizard chose this cave to house his tower."

"I don't get it." Kravek settled onto his seat.

Tina looked up at Kravek in expectation of an explanation. When he offered none, she spoke up. "What don't you get, Kravek?"

"I know magic can do a lot of things, but I didn't think that wizard was here long enough to build a tower."

Tina smiled. "A wizard's tower isn't always literally a tower, Kravek. But whether it is, wizards powerful enough to create a wizard's tower usually bind its entrance to an object." She rubbed her thumb over the face of her necklace. She didn't feel the familiar doorknob usually placed in the necklace but the rigid edges of the lava-colored crystal. "It can be placed in a rock face to form a door, summoned out of the ground to form a tower, or even be as simple as drawing a doorway in a wall with a special kind of chalk." Tina rose and folded her arms across her stomach, letting her shawl drape in the crooks of her elbows. "The tower itself sometimes resides at a fixed location in the real world, or it can even be bound in a small pocket dimension."

Kravek and Luna both blinked at Tina as if neither of them understood what she was talking about. Tina cleared her throat. "That aside... we should probably find the path leading down there and hope the wizard left the entrance to his tower behind. It's near impossible to enter a wizard's tower otherwise."

Luna nodded. "The path is this way." She looked back at Little Bit and whistled. The long strider lifted her head and looked at Luna. Luna made a fist with her hand and held it out parallel to the ground at hip height. The long strider lowered its head and lay down in the grass in response. The mink then turned away and headed for a dip on the far side of the rise of the cliffs.

Kravek held his hand out for Tina, and she quickly climbed on to get up to his shoulder. Once she was in place, he followed after Luna but turned his head to look at the mouse on his shoulder. "Do you think it likely he left his door open?"

Tina took a moment to consider while Kravek walked. "Open, no. But revealed, possibly. I wouldn't think he'd bother to hide it in a secluded place like this, especially since I doubt he was planning to be killed the last time he left it."

Kravek grunted. "Most don't expect to die in a day."

Tina sighed. "That is a truth."

The path leading down to the caves was a little wider and more direct than Tina had expected for the Maw of Kaelus. It was a flat, rough stone path broad enough to accommodate someone of Kravek's size comfortably. The coarse surface of the stones made them safe to walk on in spite of the humidity. Tina thought the path was too perfect to be natural, but with a wizard wanting to go back and forth from the cave to the outside world, she guessed he'd probably cultured it for safe passage. It wound back and forth across the face of the cliff all the way down to the mouth of the cave.

Upon reaching the cave, Tina thought 'maw' was an appropriate word for describing it. From above, the sharp outcroppings of rock resembling teeth had been evident. But the matching set at the bottom of the cave mouth had been less apparent. At an even level with the cave, the sharp rocks could easily be seen in a row which matched the sharp rocks at the top. The sides of the mouth were slanted away from one another like the jaws of a long, dragon's snout with another row of teeth which faded into the walls where the cave narrowed a little at the back.

Luna looked at Tina on Kravek's shoulder. "Why would a wizard want his tower in the body of an imprisoned dragon?"

Tina folded her hands together in her lap. "Well, there are a number of reasons, but most of the ones that come to mind have nothing to do with dealing with Maldavians. In fact, it would probably upset them if they found out a wizard had made Kaelus's body a home."

Kravek glanced at Tina. "But they won't mind us trespassing?"

Tina shook her head. "Big difference between exploring and taking up residence." She looked down to see the water splashing against the teeth at the front of the cave. "The cave mouth looks as if it would probably flood during high tide." She turned her attention to the back of the cave. "The cave slopes upward at the back, though. We're probably safe from flooding, but it wouldn't do to get trapped inside."

"The other wizard probably would have thought of that," Luna put her hands on her hips, "wouldn't he?"

Tina nodded. "I imagine so, but if it was by means of magic, any ward he placed might have faded by now. Unless specifically enchanted to be a permanent spell, a dead wizard's magic fades after death. Either way, we shouldn't linger for long." A thought occurred to Tina, and she took a moment to tap the side of her glasses. The runic circle she used to examine magical equations appeared.

She instantly pulled her glasses off and rubbed her eyes. "Mm. That was a bad idea." Tina put her glasses back on after canceling the runic circle in the lens.

Luna looked up at Tina again. "What? What did you see?"

"The magic in this area is somewhat erratic and very strong." Tina swiveled her ears forward. "I wanted to look for any lingering wards, but it's like looking for a barbed wire fence in a field of bramble bushes. And the power of it is all but blinding. I should have expected it in a dragon's grave."

"Why don't we feel anything from it?" Kravek questioned.

"There's magic everywhere in the world. Only those sensitive to it can really detect it." Tina seated herself on Kravek's shoulder. "You can learn to feel the difference, but most often, it's too subtle. A shiver running up your spine for no reason, the feeling of a breeze brushing your fur when there's no wind, even an apple falling out of a tree could be a manifestation of a disturbed magical equation." Tina giggled. "Of course, that doesn't mean all these things are disturbed magic. Sometimes, there's just a breeze. It takes talent and/or thorough training to tell the difference."

"Couldn't you tell when we approached the cave?" Luna swept her tail toward the cave.

Tina smiled. "I might have. As I said, sometimes it's very subtle. Even the notion to look could have been part of it. But since we're not inside the cave yet..." She let her statement trail off.

Luna nodded. "We should fix that and get along with this." The mink walked toward the row of teeth going down one side of the cave mouth. Kravek and Tina watched her for a few seconds as she walked toward the back of the cave where it sloped upward as if expecting something to happen. When Luna reached the back, she turned around and looked at them with one hand on her hip and the other gesturing deeper into the cave. "Well? Are you coming?"

Tina adjusted her glasses and looked up at Kravek. "And sometimes, they simply don't manifest. Much of magic remains a mystery."

Chapter 11

Luna set her backpack down and removed a pair of torches from it. After lighting them with a flint and tinder, she handed one to Kravek and put the flint and tinder away. She then headed into the tunnel.

The tunnel they passed into wound from one side to the other and back again before opening up into a much larger chamber. The tunnel leading to the chamber had only been about thirty feet long. But the chamber they entered was much larger. Comparing the room to Kravek's height, Tina estimated the ceiling was about thirty feet high, and the far end of the cave, which narrowed into another tunnel, was at least sixty feet away. The walls were curved, and the ceiling was rounded, but fortunately, the floor was mostly flat. Because of the shape of the tunnel leading into the chamber, all light from the outside was blocked which made the torches burn all the brighter.

Tina had been watching the walls of the tunnel as they'd entered. Inside the cavern, she was looking around the walls as well. "Hm. This is peculiar."

"What is?" Luna turned to look up at Tina on Kravek's shoulder.

"Well, it could be nothing, but—" Tina didn't get to finish her sentence before the sound of pebbles falling from the ceiling caught her attention. "...We need to get out of here!"

Luna raised the torch. "What? We just--"

"NOW!" Tina shoved on the side of Kravek's neck.

Luna grunted but quickly turned to run back to the tunnel entrance. The sound of falling pebbles behind them grew to the sound of rocks colliding with one another. Kravek was quick to follow Luna, but before he could reach the entrance, Luna let out a startled cry! Tina saw Luna's torch fly from around the corner and crash into the wall in front of the entrance, throwing up a swarm of embers. Luna came running back around the corner an instant later and skidded to a stop next to Kravek, using his arm to catch herself.

Kravek snorted. "Luna, what happened?"

"The rocks are moving!"

"...What?"

Luna jabbed her finger toward the tunnel entrance. "There!"

Fully illuminated by the light of Luna's dropped torch, they could all see a massive figure made from stone lumbering into the entrance. He came to a stop in the entrance and crouched down, blocking the light of Luna's torch. His body merged with the walls of the entrance and blocked the passage leading out. A head rose from the newly formed wall. Its lower jaw was lined with jagged, rocky teeth, and as it spoke, its deep, rumbling voice flooded the cavern. "You have disturbed the grave of Kaelus. So too shall it be your grave." The rumbling of its voice merged into a rumbling from the entire cave, and rocks fell from the ceiling. As they struck the floor, they shattered and sent shards flying.

Tina punched the side of Kravek's neck to get his attention. "RUN!"

"To where!?" Kravek turned about and swung the torch so he could see more of the chamber.

"There!" Tina pointed to the only exit from the room far at the back.

Luna took off quickly, and Kravek was immediately behind her as they ran for the far end of the cavern. Rocks continued to fall from the roof, each one shattering in an explosion of shards.

"Rocks aren't supposed to break like that!" Luna called

out as she ran.

"They're enchanted! Just move!" Tina watched the ceiling above them as they ran. One rock fell on a course straight for Kravek's head, and Tina threw her hands up. The rock stopped in midair and spun wildly before it exploded. The shards pelted them all but did little more than leave a stinging pain where they struck fur and skin.

The rocks falling increased in number. Tina did her best to deflect as many as she could. But twenty feet before they reached the exit at the back, a rock slammed into the ground too close to Luna. She let out a pained cry before she crashed to the ground and rolled to a stop. She managed to push herself up to her knees, but Tina could see blood coming through holes in her leather armor. Tina stopped another rock from landing right on top of her, and Kravek ducked, swinging his arm out without hesitation and looping it around the mink's waist. He threw her onto his free shoulder and ducked through the cavern's exit.

The rumbling continued behind them as Kravek ran, but as he rounded a corner, he came to a sudden stop as their path was blocked by another humanoid figure made of stone. Upon seeing Kravek, it lifted its head and growled at them. "This is your grave."

Tina rose to her feet and leapt from Kravek's shoulder. She landed on top of the figure's head, though it didn't even seem to notice her. A ripple in the air like a wave of heat surrounded Tina as she put both her hands down on the stone figure's head and rapidly chanted. The sphere around her expanded until it surrounded the creature. It then collapsed together and crushed it into a solid boulder. The creature rumbled but fell silent as it tumbled to one side. Tina dropped down onto the ground and waved Kravek on. "Come on!"

Kravek moved forward and rounded the boulder with Luna still in his arms. As he passed Tina, she grabbed the tuft of fur on the end of his tail and held tightly.

"Where are we going?! We're just getting deeper."

"Just look for an alcove, quickly!" Tina looked back at the boulder. As they ran, it suddenly rolled back into the center of the tunnel and barreled its way toward them. "I can't emphasize 'quickly' enough!"

Kravek was looking around the walls as he ran with the torch in one hand and a groaning Luna on his shoulder. The tunnel ahead turned sharply in front of them, and Kravek had to skid to a stop, put his hoof on the wall, and push off to make the turn. The metal shoes on the bottom of his hooves pounded against the stone floor of the cavern as he ran, but the rumbling in the cave was growing louder and louder. Tina glanced back to see it was not just the sound of the boulder rolling after them, but the ceiling of the tunnel was caving in behind it in a shower of rocks. She wanted to slow the rocks, but clinging to Kravek's tail, she couldn't make the somatic gestures needed for a spell. The boulder was too close for her to let go and cast a spell in time before it would have crushed her.

Kravek was looking for an alcove anywhere in the tunnel, but the walls were smooth and without an indentation deep enough for all of them. He looked ahead to see another sharp turn in the tunnel. He skidded and pushed off again to maintain his speed as he shot around the corner. But the next skid of his hooves brought them all to a sudden stop. The tunnel ahead of them was collapsing in a shower of rocks.

"Tina, the tunnel!"

Tina dropped from Kravek's tail and landed on her feet. She looked ahead and saw the falling rocks. Behind them, the boulder rounded the corner and started building momentum again as it barreled toward them.

"Tina, what do we do!?"

Tina looked back and forth between the boulder and the many rocks about to be falling on top of them. Her mind raced for a solution, but there were no alcoves, no exits, and no way out.

"Tina!"

"Brace yourself!"

The sound of the impact of the rocks crashing together was a deafening boom. And then, there was only silence and darkness.

* * *

Kravek always thought death would look like a light at the end of a dark tunnel. He blinked once and rubbed his eyes. The light was a welcome relief. But even as he lay there, staring up at it, he could feel its warmth beckoning to him. He could even hear it calling to him. He could hear the light calling his name. Its voice was so familiar. It was comforting.

"Can you hear me?"

It seemed like a strange question coming from the light of death. Kravek responded quietly. "Am I dead?"

"Close to it." Tina pushed herself up from Kravek's chin. The ball of light floating over her head rose with her. She jumped down from his chest.

Kravek sat up and looked down at Tina standing next to him. "What happened?"

Tina thumbed the platinum armlet on her left arm. The diamond in the center of it was glowing brightly. "We were very nearly crushed."

Kravek looked around to see why they hadn't been. A half-sphere of what looked like waves of heat flowing through the air surrounded them. On the outside of the half-sphere was what appeared to be a massive pile of gravel dumped right on top of them, burying them.

He looked down at Tina. "How are we not dead?"

"There's a barrier of magical force surrounding us right now. It can't hold forever, but it should hold up long enough."

"Long enough for what?"

"Long enough for me to fuse these rocks together before it collapses. And then, hopefully, I can see to Luna's wounds." Tina walked to the edge of the barrier and pushed her hands through it. She touched the rocks on the other side. "See if she has any bandages in her backpack. She's bleeding, but I don't have long enough to try healing her before this barrier breaks."

Kravek moved to Luna and lifted one of her arms. He still felt a little dazed, but urgency demanded his focus. The bull pulled Luna's backpack open and searched through it. Fortunately, there was a set of rolled up bandaging cloth there. He pulled it out, and then he slid the backpack off Luna's other arm and set her back down. There were several holes in her leather armor, but there were many more which had been stopped and were simply imbedded in the hide. Even so, he could see blood through the holes.

Kravek quickly went about pulling belts and ties on her armor before pulling it off and laying it aside. He looked at the bloodied fur on her body. She wasn't bleeding profusely, but the number of wounds made him worry. "Tina, she's pretty badly hurt."

As Kravek started wrapping wounds, Tina nodded. "I'll see to her. Now, be quiet for a minute. This is harder than it looks without my glasses." Unable to see the exact equations pertaining to the pebbles, their number, their weight, the force pressing down on her sphere, or how deep they ran, Tina had to make estimates and work slowly. As she multiplied her own organic variable, she cast the product into the rocks. With the sound of shifting gravel, the pebbles merged in front of her hands. The fusing process slowly expanded outward as the wizard worked carefully. It took a few minutes, but once she was finished, the rocks around them had solidified into a single, solid half-sphere.

Tina stepped away from the rocks and sank to the ground with a sigh. The diamond set on her armlet cracked just before the half-sphere of pure force faded. She looked down at it and slid the armlet off. It wasn't going to be easy to replace, but it had saved their lives. Tina picked up her rucksack, tucked the armlet into it, then moved to where Kravek was tending Luna. He had bandages wrapped around her middle, her chest and shoulder, and her right arm at the bicep and forearm. The bandages were already stained with her blood.

Tina climbed up onto Luna's chest, being careful of her wounds, and looked at her head. Fortunately, it looked as though the blast had caught only her right side. "No head wounds. Small miracle, but one for which I'm very grateful."

"There are two holes in her belly." Kravek's expression looked grim. "Those need tending first, or she'll be dead before you can get to the rest."

Tina turned back around and moved to Luna's stomach. She rubbed her face. "Kravek, I can't mend wounds of that kind without my glasses. Wounds like this... it's much more meticulous than making a wall of stone. Even if I'm careful, I run a high risk of doing more damage than good."

Kravek narrowed his eyes at Tina. "You have to try, Tina."

"Kravek," Tina looked up at him, "I can't be sure it will help."

"You still have to try." He touched Luna's shoulder. "She came here to help you. Now, she might be dying." Kravek's gaze was fixed on Tina's face. "It may not be perfect, but you have to try."

Tina hesitated as she looked at Kravek. She knew the damage she could do if she wasn't careful. Her ears pressed back against her hair. "Kravek, if I don't get this right, she could end up with any number of--"

"Are any of them worse than death?" Kravek's expression was stern as he interrupted Tina.

Tina looked up at him again and saw Kravek's hard eyes. It was an expression she hadn't seen before. But she was afraid. If she didn't heal Luna's wounds perfectly, the mink could end up living in pain for the rest of her life. If Tina got it wrong, Luna might even wish for death.

Tina's hands trembled. "Kravek, there are worse fates than death."

Kravek sat straight up. His stern glare turned to one of disappointment. "Well... that's it then, is it?" He looked away from her. "And here I thought I was the coward."

Tina felt the blood leave her face. "Kravek..."

Kravek shook his head. "Every minute you wait, she draws closer to death, Tina. Maybe you will screw up. Maybe she will hate you. Maybe she will wish to die." He hesitated for a moment before he spoke again. "She might even want to kill you before the end." He fixed his gaze back on Tina. "But at least her end won't be here."

Tina closed her eyes. There were so many risks. She opened her eyes again and looked back down at the bandages on Luna's belly. Wizards did not normally possess the power to heal, and while what Tina did was not the same as a healing spell, she did have the ability to at least get Luna out of danger from her stomach wounds. But without her glasses, she would be flying blind.

With a sigh, Tina moved to Luna's stomach and pushed the bandages down to reveal the holes in her skin. "Kravek, I need your help. This isn't going to be easy for either of us. Tear off a few pieces of the bandages, and then hold her down and pray to whatever deity you worship that she doesn't wake up."

After Kravek set a few torn pieces of bandage across Luna's stomach, he put one hand on Luna's shoulder and the other on her hip. Tina leaned over the larger of the two wounds and picked up one of the torn bandage strips and wrapped it loosely around her hands. She pushed her hands into the hole in Luna's skin, and the cloth quickly became soaked with Luna's blood. Tina used the cloth to wipe the blood away several times before she pushed her hands in more deeply. Though the wound looked large, the rock shard had not gone as deep as it could have. Wrapping her fingers around it, she manipulated the stone until she could slide it out of the wound and tossed the shard aside.

Pushing her hands back into the wound, Tina drew on her gift and poured it into Luna's skin. A flicker of flame rose from the wound as Tina cauterized it to stop the bleeding. But as soon as the flesh had mended, she used her claws to rake at the skin and open it again. Manipulating Luna's natural healing process, she accelerated it and carefully watched as the flesh started knitting. Within a few seconds, she had to burn the wound again as pathways for blood were restored without the skin to cover them. The shard hadn't penetrated the muscle in Luna's belly, but it had ripped several fibers. Tina had to burn the wound many times over the course of mending it and then poured her gift into Luna's stomach to accelerate the healing process.

It took two minutes to mend the larger wound. Tina had hoped the larger one had been the deeper wound, but it had merely been caused by a larger shard. Once she pulled her hand away, she tugged the bandages across Luna's belly up to cover the wound again.

"Why do you keep burning her?"

"Kravek, I really need to focus right now." Tina moved to the smaller of the two wounds which was farther to one side on Luna's body. She wiped her hands, dabbed the wound, then wrapped her hand again. She could only fit one hand through the small hole, but it was much deeper. The pathway through Luna's muscle was less rigid and torn. Tina felt her arm push all the way through it before she pulled it back out again. Using another one of the bandage strips, she cleaned up the resulting blood, wrapped her hand more tightly so the bandaging wouldn't come off in the deeper wound, and then pushed back in again. Her arm went in all the way up to her elbow, and Tina had to change position to press deeper.

"Can't you burn the wound to stop that bleeding?" Kravek questioned.

"If I do before I find the shard, I run the risk of sealing

it in her body. Now be quiet Kravek, please." Tina pushed her arm in deeper and carefully tried to feel around for the stone. Feeling around inside Luna was making Tina's stomach turn, but she didn't have a choice. When her hand finally brushed against something stiff, she grasped for it. She could feel the shard had sharp edges on it, but it hadn't begun to dissolve, and she had a firm grip on it.

As Tina pulled her arm back, she felt the muscles of Luna's stomach suddenly flex. They tightened around Tina's arm, and the wizard gasped in pain. Biting her lip, she tried to pull her arm back again, but the muscles tightened as Luna let out a groan. Tina had to get free before Luna woke up, or the restricting muscles could break her arm. She twisted the shard to try to get it to move, but that only made the problem worse as the pain brought the mink closer to consciousness. Tina's tail slapped the ground hard as she fought the feeling of her arm being crushed. She wanted to put a sleep spell on Luna to knock her out again, but the mouse couldn't focus.

Tina stopped pulling on her arm. She kept her grip on the small rock shard tight, but she stopped moving in Luna's body. The feel of Luna's muscles squeezing on her arm was painful, but all of Tina's moving around was only agitating the situation. Tina pressed her incisors against her bottom lip to keep from crying out. But as she stopped moving, Luna slowly relaxed. Tina turned the shard so the sharp edge was against her palm and then managed to slowly slide her arm free. With a small puff of flame, she cauterized the wound and dropped the shard. "It's out."

Kravek quickly wrapped up the wound on Luna's side again. He placed his hand on her shoulder, but she had stopped moving around. Kravek looked down at Tina on the floor next to Luna. "Are you all right?"

"I'll be fine." She looked down at her bloody hand. It was all Luna's blood, and Tina had fortunately escaped getting any cuts from the sharp edge of the stone shard. The mouse lay back on the ground and closed her eyes. She'd removed the shards and hadn't felt any cuts in Luna's bowel around the shard which had penetrated the muscle. Luna was going to be all right.

Chapter 12

Tina leaned against Kravek's backpack and put her blood-soaked hand down in her lap. Her stomach grumbled. Working with magic had drained a good deal of her energy. "I need something to eat."

Kravek glanced at Luna to make sure she wasn't in distress before he retrieved the food Tina had given him. Pulling it out of his backpack, he removed a piece of bread and broke off some of the crust. "Will you be able to get the other shards out?"

"I can, but they shouldn't be nearly as difficult. And there's no immediate risk. Once I've eaten, we can remove them, and I can sear the wounds so she won't keep bleeding once the shards are out." She started to reach for the piece of crust in Kravek's hand but saw the blood on her own. "Don't suppose you brought a water skin, did you?"

Kravek withdrew a water skin from his backpack. "Soldier's habit." He pulled the stopper from the water skin and poured out a little water for Tina to wash her hands.

Once the blood was out of Tina's fur, she wiped her hands on a piece of clean bandage and then took the piece of bread Kravek had offered. "Are there any surgeons in the city?"

Kravek looked at the piece of bread from which he'd broken the crust and put it back in the cloth. "Three. They're all former combat surgeons."

"Benefit of having a lot of ex-military around." Tina took a bite out of the bread crust.

Kravek looked down at Tina in consideration. "You're not a coward, Tina. I shouldn't have said what I did."

Tina paused, then lowered the piece of crust from her mouth and folded her hands in her lap. "No, Kravek. You were right. I was being cowardly." She laid her tail across her lap. "Luna's wounds weren't as serious as they could have been, but I made up this scenario in my head where I would have to try to heal a grievous injury." Her gaze lowered to the ground. "I was afraid I'd be risking her life. After seeing that dragon's injury, I just... leapt to the worst possible conclusion."

"Dragon?" Kravek flicked one of his large ears.

"There was a wounded Maldavian near Lazur Thulfa's farm. I went to see if I could save him." Tina wrapped her fingers around her necklace and rubbed her thumb over the lava-colored crystal it held. "I couldn't, but his Albatross is with me for now. He'd been too badly wounded. It was a stomach wound as well."

"I'm sorry." Kravek looked down at Luna. "Will she be all right to move about with pieces of those rocks still in her skin?"

Tina sighed. "No. But once I have my strength back, I'll remove them as well. As hard as it is to believe, wizards aren't all-powerful, Kravek." She wrinkled her muzzle.

Kravek looked back down at Tina. "I didn't mean--"

Tina held her hand up to stay his statement. "I'm worried too." She flicked one of her ears when she heard Luna groaning. "Make sure she doesn't try to get up, will you?"

Kravek nodded and moved to Luna's side. As the mink began to stir, he rested his hand on her uninjured shoulder. "Don't get up."

Luna blinked a few times before her eyes were open. "Kravek? What happened?" She looked around the room. "We're still in the cave."

Kravek nodded. "Tina was able to keep the rocks from falling on us. You have a few wounds from a rock that shattered too close to you. Just lie still for now."

Luna closed her eyes and began to tremble. It looked to Tina as though the mink was fighting to keep herself from rising.

A thought occurred to her, and Tina rose. She walked to the side of Luna's head and rested one of her hands on the mink's temple. "Shh, it's all right. You're going to be okay."

Luna was still trembling, and Tina could tell with the way Luna had started growling that keeping her down wasn't going to be easy. Whispering quietly, she called on a small portion of her gift and let it flow into Luna's mind. "Rest now. You need your sleep."

The growl in Luna's throat slowly abated, and her eyes closed again. Within moments, Luna was asleep once more.

Tina drew her hand away and walked back to seat herself against Kravek's backpack.

Kravek glanced at Tina. "Why did you put her back to sleep?"

Tina looked up at Kravek. "Two reasons. First of all, I don't want to risk getting my arm broken again if I have to dig as deeply as I did before to get shards out of her body. And second... I think she might be claustrophobic."

"Claus... what?"

Tina gestured to the room around them. "It's a fear of being in a closed space. I guess she was all right inside a larger cave, but this room barely has enough space for the three of us."

Kravek glanced at the ball of glowing light still levitating above Tina's head, then looked back down at Luna. "How did all of this happen, Tina?"

Tina picked up the piece of bread crust and returned to munching on it. She was quiet for a minute while she finished eating as she considered how to answer. Kravek could apparently see she was thinking because he didn't press the question. Tina wiped her hands and settled them in her lap. "That's a good question, Kravek. It doesn't make any sense."

"What do you mean?"

Tina rose to her feet and looked at the walls around them. "The cavern collapsed on us as the result of a spell. Those two stone creatures you saw were part of the spell meant to trap any-one who entered the cavern so it could be brought down on top of intruders. But that's the part which doesn't make any sense."

Tina reached up to adjust her glasses on the bridge of her muzzle but felt they were still missing. Her eyes were tired, and she rubbed them. "I can understand a wizard leaving traps and wards to prevent someone from finding the entrance to his tower. But to leave a spell behind to bring down the cavern his tower was in is a step too far. He'd literally be burying the entrance to his tower under a mountain."

"What does it mean?" Kravek leaned back from Luna and seated himself again.

"It could mean a lot of things, but the reason which makes the most sense is that he never intended to come back. In which case," Tina pinched the bridge of her muzzle, "he knew he was go-ing to die when he left. But that just raises more questions. If he wasn't planning to come back, why would he leave behind a spell to kill anyone coming into this cave?"

"Could it have something to do with the story of Kaelus?" Kravek questioned.

Tina shook her head. "The spell would have triggered be-fore he ever placed his tower. I don't think this was a trap set by the Maldavians to keep Kaelus's grave undisturbed. If noth-ing else, Shahdazhan would not stand for Kaelus's grave being de-stroyed and his soul released." She rubbed her face. Rising from the ground, she touched the light over her head. It grew brighter. "It just doesn't make sense."

Kravek looked at the light. "What are you thinking?"

"I don't know yet." Tina looked back at Kravek. "Can you see my glasses anywhere? They were thrown off when I activated my armlet, and my eyes aren't good enough to spot them without wearing them."

Kravek looked around the small cavern. "I'm sorry Tina, but I..." He paused. "Wait. What's that?"

Tina looked back at Kravek. He was close enough she could see where he was pointing, and she turned her head. She moved closer to the wall, and the light glinted off something. Stepping closer, she ran her hand over the wall until it brushed against something jutting from it. She tugged once, but the small piece of metal was lodged in firmly.

Tina sighed. "Those are not easy to make. I must have trapped them in the wall when I fused the rocks together."

"Can't you magic them out?"

Tina looked back over her shoulder. "You remember what I said about the door to the Stumble Drum and your horns? Think of that happening in here."

Kravek nodded. "Right. Do you have a spare set?"

"Only one. I probably destroyed this pair when the rocks came together. And it looks as though I'll need to make another spare set once I return to Kerovnia." Tina walked back from the wall and seated herself. She looked up at the center of the ceiling.

Kravek looked up when he noticed. "What are you looking at?"

"Nothing, really. I was just thinking about how long we can survive in here before the air runs out." She rubbed her fingers against her brow. "And about what it's going to take to get us out of here. I'm also thinking about how much magic it's going to take to get the stones out of the rest of Luna's wounds and how much I will be able to endure before it kills me."

"Can't you just blow a hole to the surface from here or something?"

Tina shook her head. "Far too many risks, and even putting the immediate ones aside, there's too much rock between us and the surface. Even if I could conjure enough magic right now, a lot of it would fall back down on top of us." She sighed. "On top of that, the longer I take to think about it, the more air we use up." Turning back to Kravek and Luna, Tina walked to the two of them and climbed up onto Luna's stomach. "This may be pointless if I can't get us out, but at least if we die down here, Luna can do it without those rocks in her body."

* * *

Tina pulled the last rock shard from Luna's shoulder and set it down with the others she'd removed. There had been almost a dozen lodged under Luna's skin. Sitting back down, Tina picked up the last piece of clean gauze she could find to wipe her hands. "That should do it. Wrap her shoulder back up while I work on getting us out of here."

Kravek pulled the bandages over Luna's shoulder and across her chest to redress them. "You have a plan?"

"Maybe. I was thinking while I was working on Luna's wounds." Tina looked up at the side of the dome she knew to be facing the tunnel which led back out to the cave mouth. "It occurred to me it would take a truly exceptional wizard to collapse an entire mountain. I think it far more likely only the surface rocks fell on us. And if that's the case--"

"Then there'd be a gap." Kravek paused in wrapping Luna's shoulder. "You think maybe it left behind another tunnel?"

Tina nodded. She felt a mild sense of reassurance that Kravek had picked up on the same idea. "It's possible. Of course, the loss of support could have caused a greater cave in. But if I can bore a hole large enough for you to get through, we might be able to find that gap, if it's there, and get out of here."

Tina reached for her glasses again and had to remind herself they weren't there. She rubbed the bridge of her muzzle. "It's risky, though. What I've basically created here is just a shell. If I start boring holes, it could give way and bury us."

Kravek laid Luna back down after finishing with her bandages. "It's a risk. But the alternative is worse."

Tina thought back on Kravek's last assessment of risk. It was worth a shot. "All right, Kravek. Do you mind acting as a bit of a body shield for Luna while I do this?"

He shook his head. "Of course not. You do what you need to. I'll keep her safe." Kravek leaned over to pick up his and Luna's backpacks. He put his own on and slung hers onto the front of his load-bearing harness. "When you're ready." Kravek leaned over Luna with his back to Tina.

Tina scooted back until she was on the opposite side of the dome and raised her hands. She had a few hopes to express, but it wasn't the time for wishing. Drawing on her gift, she put the thumbs and forefingers on both hands together and focused on the spot she could see on the other side. From her hands lashed out a ray of pure force which struck the stone. She sustained the ray which cast off chips of stone as it chewed away at the rock. The ray then made rapid, circular sweeps. It cut away at the rock in a growing spiral until there was a circle an inch deep with a four foot diameter.

For what came next, Tina would need control. She pressed her hands together to form a sphere of pure force. Spreading her hands from one another, she let the sphere grow in size until it matched the size of the missing layer on the wall. She then looked at Kravek. "Luck to us all."

She drew in a deep breath, and then forced it from her lungs in a cry. The sphere slammed into the weakened layer of stone and cracked it outward. Tina held the ball of force in place with one hand raised and drew the other one back. She punched the back of her hand, and the ball lodged itself deeper into the break. Another punch and it broke through the weakened wall, and Tina stopped. There was nothing on the other side. Putting both hands together, she shoved firmly, and the ball of force broke through, scattering the pieces of the weak spot into the darkness.

No rocks fell into the dome. Tina moved closer to the wall, but realized she didn't have a way to reach the hole. "Kravek, Luna's out of danger now. Quickly, lift me up."

Kravek rose from Luna and put his hand down on the

ground so Tina could step into it. He then lifted her through the hole. "Do you think we can get out?"

Tina looked as far as her eyesight and the light would let her. Stretching on in both directions was a passageway almost as large as the tunnel had originally been. But the floor was covered in gravel several feet deep. Even so, it would do. "Yes, Kravek, I think we can." She leapt from Kravek's hand onto the gravel and stood up. Pointing at the light above her head, she cast it back through the hole. "Get Luna out."

It took Kravek less than a minute to push Luna through the hole. He then tossed both backpacks through it and grabbed hold of the top of the dome to lift himself up and pull himself out.

The light followed Kravek out, and then floated to Tina with her rucksack sitting on top of it. She pulled the rucksack off and tied it back around her shoulders. "Time to go."

Kravek reattached both backpacks to his load-bearing harness and scooped Luna up. "Hop on."

Tina jumped onto Luna's stomach as Kravek stood up. She cast the light out in front of them to illuminate the path ahead. Kravek had run halfway down the tunnel to the first bend when they heard a crash and shifting gravel behind them. He looked back over his shoulder.

Tina's ears flattened against her hair. "Thank goodness the dome held long enough."

"Thank you, too." Kravek turned and continued down the tunnel.

The gravel was at a relatively even level as Kravek moved along. Tina's light led the way and rounded the next bend, and they would reach the main cavern before long. The condition of the large cavern wasn't much different than that of the tunnel, but Tina sharply whistled before Kravek could enter.

The light stopped as did Kravek, and he glanced down at her. "What? What is it?"

Tina beckoned the light back to her, and positioned it

131

above Kravek's head. "You remember what the rocks in here were doing before?"

Kravek grunted. "Exploding."

Tina nodded. "I'll levitate us across this room. Just keep a firm grip on Luna and try not to move around too much. Levitation spells are simple but can easily be disrupted. How much do you weigh, Kravek?"

"About five hundred pounds."

Tina wrinkled her muzzle. "I'll estimate Luna is around a hundred and forty. She's got some muscle." Tina held her hands out together in front of her and spread them in a circle before they met again closer to her body. She rolled her hands over and lifted them. Kravek's feet rose from the ground slowly. "Steady your feet." Once Kravek had widened his stance, Tina pushed her hands forward, and the three of them moved forward.

"I didn't know you could make us fly."

"I can't." Tina kept her hands held forward as they drifted across the chamber. "Levitation is easy. Flight is much more difficult, and it usually takes a sustained modification to a levitation spell keyed off an object, like a broom or a boat."

"A boat?" Kravek glanced down at Tina.

"That's more theory, but such a project is being worked on in Kerovnia right now. If it works, we'll see the first flying ship ever created." Tina smiled at the thought of a flying ship. "It would be a huge step in the advancement of magic."

Kravek chuckled.

As they crossed a third of the chamber, one of Tina's ears flicked. She kept her hands forward, but turned her head to look back. All she could see was Luna's backpack strapped to Kravek's chest. "Do you hear that?"

Kravek looked back over his shoulder. "Something's rumbling." He looked down at Tina. "Another cave in?"

"It's too constant."

The sound of rumbling grew louder, and as Kravek looked

back to see what was causing it, a large, rigid sphere of stone rolled into the mouth of the tunnel behind them. It unrolled into the large stone figure which Tina had trapped.

"It's that stone monster!" Kravek looked down at Tina. "It's following us!"

"If it starts walking on these rocks, they could start shattering again." Tina wanted to think of a solution, but she needed to concentrate on her levitation spell. Thrusting her hands forward, Tina doubled their pace in crossing the cavern.

The stone figure rumbled. "This is your grave." It curled up into a ball again and rolled out onto the rocks. Barreling after them, it crushed rocks beneath it, and as Tina suspected, the rocks crushed under it started shattering one after another, setting off a chain reaction. Blast after blast erupted around the rolling stone, but the explosions didn't seem to do more than cause the boulder to bounce as it remained on its path straight for the three of them.

Tina didn't know how close it was, and she couldn't look back with Kravek blocking her way. But they were close to the cavern's entrance, and as they passed through it, Tina set them down on the ground. "Get us out of here!"

Kravek lunged to take a step forward, but as he did, he felt something grab his ankle. He threw Luna forward to keep from falling on top of her and managed to soften his own landing with his hands. Turning over, he saw a stone hand sticking up through the rocks. A mound of gravel rose next to the hand as the other stone figure, the one which had blocked their exit before, emerged. It growled at Kravek.

Kravek lifted his other foot, showing the creature the metal shoe on the bottom of his hoof. The black bull snarled and slammed the metal shoe into the creature's head. It jerked back with a crack in its forehead. Kravek slammed his hoof into its head two more times before it broke into pieces, and the hand grasping his ankle let go.

Tina rose from the gravel. The second creature was still

rolling after them. She saw the body of the first creature as Kravek scrambled away from it. With an upward thrust of her hands, Tina slammed the creature's body into the ceiling of the tunnel and kept one hand in the air. The ball remained levitating as she spun her other hand in a circle. "I've had just about enough of you two."

The creature reformed into a large boulder and started spinning. After a few seconds, Tina dropped her hands and the boulder hit the ground rolling. She then threw her hands out to the sides to form a wall of force in the tunnel entrance, and as the boulders collided, they careened off of one another in several pieces. The shattering stones in the chamber pelted the wall of force, throwing ripples throughout it. But the wall held. After a few moments, the shattering of the stones died down, and Tina let the wall fade. She released a sigh of relief. "We made it."

Chapter 13

While Tina was aware that Kravek could have made the run back to town carrying Luna and her on his own, she had summoned Shasta to hasten their return to Likonia. With Little Bit in tow behind the construct, their return had been swift.

Upon arriving back at the city, Tina had then dismissed Shasta, and Kravek led the way to the nearest of the three surgeons in town, a tall, thin, male weasel. While Luna was mostly out of danger, it would take a more practiced hand than Tina's to minimize the damage to the mink's body. At least the surgeon didn't have to worry about removing explosive rock shards while he worked. The surgeon's home was small, but there was a room set up in the back of his house for just such an occasion. Tina was thankful for there being so many ex-military in the town with useful skills.

Tina and Kravek waited outside in the surgeon's living room while the surgeon worked on Luna. The surgeon's wife, a middle-aged badger woman, had joined him in operating on the mink. Tina guessed the badger must have been a field nurse by the way she and the surgeon had begun to work immediately once Tina, Kravek, and Luna had arrived.

Tina sat on the arm of a rocking chair next to a larger cushioned chair, both of which faced the fireplace in the surgeon's home. Kravek, unable to find a chair which might not collapse under his weight, remained standing while he leaned against a kitchen counter. His arms were folded, and his tail was brushing the wooden front of the counter.

"She's going to be all right, isn't she?" Tina asked from her position on the arm of the chair.

Kravek nodded. "You did a good job. She wasn't bleeding any more, and she was still breathing. The surgeon can handle the rest."

Tina rubbed her fingertips across her brow and sighed. "I can't help but feel responsible."

Kravek pushed off the counter and walked to the rocking chair to rest his hand on the back of it while he looked down at Tina. "Put it on the one who set the trap."

Tina huffed. "Too bad he's supposedly dead."

Kravek's eyebrow arched. "Supposedly?"

"I had more time to think on the ride back." Tina rested her elbows on her knees and steepled her fingers in front of her muzzle. "It's only speculation, but I can't come up with any logical reasons for the wizard to leave a trap like that behind unless he didn't want someone who was poking around to find anything, or if they did find something, to be able to leave with it."

"Why would he do that?" Kravek's tail swept around to slap the tuft of fur on the end of it against his side.

Tina was briefly silent before she settled her hands in her lap. "Kravek, do you know where the wizard died?"

"No. I wasn't there." He raised his hand to pick at the tip of one of his horns. "There was a handful of town folk who were, though. I think Lazur was there."

Tina snapped her fingers. "Lazur. Beth told me last night he wanted to see me about something." She folded her hands in her lap. "Once we're sure Luna's all right, I need to go see Lazur." The mouse looked up at Kravek again. "Would you mind being my feet a little while longer?"

Kravek chuckled, "Why not. You've paid me up through lunch, after all." He gestured toward his backpack sitting next to the front doorway wherein lay the package of food Tina had provided.

Tina giggled. "I'll buy more from Mr. Kilba for you if

that's not enough. I imagine someone of your size has a healthy appetite."

Kravek chuckled before the two became quiet again.

Tina broke the silence as she rubbed the bridge of her muzzle. "Before we go anywhere, I should retrieve my spare set of glasses. We're still dealing with magic, and I need to be able to see it." She laid her hand back into her lap. "Not to mention wanting to be able to see the rest of the world as well."

"How bad are your eyes?"

Tina shrugged. "Not bad enough I can't live without my glasses, but enough to make my eyes tired without them."

The surgeon's wife emerged from the back room with a rag turned red with blood and threw it into the sink. She opened one of the cabinets built above the counter and pulled out a small handful of clean rags before she headed back to the doorway.

Tina stood up. "Ma'am."

The badger woman stopped and looked back. "Vira."

"Vira, how is she doing?"

"Well enough." Vira rested her hand on the door. "She's going to be fine, but she needs to rest for a few days. A couple of the wounds needed to be opened again for proper stitching," the badger woman smiled comfortingly, "but you don't need to worry. It was smart to burn the wounds so she wouldn't bleed out on the way back. You did well." She then turned and disappeared into the back room again.

Tina watched the door close and then seated herself as she turned her gaze back to the unlit fireplace. Her thoughts turned to her own fireplace wherein rested a bottle full of everglow flames. She rubbed the bridge of her muzzle again. "I have things I need to do," she put her hand back down in her lap, "but I'd like to be here when Luna wakes up."

Kravek looked down at Tina with his arms folded across his chest. "You want to make her pain worthwhile, you do what it takes to put the monsters to rest."

Tina looked up at Kravek standing next to the chair. The corners of her mouth rose slowly before she wiggled her whiskers and got to her feet. "I need my glasses. And then, we need to go see Lazur Thulfa."

Kravek nodded and offered his hand down to Tina. She stepped onto it, and Kravek lifted her to his shoulder. "Back to the Stumble Drum, then?"

Tina took a last look over her shoulder at the closed door leading to the room where Luna lay. She drew in a deep breath and then let it out. "All right. Let's go."

* * *

The walk back to the Stumble Drum had been less eventful than Tina had expected. The guards had seen Luna's condition when the three of them returned, and Tina expected Captain Cephalin wouldn't be happy that one of his lieutenants had been hurt on a venture with a wizard. But from what the nurse had said, Luna was going to be all right, and there was work to be done.

Back at the Stumble Drum, Kravek stepped through the doors at the front of the dining area and headed for the counter. Tina could hear muttered conversation among the gathering lunch crowd and noticed one or two patrons glancing her way. The sailors from the Thorn's Side were among those who were not looking at the pair, with the exception of the grey-furred Kylathian Captain Jessica Morgan, who was seated in a corner booth with her Madrian Shepherd first mate, Allister, and her black cabin cat, Thomas. Captain Morgan waved Tina over at seeing her on Kravek's shoulder. Tina shook her head at the captain. She didn't have time for socializing at the moment.

Kravek stepped up to the bar counter and put his hand down on it. Tina climbed down his arm onto the countertop and started for her door. She noted Mr. Kilba was behind the counter pouring water into a mug in front of a badger. She rounded the mug to head for her door but was surprised when she heard Lazur Thulfa's voice. "I was just waiting for you, wizard."

Tina stopped and looked up at the stocky badger. She hadn't recognized him in passing without her glasses. "Oh, Lazur. We were just about to seek you out."

Lazur lifted one eyebrow. "We?"

Tina pointed to Kravek who had seated himself at the counter. Mr. Kilba stepped up in front of the black bull, but Kravek shook his head and waved the weasel off. A curious smile appeared on Tina's mouth, but she shook it off and looked back up at Lazur. "Kravek has been accompanying me this morning. He has a much longer stride than I."

Lazur raised both eyebrows and nodded. "I see. Did Beth tell you I was looking for you?"

"She did." Tina reached up to adjust her glasses and came just short of hitting herself in the face in consternation for not being able to repress the personal tic. "I had errands to run this morning; and to be honest, I was a little unsure of how I should react to your telling Captain Cephalin where I was rooming. I had wanted to keep my presence secret a little longer."

Lazur folded his arms on the counter. "You mean, you hadn't told Idori that you were here yet?"

Tina wrinkled her muzzle. "No, I hadn't." She hesitated for a moment to tell Lazur it was practically his fault Luna had been hurt since Governor Keldo had insisted Tina have an escort. But she knew better than that, and she was the one who had picked Luna in the first place. "But it's no matter. I wanted to ask you about something, and Beth said you wanted to tell me something as well."

Lazur gestured to Tina with his hand. "Ladies first."

Tina wiggled her whiskers. "Well, I have a couple of questions, actually."

"Fire away."

"First of all," Tina swiveled her ears toward Lazur, "the governor mentioned to me that the wizard had a pair of assistants with him, a couple of Kamadene women. The Kamadene aren't common in this area, and I was wondering if you knew anything about their whereabouts right now."

Lazur shook his head. "I know who you're talking about, but I can't say I've seen them since the wizard died." He rubbed his chin, "Come to think of it, I don't recall seeing them much after the Dragon Eaters appeared, either. Though they did once come out to Garina's farm to help her till the land."

"Yes, the governor did tell me they lent a hand on the farms once in awhile." Tina wrinkled her muzzle again. It seemed odd to her that the wizard would lend his assistants out to do farm work, but she pushed the thought aside for the time being. "If you come across any information about them, I'd appreciate it if you let me know."

Lazur nodded. "I'll keep an ear up."

Tina returned the nod. "Thank you. The next question concerns the wizard directly. Do you know where he died?"

Lazur nodded. "I do. Me and a couple of the others in town were trying to convince him not to go out and face those things on his own in an open field. But he seemed insistent on doing it."

"You saw him die, then? How did it happen?"

Lazur leaned back from the counter. "Didn't think you the morbid type, wizard."

Tina shook her head. "It's not out of curiosity that I ask. Details of how he died might help me determine what he was trying to do and to avoid possibly attempting the same thing myself."

"Ahh, that makes sense." Lazur picked up his mug of water and took a drink of it. He wiped the back of his arm across his muzzle. "Garina and I were standing at the edge of the woods watching the wizard while he was walking out into the middle of the fields between here and the mine south of the city. We'd tried to convince him not to go, but like I said, he was insistent. The others with us didn't even want to get close to the tree line."

"If you don't mind my asking, what were you doing there in the first place?" Tina seated herself in front of Lazur with her legs crossed and her arms folded. "Surely, you didn't follow him all that way just to tell him it was a bad idea."

Lazur shook his head. "He'd hired a few folks to help him set up some 'magic trap' for the things. There was this big stack of wood, looked like he was setting up for a bonfire. But he wasn't burning any of it. Last thing he did before moving back into the trees was chant some words out and make some kind of purple smoke rise from it. But the whole time, we couldn't see any fire. He'd had us clear an area of tall grass about twenty feet all around the pile of wood so he could draw some odd marks. Took him almost an hour to get all of the marks he wanted drawn."

"Anyway, it was already starting to get dark when those monsters decided to show up. It's the earliest I've ever seen them walking around. It was like they were drawn to that pile of wood because they went right for it. They even started shoving it in their mouths." Lazur took another drink of his water and put the mug back down. "It was pretty strange, the whole thing. I thought they ate dragons, not wood." He waved his hand. "But they just gobbled it all up. Then the wizard moved out in front of all three of them and stood right in the middle of that drawing."

"We thought they were going to eat him, but whatever that circle and those drawings were for, they didn't want to move any closer once the wood was gone. It looked like he was talking to them or something after that, maybe trying to calm them down. I don't know. But it didn't work. The big, red one let out this loud roar, and I saw something like heat rising off the ground on a hot day swirl all around the wizard just before the red creep snatched him up and ate him."

Tina cringed. It was hard to get any more dead than that. "Thank you, Lazur. I think that's all I need to know."

"It might not be. And that's what I came to see you about." Lazur leaned down from his stool and picked up a rectangular object with cloth wrapped around it. He laid it onto the table next to Tina and folded his arms again. "I saw something fall from the wizard's robe when the Dragon Eater grabbed him. This was lying in the middle of the circle."

Tina looked at the cloth-wrapped object. She lifted one edge of the cloth. It was a book. "The wizard had this with him when he went to confront the Dragon Eaters?"

Lazur nodded. "I thought it was odd for him to have a book with him, but what do I know of what wizards carry around."

"Too true." Tina rubbed the side of her muzzle. "Lazur, why didn't you tell me about this before?"

Lazur shook his head. "You didn't really give me a good first impression, wizard. Being judgmental about the people here and the governor and sneaking around in the shadows, I wasn't sure what you were up to. But after seeing what you did for that Maldavian, it just seemed strange."

Tina's ears stood up. "Strange?"

Lazur put his finger on top of the book. "That circle you drew in the ground was a lot like the one the other wizard drew. Just a lot smaller."

Tina wiggled her whiskers. The spiral Angelica had drawn was meant for the casting of a Ritual of Preservation. It wasn't an unusual practice for a wizard to draw a spiral like that, but she doubted Lazur had the knowledge in magic to really recognize the difference. But it did tell her the wizard was using a spell of some sort.

Tina stood up. "You're right, Lazur. Seeing it from your point of view, I must have seemed a bit like a thief sneaking around in the shadows. As far as being judgmental goes, I've learned in my line of work I have to be careful of people. Investigation is largely a matter of observation, so I've gotten used to trying to figure people out from a distance." She sighed. "But I do see your point." She put her hand on the edge of the book. "Thank you for bringing this to me. I take it from this you've decided to put a little more trust in me, hm?"

Lazur snorted. "Don't go too far, wizard. I trust you enough to try to put this thing to rest." He leaned back from the counter. "Don't start thinking that means I'm ready to put my life in your hands."

Tina smiled. "Fair enough." She considered for a moment before asking her last question. "Lazur, how long ago was it that the wizard died?"

Lazur scratched the underside of his chin. "It would be around five months ago, so right in the middle of autumn."

Tina supposed there would be no chance the spell spiral would still be visible since autumn was a rainy season. The winter had surely brought enough snow for the spring thaw to wash the spiral away even then. She nodded. "Thank you, Lazur." She put her hand on the cloth wrapped book. "I'll see what I can find out from this book. Though, I am curious about one thing. Why were you holding onto it? I would have thought you'd hand it over to the guards or the governor."

Lazur shrugged. "Idori might have destroyed it." He thumbed toward the governor's house at the northern end of town. "And while I trust Governor Keldo to do what's right for the people, I'm not sure I trust him enough to put an implement of magic in his hands. I wasn't sure of what to do with it until I heard the governor was going to the Council of Stars for help."

Tina nodded. "I think I can understand that." She smiled at Lazur. "Thank you again, Lazur. You've been very helpful."

Lazur gestured toward the book. "You need any help moving that somewhere safe?"

Tina shook her head. "I will handle it."

Lazur nodded and rose from his seat. "Be careful, wizard."

As Lazur walked away from the counter, Tina turned her head toward Kravek. She could see he had been keeping an eye on her, but he had stayed far enough away for her to handle business privately. She beckoned him over.

Kravek rested his hand on the counter next to Tina once he'd moved from his seat. "Guess we don't have to go looking for him, huh?"

Tina giggled. She pointed at the covered book. "Is there room in your backpack for that?"

Kravek started to lift the edge of the cloth covering the book, but Tina swatted his finger with her tail, and he moved his hand away. "Dangerous?"

"Potentially. Just leave the binding on and don't open it."

Kravek nodded. "It'll fit in the back pocket." He put his backpack down on the table and opened a large flap on the back. The book fit inside snuggly, and Kravek tied the flap. He then slung his backpack onto his shoulders again. "Since Lazur came to us, where do we go from here?"

"Before we do anything else," Tina pinched the bridge of her muzzle, "I need my glasses."

Chapter 14

After Tina emerged from her doorway in the wall of the Stumble Drum, she found herself walking into an almost empty inn. Captain Morgan, Mr. Kilba, and even Beth were nowhere to be found. Standing at the doorway to the outside, Kravek looked anxious. His tail lashed about behind him in agitation as he stood with his hand on the door frame. Tina noted he was looking out-side. "Kravek?"

Kravek looked back at Tina and then quickly moved to the counter and put his hand down on it. "Something's been spotted at the edge of the woods, Tina. Something big."

Tina stepped onto his hand. "One of the Dragon Eaters?"

Kravek shook his head. "I don't know. But it's got every-one running for cover, and the guards have loaded the trebuchets. We better get out there." He lifted Tina up to his shoulder, and she stepped off onto it.

Outside the inn, the streets were quickly emptying. Tina adjusted her glasses on the bridge of her muzzle as she watched guards running from the port to the western gate leading out of the town. "Take me to the gates."

Kravek nodded and was quick to leave the tavern. He sidestepped a family of foxes, a mother and two boys, as they ran in the direction of the port. The black bull made his way to the gate swiftly, but even with Kravek's towering height, Tina couldn't see over the wall.

"We need to get up there." Tina pointed up to the walkway on the inside of the wall.

"I'm not a guard, Tina. Town folk aren't allowed up on the

battlements." Kravek looked at her on his shoulder.

"Then just put me up on the stairs." Tina ran down Kravek's arm. He lifted his hand to the platform at the top of the first set of stairs where they turned to lead up to the walkway. Tina leapt off and climbed the stairs until she could reach the wall itself. Guards were already in position on the wall as Tina climbed up to the top to perch between two of the carved spikes. She adjusted her glasses as she looked outward.

At the edge of the woods, she could see something moving in circles. It looked like a mound of soil. Next to it was another massive mound of soil, but it was unmoving. The runic circle appeared in the right lens of Tina's glasses, and it didn't take long for her to figure out what was moving the soil. "Belthazuul?"

Governor Keldo, who was standing on the bridge over the closed gateway of the town, turned his head at hearing Tina's voice. "Wizard!" He quickly moved to the end of the bridge where Tina was perched. Tina could see Captain Cephalin standing behind him, but the wolverine's attention was entirely on the mound of soil on the other side of the open field.

"Open the gates." Tina jumped down from the wall and landed on the walkway in front of the governor.

"What?"

"Open the gates. They won't do much good either way. That's a Maldavian of Cerra out there. Maybe he wants to talk, and I want to be able to talk back. And stand your men down."

"But Wizard--"

"Governor, I'm here to deal with the problem of the Dragon Eaters. If the dragons can help, I wish to speak with them."

Keldo considered Tina for a moment, then turned and called out to Captain Cephalin. "Captain, open the gates."

The wolverine turned his head to glare at the governor. "I don't think I heard you right, Governor."

"I said open the gates. Now do it, Captain."

Captain Cephalin grunted, but his glare melted, and he

called down to the guards standing inside the gates. "Open the gates!"

The guards looked confused but knew better than to question the order. They lifted the board barring the gates and pushed them open.

Tina ran down the stairs and jumped back onto Kravek's shoulder. "Take me outside."

Kravek nodded and walked through the gates. "Where are we going?"

"Take me to that mound of soil."

Kravek nodded, but before he could take three steps, he stopped. "I might not have to."

On the far side of the field, the mound of soil had suddenly started on its way to the city. It wound back and forth like a giant snake moving beneath the soil as it rapidly approached. The other mound of soil which had been moving around in circles remained at the edge of the woods but had finally stopped circling.

"Farther out. Let's keep him away from the city." Tina climbed to the top of Kravek's head and seated herself with her hands gripping his hair.

Kravek hesitated but ran away from the city. Once he'd gotten about a hundred feet away from the walls, the moving mound of soil had redirected its path straight for him. The black bull snorted as his pace slowed. "I think we're far enough out, Tina."

Tina tugged on Kravek's hair. "This will do, then." She climbed down his body and dropped to the ground. Tina ran a few feet in front of Kravek and threw her hands up before calling out in a voice amplified well beyond her normal speaking range. "Belthazuul!"

The mound of soil came to a slow stop thirty feet in front of Tina and collapsed back into the soil. The ground shook. A being much larger than the initial mound of soil emerged from beneath the ground. The top of its head was flat and sloped forward into a gigantic maw of stone filled with hundreds of crystal teeth. Its eyes were golden as it looked down at Tina and placed one of its massive arms on the ground. It pushed itself up from the soil as if emerging from water with rocks falling all around it. Its other arm, easily twenty feet tall up to the elbow, settled on the ground as it rose. The dragon's entire body was made of stone with plates of raw, metallic ore covering its chest, the backs of its arms, and the top of its head. Even its wings, which had a massive span of more than sixty feet, had plates of raw ore covering the backs. They slammed down against the ground as the Maldavian's upper torso emerged, and it looked down at Tina.

The Maldavian's voice was deep and firm as he spoke slowly, and his bass tone resonated outward like a wall of air. *"Tina van Schtoffen."*

Tina had to pick herself up after Belthazuul's wings had shaken the ground. She dusted off her robes, folded her arms, and bowed to the stone dragon. She replied in fluent Maldavian. *"Belthazuul, it is good to see you again."*

"Perhaps not so good once you learn of my purpose here." Belthazuul straightened up, though his lower torso remained hidden beneath the soil. He then spoke with equal fluency in the trade language. "I have been sent by the Word of Shahdazhan to force these interlopers to flee. And then, I am to destroy their town, their farms, and their port." In spite of what he said, Belthazuul spoke calmly.

"Belthazuul, these people are not the enemies of Maldavia." Tina straightened up as well. "Why has the Word of Shahdazhan sent you to destroy their town?"

Belthazuul shook his massive head which threw dirt and rocks away from the top of it. "It is not mine to ask the reasons of the Word of Shahdazhan, Lady van Schtoffen. It is only mine to carry out his orders."

"Shalizan was the Word of Shahdazhan before his death, Belthazuul. Who is the voice of the dragon All-Father now?"

148

"The Word of Shahdazhan has passed to another. You know of Vistru, the Cloud Hider. He is the new Word of Shahdazhan." Belthazuul leaned forward slowly, and his head came within a few yards of Tina. "Though you are a friend of Maldavia, Lady van Schtoffen, I cannot turn away from the duty to which I am bound."

Tina pulled her necklace off over her head and held it up so Belthazuul could see the lava-colored crystal held within it. "I bear Shalizan's Albatross with me, Belthazuul. If not on my word, then at the request of Shalizan. He, like others, has asked me to undo the damage done by the Eaters of Magic. If you cannot hold on my word, then I ask you to send your Albatross to the Ring of Fire and inform them that I am here and that I am working to bring about the end of the Dragon Eaters."

The ridge of rocks above Belthazuul's eye rose. He then remained as still as a statue, motionless as the rocks from which he was made. After a brief consideration, he turned his head and bellowed at the mound of soil at the edge of the trees. It burst upward as a Maldavian Albatross with black skin and a pair of brown and white speckled wings took to the air. Belthazuul then turned to look down at Tina again. "Until Norita returns, I will wait. But I will wait at the gates of the city. For if Norita returns with word I am to carry out my orders, I will not wait longer."

Tina let out a sigh of relief. She put her necklace back on and turned away from Belthazuul. Even with the expectation of dealing with creatures powerful enough to be called Dragon Eaters, this was going to be much harder than she had anticipated.

Chapter 15

Belthazuul had come to rest in front of the gates of the town of Likonia with his hands spread in front of him. As still as the ground beneath him, the dragon's torso looked like a giant, imposing statue. The level of tension it produced in the town itself could be felt in the air. A dragon on anyone's doorstep could easily cause such an effect.

Tina, riding on Kravek's head, crossed back into the town to be met by Governor Keldo and Captain Cephalin. Captain Cephalin didn't look happy, but from the way he glared at Tina, she guessed it wasn't just because of the dragon on their doorstep.

Governor Keldo stepped forward and sighed. "So, now we have the Maldavians pressing on our little town as well."

Tina folded her hands in her lap. "I would not worry about the Maldavians so much, Governor. I have had encounters with them before. They will listen to me."

Keldo nodded. "I trust you to try to speak some sense into them, Wizard. But we have had our own encounters with the Maldavians as well." He sighed again. "The arrival of the Dragon Eaters was almost a blessing for awhile. The Maldavians were on the verge of trying to drive us off this land before." He raised a finger. "Mind you, almost a blessing. The Dragon Eaters must be dealt with because they still pose a threat to both our peoples. Perhaps some common ground may be found there."

One of Tina's ears twitched. She then nodded. "It is likely. Once the Albatross returns, I hope to have a chance to speak with Belthazuul." Tina adjusted her glasses. "If I may, Governor, since we have some time before the Albatross returns, I had a question

I've been meaning to ask you."

Governor Keldo showed that smile which hid too many teeth. "Of course, Lady van Schtoffen."

"Why did you believe you specifically needed to bring a wizard here to deal with the Maldavians?"

Governor Keldo folded his hands together. "This is a question you have asked before, Lady van Schtoffen. Was my answer before not sufficient?"

"It was, but with a little more information, I'd like to know why you thought specifically that a wizard would be of benefit."

Governor Keldo nodded. "Of course. I hired a wizard because I have been told several times that wizards regard the Maldavians as magic incarnate. I thought perhaps the wizard could find more in common with the Maldavians, find some way to relate to them." He gestured to Tina. "I wish I could have had a wizard like you who has dealt with them before, in truth." Keldo sighed and folded his hands together behind him. "But alas, my requests for intervention from the Council of Stars were denied, as you are well aware."

Tina nodded. "Was he able to find common ground with them?"

"It seemed like it, at first." Governor Keldo leveled his ears out to the sides. "Unfortunately, when it appeared he was making progress, the Dragon Eaters arrived. Shortly afterward," the governor's ears lay straight back, "he perished. That was a little more than five months ago."

"And how many times have the Dragon Eaters appeared since then?"

Governor Keldo rubbed his chin in thought. "Well, they have only been seen on the nights surrounding when Cerra's Grace is at its brightest."

"The nights around the full moon?"

Governor Keldo nodded. "Of course."

Tina was about to ask another question when she saw a

short, black-furred rabbit boy suddenly run past. She saw him heading for the main gates which were still open.

"Aiden!" Not far behind the boy was Beth with her ears laid back against her black hair.

Kravek looked at Tina on his shoulder. "Shouldn't we stop them?"

Tina shook her head. "No. But I would like to observe this."

Kravek's eyebrow rose in curiosity. He turned and walked to the front gate where Beth stood, frozen in fear, with one hand on the open gate and the other reaching for Aiden. He had escaped her grip, but Beth stood trembling as she watched Aiden run toward the dragon.

Tina stood on Kravek's shoulder and leapt down to Beth's. Beth felt the weight land on her shoulder and turned her head. She whimpered as she looked at Tina. "Please, Tina, save him!"

Tina could feel Beth trembling as she stood in the gateway. As much as she knew Beth wanted to run out, fear of the dragon was all but pinning her feet to the ground. Tina gently rested her hand on the side of Beth's neck and smiled reassuringly. "You don't need to worry, Beth. That's your little boy?" Beth nodded in response to the question, but Tina could still see the fear in her eyes. Tina gently stroked the fur on the side of her neck. "Aiden is safe, Beth. Dragons of the soil and stone are quite patient." She gestured for Beth to look at Aiden as he stopped in front of the statuesque dragon.

Aiden looked up at the dragon with wide eyes. "Wow! You're one of the dragons!"

Belthazuul turned his head with the sound of grinding stone and shook the rocks free from his neck. He then nodded at the little black rabbit boy. "I am a dragon of soil and stone, young one." The dragon lowered his head and turned it to one side so he could look more closely at Aiden. "My name is Belthazuul."

Aiden pointed at his own chest. "I'm Aiden, sir. You're

really big!"

Belthazuul's voice rumbled out as a chuckle which reso-nated throughout the area. "And you have quite a small body, Aiden. But to approach a dragon, I sense you are much larger than you look."

Aiden grinned at the dragon. He looked at the stretch of the dragon's wings and stepped back. "You're wings are huge! Can you fly for a long time, sir?"

"I cannot fly at all," Belthazuul replied as he stretched his wings apart, "but my wings are meant to protect me, not to fly."

Aiden's ears swiveled forward. "Oh. I'm sorry. Are you sad that you can't fly, sir?"

Belthazuul raised and shook his massive head. "I am not. But, young Aiden, other dragons may not swim through the earth as I. So I do not envy them the sky."

Aiden grinned. "That rhymed! Do you like rhyming?"

Belthazuul chuckled again. "I'm afraid I do not have the gift, young Aiden. Do you have a rhyme you would wish to tell me?"

Aiden turned his head to one side and folded his hands in front of himself as he thought. "Well, my mom told me a rhyme."

Belthazuul bowed his head to Aiden. "I see. If you wish to tell me of this rhyme, young Aiden, I will listen."

Aiden took hold of his long ears and pulled them down on the sides of his head. He held them still as he tried to remember his mother's rhyme.

> "Sewed and sewed did old lady Ren,
> But never sewed did the old hen.
> Many clothes, she did make,
> And many muffins, she wished to bake.
> But never made them, only stared,
> Never cooked, only prepared,
> Sat upon the porch to wait,

And wait she did until too late.
Sewed and sewed did old lady Ren,
But never sewed did she again."

When Aiden let go of his ears, Belthazuul bowed his head once more. "A clever rhyme, young Aiden. Do you understand its meaning?"

Aiden tilted his head to one side with one ear standing straight up while the other swiveled out to one side. "Meaning, sir?"

Belthazuul nodded. "Its meaning. Many rhymes have a meaning, young Aiden. The rhyme you recited talks of an old woman named Ren." Belthazuul folded his arms and gently rested his massive wings on the ground. "From what I have heard you say, it sounds to me as if this woman Ren planned for the future, but waited far too long to act. There is a moral in that, young Aiden. Can you discover it?"

Aiden shifted his large feet in the dirt, but eventually shook his head. "I don't know, sir."

Belthazuul bowed his head once more. "Men and women can plan for the future all they like. But things do not always go as planned. Simply sitting around and waiting for the chance to act will get you nowhere but where you sit."

Aiden's ears both straightened up, and he smiled at the dragon. "You're smart, Mr. Bel." He waved his hand in the air then and turned back toward the town. "I should get back to Momma, sir. It was fun talking to you!"

Belthazuul nodded at the boy. "I am sure she is waiting for you, young Aiden."

Beth caught Aiden as he came running back to her, and Tina had to leap into Beth's hair to keep from falling as the rabbit woman threw her arms around Aiden. Kravek stepped up behind Beth and held his hand out for Tina who dropped out of Beth's hair and onto Kravek's palm. She fixed her glasses on the bridge of her muzzle.

The runic circle appeared in Tina's right lens as she looked at Aiden. It faded shortly after, and a faint smile crossed her lips. "Intriguing." She cleared her throat and looked up at Kravek. "Kravek, I'd like to go to the Thorn's Side."

Kravek looked at Tina curiously. "Captain Morgan's ship?"

She nodded. "Yes. Captain Morgan was trying to get my attention in the Stumble Drum, and I would also like to take a look at that book on board her ship."

Kravek deposited Tina onto his shoulder. "I can do that."

As Kravek started to walk off, Governor Keldo stepped forward. "Wizard, where are you going?"

Tina tugged on Kravek's ear, and he stopped. She stood up so she could turn around on Kravek's shoulder and look back at the governor. "I'm going to continue my investigation. We likely have a few hours before Belthazuul's Albatross returns. He will not harm the city until then." Tina patted Kravek's ear, and the bull swept his tail around to slap the tuft of fur on the end of it against his side before he continued on.

"And if he does?" Governor Keldo took a step forward.

"Then I suggest you be prepared to evacuate the town. The Maldavians only want to destroy the city, not its people, but refusing to get out of the way would not stop Belthazuul from carrying out his duty."

"And you're going to do nothing?"

"I am going to do the only thing which will likely keep them at bay; I will try to determine how we can get rid of the Dragon Eaters."

* * *

"Permission to come aboard!" Tina called up to Allister who was standing at the top of the gangplank leading onto the Thorn's Side.

155

The Madrian Shepherd looked at Kravek, then to Tina on his shoulder. "I've been told not to allow anyone from Likonia aboard the ship without the captain's express permission, Lady van Schtoffen."

Tina wondered for a moment why Captain Morgan would give such an order, but with a Maldavian perched in preparation to destroy the town, she guessed the captain didn't want people trying to rush to board the ship and overcrowd it. Tina bowed her head. "I think you can make an exception for Kravek. He is from Akoa, after all."

Allister cocked an eyebrow and turned to address one of the crew, but Captain Morgan came down from the quarterdeck. "Let them aboard, Allister." She put her hands on her hips and grinned. "Any guest of Tina's is welcome on my ship. Especially one as good-looking as him." The grey-furred cat winked her one good eye at Kravek and turned away from the railing, her thin tail sweeping to the side as she headed for her quarters.

Tina giggled at the captain's statement. She then looked up at Kravek, who seemed to be hesitating. "Kravek? Is everything all right?"

Kravek's eyes widened, and he shook his head. "Uh. Yes. Yes. I'm fine." He looked down at the gangplank and stepped onto it.

Tina eyed Kravek briefly. "You haven't been drinking this morning, have you?"

Kravek kept his attention on the gangplank as he walked up it. It wasn't particularly wide, but the coarse underside of his metal shoes gripped the wood well. Tina thought he might have wondered if it would support his weight before he spoke. "No, I haven't. I'm all right, Tina. Just... not used to being called good-looking."

Tina giggled. Once on board the Thorn's Side, she directed Kravek to the captain's quarters. "Go ahead and knock."

Kravek did so, and the door to the captain's quarters swung

open a moment later. On the other side, Captain Morgan smiled at the two of them. "Come in." She stepped away from the door and walked to the round table sitting in the middle of her quarters.

The back of the captain's quarters was all window which gave a clear view of the open sea behind the ship. In front of the window was a fairly lavish bed with four tall posts, one of which had a little carpeting wrapped around it. Captain Morgan reached up and unsheathed her claws, raking the post once in passing on her way to a dresser next to it. She stopped at the dresser and picked up a bottle of scotch. "Can I offer either of you a drink?"

Tina was about to answer when Kravek cut in. "No. Thank you."

The captain nodded and poured herself a glass. She turned back around to face the two of them and leaned against the dresser. "I had something I wanted to talk to you about in the Stumble Drum earlier, Tina. I've been chatting with the foreman, and I found something you might want to see." She gestured to a piece of paper lying on the table. "You remember on our arrival, I told you about one of my sailors having talked to another from the Water Walker?"

Tina nodded. "I do. You've been doing a little digging, I take it?"

"I told you I'd keep you informed if I found anything, and I just thought I'd follow my curiosity since we had information about another wizard coming to Likonia." Captain Morgan set her glass of scotch down on the dresser and walked to the table. She tapped the piece of paper. "I know most trade goods which are shipped in and out of the ports in Madrigaarde and Levansia. But what I found in the foreman's records was one shipment of supplies coming here which I do not usually see moved unless they're being accompanied by a magic user. Since we really didn't have any information about the wizard, I thought I'd look into it."

Tina looked down at the slip of paper, but before she

could ask, Kravek lifted his hand to his shoulder. Tina smiled and stepped out onto it. He lowered her down to the table, and Tina stepped off so she could walk over to the piece of paper. On it, she saw written an interesting collection of occult items. Most of them were fairly common and had multiple functions. But one item on the list stood out among all others.

"Three flasks of Milk of Cerra?" She looked up at the captain. "When were these items shipped?"

Captain Morgan thumbed the corner of the paper where a date was written. "According to the foreman's records, this shipment arrived in Likonia about nine months ago." Captain Morgan folded her arms and smiled in the way only a self-satisfied feline could. "But here's the part where it gets interesting. These items weren't on the foreman's regular receiving list. This is a copy made from his second set of books."

Tina looked up at Captain Morgan. "Second set of books?"

Captain Morgan nodded. "I'm sure you're aware there are some items banned from open trade. Usually, it has something to do with the items being dangerous to transport on a ship. There are a few items which have to have special care, and it takes a special dispensation from the courts in Madrigaarde for them to be legally shipped on a transport capable of carrying them through the proper means. Other items are simply banned because they're illegal in any form."

Tina looked over the list. "I'm familiar with the trade practices in Madrigaarde. But why do you bring it up? As far as I can tell, these reagents are all fairly safe on their own."

"The foreman of any port or dock is responsible for items received, including those which shouldn't have been shipped." Captain Morgan let her tail sweep back and forth slowly behind her. "But one of those items on a foreman's books can get the foreman in a lot of trouble with the trade guilds, especially in Madrigaarde." She held up two fingers. "Those foremen who receive items like that usually keep two sets of books. But that's what's unusual."

Tina looked up from the list. "How so?"

Captain Morgan walked back to her dresser and opened the top-middle drawer to withdraw a small, leather bound, red book. She tossed it onto the table. "You can check the list yourself if you like, but as far as I can tell," Captain Morgan folded her arms and leaned against the dresser again, "none of those items are on it."

Tina blinked at the red book sitting on the table next to the list. She didn't need to double-check the list, though. Tina had known Captain Morgan long enough to trust both her and her thoroughness. "If the items aren't illegal, then why would the foreman be keeping them on a secret set of books?" She looked up at the captain. "For that matter, how did you get him to show you his second set of books, knowing you're a Madrigaardian trader?"

When Captain Morgan offered back only her feline grin, Tina rolled her eyes. "Right. Feline persuasion." Tina returned her attention to the list of items which Captain Morgan had copied from the foreman's books. Her attention was drawn back to the three flasks of Milk of Cerra. While there were plenty of uses for Milk of Cerra outside of a wizard's needs, within the scope of a wizard's interest, Milk of Cerra really only had one function.

Tina looked up at Captain Morgan as she moved the list to one side. "Thank you for this, Captain. I do think this will be useful. I'd like to confirm something in a book I've been given by one of the Likonians, and I think this list will be important." She looked up at Kravek and curled a finger at him. "Kravek, will you get out that book, please? Set it on the table, but don't open it or remove the wrappings."

Kravek put his backpack down on the floor and opened the back flap. He removed the book and laid it onto the table next to Tina. He did as instructed and left it closed with the wrappings still around it.

"Kravek, take a step back, please."

Kravek looked at Tina curiously but did as he was told and moved back from the table.

Tina rested her hands on the cloth wrappings, and the runic circle appeared in the right lens of her glasses. She carefully sheathed the entire book in a field of force. Then she looked deeper into the equations surrounding the book. It took her only a moment to confirm her suspicion. "Captain Morgan, open your back window, please."

The grey-furred Kylathian pushed off the dresser and moved to the back window to undo the latch. She pushed both windows open. A moment later, the book sailed through the window and splashed into the water. Tina pressed her hands downward, and the book sank rapidly.

"What did you do that for?" Captain Morgan looked where the book had sunk.

Tina pushed her hands forward, and then curled her fingers as she swept her hands toward herself. The windows closed in front of Captain Morgan who stutter-stepped back from them. "Because I didn't want to mess up your pretty bed."

A loud WHOOMP came from behind the ship before a plume of water rose into the air. It drenched the back of the ship, and Tina was certain the quarterdeck would be soaked. But at least the ship was in one piece. "That's what I thought." Tina lowered her hands and seated herself on the table. "Lazur's rhabdophobia might have actually saved his life."

Kravek's startled manner slipped away as the plume of water dissipated behind the ship. "What on Cerra...?"

"The book," Tina adjusted her glasses, "was a trap. And that's enough evidence for me." She gestured to the list next to her. "Since none of these items would normally be concealed on a trade list, because the Maw of Kaelus literally collapsed on us simply because we entered, and as a result of that book being armed with an incendiary trap, I have come to the conclusion that, like my Shasta and the Maldavian Albatrosses, the Dragon Eaters are creations of magic. It would explain the Milk of Cerra being brought to Likonia with that shipment as well. And I would bet my glasses that the wizard Harkon Keldo called here to 'help' is the one who created them."

Chapter 16

The sound of footsteps running up the hallway drew the attention of the captain, and she moved to the doorway to see Thomas, her cabin boy, being followed by the first mate. Thomas burst through the door and threw his arms around Captain Morgan's waist. "Captain! You're all right!"

She put her hand on top of Thomas's head and stroked her fingers through his black fur. "Yes, Thomas, I'm just fine."

Allister stopped a few feet away from the captain. "Captain?"

"Everyone's all right, Allister. An item of magic exploded underwater behind the ship. Tell the crew not to worry."

The first mate straightened up and cut a brisk salute. "Aye, Captain."

Captain Morgan led Thomas back to her bed and seated herself on the edge with the young cat next to her, his arms still around her waist. She turned her attention to Tina. "You might have warned me you were bringing something explosive onto my ship, Tina."

Tina bowed her head. "I'm sorry, Jessica. I didn't have any reason to believe it would detonate until I saw your list and got a look at the magic surrounding it. I also preferred to look at it in a place private from the rest of the city." She raised her hand toward Likonia. "Too many wandering eyes, and now that I believe the Dragon Eaters were created by a wizard working for the governor, I'm not certain who I can trust." Tina glanced up at Kravek. "You, though, I'm not so worried about."

Kravek lifted his eyebrows and folded his arms with a

smile on his face. "Don't think I'm smart enough to be a co-conspirator?"

Tina giggled. "Oh, nothing so insulting as that. Your arrival time doesn't fit a co-conspirator. Willa told me you didn't get here until six months ago. The Dragon Eaters appeared eight months ago." She lowered her gaze and tapped the end of her muzzle. "Though, something about that doesn't make sense. Didn't you say before you had carried supplies to the Maw of Kaelus at one point?"

Kravek nodded. "I did. Wasn't long after I got here."

"And you didn't go inside the cave."

Kravek shook his head, then paused. "Well, I went into the mouth of the cave. Not much deeper."

Tina steepled her fingers in front of her muzzle and looked down at the table. "I don't suppose you know what it was you were carrying, do you?"

"Sorry." Kravek's tail swept around to slap the tuft of fur on the end of it against his side. "The foreman said go, so I went. But whatever was inside wasn't all that heavy."

"No?"

"Felt mostly empty. I could hear something shifting inside, but it was like I was carrying an empty crate. Probably something fragile with a lot of packaging."

Tina rubbed the side of her muzzle. "How big was it?"

Kravek held his hands up to show the size. "Maybe two and a half, three feet tall, rectangle-shaped. But like I said, it wasn't heavy at all."

Tina narrowed her eyes as she thought. "If the Dragon Eaters appeared eight months ago, but the wizard wasn't killed until five months ago, perhaps something went wrong." She looked up at Captain Morgan sitting on the edge of the bed with Thomas. "It's possible the wizard made the Dragon Eaters to gain some leverage with the Maldavians, but then he lost control. If that's the case, he might have had something delivered to the city to help control them. Captain, is this list everything from eight months ago?"

Jessica, who was purring to Thomas, turned her head. "It is. You want me to have another talk with the foreman?"

Tina straightened her head and rested her chin on her hands. "Mm. No, I don't think so. You start asking too many questions, and the foreman might get suspicious about your intentions and completely shut down. But knowing what was in that crate could be helpful in unmaking the Dragon Eaters." She rubbed her forehead. "And I would very much like to find out what happened to the wizard's assistants, the two Kamadene women."

Captain Morgan's ears lay back against her brown hair. "Tina, is it possible the wizard used them to create the Dragon Eaters, sort of like these reagents?"

"I haven't dismissed the possibility, and it would certainly account for why they haven't been seen in a long time." Tina sighed and put her hands down in her lap. "From what I've heard of them, though, they seem kind-hearted what with helping the farmers. It's possible he used them to create the Dragon Eaters thinking he would be able to control them more easily, but something went wrong." She scratched behind one of her ears as it twitched. "But that's also something which doesn't make sense. There weren't only the two Dragon Eaters. Shalizan said there are three of them, and his people have only ever seen the three." She rose from the table. "I should make a report to High Theorist Mythran. If it's true that wizard created the Dragon Eaters, this matter may have just escalated considerably."

* * *

Kravek stepped off the gangplank leading to the deck of the Thorn's Side. "The Stumble Drum, then?"

Tina shook her head. "Not yet. My report to the High Theorist will have to wait until the safety of the city isn't in ques-

164

tion. But we do have some time before Belthazuul's Albatross returns. I'd like to check on Luna."

Kravek glanced at Tina and nodded. "I'd like to know how she's doing, too."

Tina looked up as Kravek headed off the pier toward the surgeon's home. She saw Belthazuul looming over the town even from the port. He must have looked to the townspeople like the harbinger of doom, but there wasn't much to be done about it. She knew Belthazuul well enough to be aware he wouldn't be moved without word from the Ring of Fire. It wasn't so imposing to her to see him there, but that was simply because she was used to the Maldavians' manners from her previous visits. When it came to what they felt they needed to do, even those not so committed to their duties as Belthazuul were hard to convince otherwise.

As Kravek walked down the street, however, the Likonians were coming out of their houses to look up at the impressive stature of the dragon. Tina's ear twitched as she listened to their conversations. A few of them were expressing fear concerning the dragon, but she heard Aiden's name being spoken and how the young rabbit had simply approached Belthazuul. She even heard one conversation coming from a familiar voice. Tina turned her head to see Lazur talking with another badger with what looked like her own pup in her arms.

Kravek glanced at Tina on his shoulder. "You're quiet, Tina."

Tina looked up at Kravek a moment later and rubbed the back of one of her ears. Putting her hand at the base of her ear, Tina pushed back her hair and used the other hand to brush the fur inside her ear to one side. Concealed in the fur was a pair of golden studs which she removed. She then took a thin, golden plate off the back of her ear and rubbed the spot from which she'd removed the plate. "I'm sorry, Kravek. I was just thinking and listening. I wonder a little bit about how much contact the townspeople have actually had with the Maldavians. From the conversations going on around us, it seems to me as though they've had little to none. They feared Belthazuul when he first arrived, and rightfully so. But now... they seem more in awe of him than anything else."

"What's that in your hand?" Kravek tried to look a little more closely at the golden plate Tina held.

She glanced at it, then held it up so Kravek could see the runes inscribed on it. "They're meant to augment my hearing."

"You have bad eyes and bad ears?" Kravek cocked one eyebrow curiously.

"Not so much bad as too small." She put the plate onto the back of her ear and replaced the studs. The long furs in Tina's ears hid them well. "I discovered a long time ago when I was transformed to this size that it affected my hearing, my voice, even my eyesight. My eyes aren't even all that bad. They're just very small, and my vision wasn't perfect beforehand." She rested her hands in her lap. "Without those plates, I can't make out speech very well unless it's someone with a very high-pitched voice."

"What about your voice? You have a plate for that too?" Kravek turned his attention back to the street and spotted the alley leading to the surgeon's house.

"Speech is easier to handle." Tina pulled her hair to one side and brushed her fingers through the fur. "It's probably too small for you to see very easily, but there's a rune tattooed under the fur on the side of my neck which lets me project my voice as if I were normal-sized."

Kravek chuckled. "I'll take your word for it." He stepped up to the door of the surgeon's home. "So I guess you couldn't really function without magic, huh?"

Tina shook her head. "Not anymore. Seems fitting magic made me reliant on magic, doesn't it?"

Kravek paused as he put his hand on the door and considered. "Maybe." He looked at Tina on his shoulder. "Have you ever wondered what your life would have been like if you'd never become a wizard, Tina?"

Tina wiggled her whiskers. "I have. There are a lot of possibilities. But I do know one certainty."

"What's that?"

"It would have been much shorter, even if I'd spent it taller." Tina inclined her head toward the door. "You should probably knock first."

Kravek turned his attention back to the door, curled his fingers into a fist, and knocked gently.

The door opened, and on the other side was the badger nurse whom Tina and Kravek had spoken with earlier. "Oh! Welcome back. Did you come to check on Luna?"
Tina nodded. "Yes. How is she doing, Vira?"

Vira smiled. "She is doing just fine. She's still a little exhausted from the whole ordeal and the loss of blood, but she is out of danger. I can ask my husband if she's strong enough to see you, if you'd like."

"It would be greatly appreciated." Tina bowed her head in thanks.

The nurse smiled. "Just wait here a moment. I will be right back." She let the door close, but not enough to latch it. Tina could see her walk to the back room from the doorway. The nurse stuck her head in and spoke, but Tina was too far away to hear the short conversation. When the nurse returned, she pulled the front door open as the surgeon stepped out of the back with a rag in hand. Vira smiled. "Luna's awake, and she can see you, but try not to keep her very long. She does need her rest."

"We appreciate it," Kravek replied. He walked through the door and came to a stop in front of the back door. He put his hand on it, but glanced at Tina on his shoulder. "Do you want some time alone with her?"

Tina looked up at Kravek curiously. He wasn't wrong about her wanting to be alone with Luna for a little bit, but she wondered how he'd picked up on it. "If it's all right with you, I would."

Kravek nodded. He lifted his hand to his shoulder, and Tina stepped off onto it. Kravek pushed the door open and walked inside to set Tina down on the edge of the bed. He turned his attention to Luna who was covered up to her chest by the blanket, though her arms lay on top of it. "Glad you're doing better, Luna. Tina wanted to talk to you alone for a few minutes."

"With my state of undress, I'd like to talk to her alone too." Luna's voice was quiet, but steady.

Kravek rubbed the side of his muzzle for a moment, then turned away and walked back out through the door.

Tina walked up along the bed until she was standing next to Luna's chest. She put her hand on the mink's arm. "How do you feel?"

Luna turned her head to look down at Tina, though it put her neck in an uncomfortable position. She straightened up again. "Like I was trampled by a thunder lizard. Everything aches."

Tina could see that while the cuts she'd mended had been bandaged and were probably stitched up underneath, there were several bruises showing through Luna's white fur. She adjusted her glasses and glanced around the room. Seeing a spare set of sheets sitting on the counter across from the bed, Tina rose. "I'll just be a second." She leapt onto the end table next to the bed.

Climbing onto the counter next to the end table, Tina settled down on her knees next to the sheets. She disrobed, removing her ear plates, her necklace, the armlet which hadn't been broken, and her robe, though she kept her necklace in hand. She looked at the lava-colored crystal it held briefly but then turned the necklace over. On the back of it was a diamond-shaped plate.

Tina slid her claws under the plate and pried it loose. It came off with a soft 'tink,' and she set it aside. Inside was a wide pocket which held three small, black spheres. Tina removed one of them, then replaced the plate on the back of the necklace.

Leaving her robe and accessories on the counter, Tina unfolded one of the sheets and climbed under it. She popped the small, black sphere into her mouth and crunched it between her back teeth. It tasted like licorice.

Tina felt a familiar moment of vertigo and disorientation. It had come quickly. The world had darkened for her within seconds. Her eyes drifted shut, and she slumped against the sheets.

When her eyes opened again, it was as if she had just awakened from a long sleep in a pitch black room. She felt disoriented and unsure if she was actually awake. Tina knew she was, but it was as though her mind was hesitating to acknowledge it. That hesitation faded as the room came back into view.

Tina pushed herself up and felt the sheet pressing against her body. Looking down, she had to take a moment to recognize where she was, what she was doing, and who was nearby. When she saw Luna's wide-eyed stare, everything finally came back to the wizard.

Tina slid her legs off the counter and stood up as she pulled the sheet around her shoulders to cover herself. Looking down at the counter, she saw her tiny robes and all of her accessories lying there in a neat pile. Her gaze then moved to her feet as she saw them resting on the floor five feet below.

Tina heard Luna try to sit up, but she moved to the bed and put a hand on the mink's good shoulder to usher her back down. "Don't worry, Luna. It's just me." Tina seated herself on the side of the bed as Luna lay back down.

"Tina, you're--"

"Big?" Tina smiled at Luna in a friendly manner.

Luna smiled back weakly. "I was going to say thin."

Tina looked down at herself underneath the sheet and sighed. "I should probably eat more often than I do. But I get on a job and get so focused, sometimes I just forget."

Luna held up one of her hands, and Tina slid her hand into it. "Why did you do this?"

Tina put Luna's hand into her lap and covered it with both

of her own. "I'm the reason you were hurt, Luna. There are a few reasons, but... I wanted you to be able to see clearly who was responsible."

Luna quietly laughed as she laid her head back down and closed her eyes. "Are you always a martyr, Tina?" Tina looked confused at Luna, but it only broadened the mink's smile. "I was the one injured, but you're the one who looks wounded."

Tina lowered her gaze to Luna's hand in her lap. "I'm the one who asked you to come along with us. I did my best to mend your wounds, but without my glasses, I--"

"You did enough." Luna tapped one of her fingers against Tina's palm. "The surgeon says I'll eventually make a full recovery." She sighed quietly. "Besides, I've had worse injuries. Price of being a soldier."

Tina laid her ears back against her hair. "I have rarely seen women being soldiers outside of the Khanifran tribes and the Braka. How did you ever manage to become one?"

Luna smiled in a self-satisfied manner. "By being a better archer than any man in the whole of the Vulfin District." She then looked up at Tina. "How about you? How did you become a wizard?"

Tina rubbed the back of Luna's hand gently. "Another wizard spotted I had the talent for it. But that was a long time ago."

Luna closed her eyes. "I've heard about you before, you know."

Tina wiggled her whiskers and looked at Luna curiously. "You have?"

"You've got more of a reputation than you might realize, Tina." She laughed weakly, but stopped with a wince. "Do you even know what the Mateesh people, your own kind, call you?"

Tina nodded. "*Kedish Kerasta*. The Tiny Tempest."

"You may not have known it at the time, but when you requested me to go with you to Dragon's Mouth," Luna opened her eyes and looked up at Tina, "I was honored. So don't feel bad that

I got hurt." She grinned in spite of the bruises on her jaw. "I will be able to tell my family someday about how I was once asked for, personally, by a famous wizard."

Tina quietly laughed. "Are you still in touch with them, even here in Likonia?"

Luna nodded. "I am. We send letters whenever there's a ship in port. There's one in my room at home right now I wanted to send on the Thorn's Side when it goes back to Madrigaarde." She squeezed Tina's hand. "If I'm not well enough by the time the ship leaves, would you make sure to send it for me, Tina?"

Tina nodded. "I will. Are you sure you want me going into your room alone, though?"

Luna shook her head. "I don't mind it. I'd rather you went in than Idori or any of the other guards." She laid her head back down and closed her eyes. "He's not going to be happy about this, Tina."

Tina hesitated. "Why would Captain Cephalin have any more reason to be unhappy than any of the other guards?"

Luna frowned. "It's... complicated." She turned to look up at Tina again and noted the mouse's curious expression. "I've known Idori longer than any of the other guards in Likonia, Tina. I know it's technically fraternization, but... we're not exactly regular military anymore."

"Oh. I see."

Luna laid her head back. "You've seen how he is these days. I wish you could have known him three years ago, before—" She caught herself. The mink looked as if she'd almost said something she shouldn't. "Well... before we came to Likonia." Luna squeezed Tina's hand. "I'm just warning you because he'll probably take this out on you."

Tina lowered her head, ready to say something when the door to the room opened, and Kravek stuck his head in. "Are you two doing al—"

Before Kravek could finish his sentence, the heel of a flying boot smacked him right in the forehead. He recoiled from the blow and slapped his hands over his face, letting the door shut behind him. "Ow ow ow!"

Luna sighed and let her arm fall back to the bed as her shoulders hit the pillow again. "Women talking in here!" She called out.

Tina covered her mouth with her hands, then quickly uncovered it and called into the living room. "Doctor, I think you have another patient out there!"

Luna and Tina both shared a brief fit of laughter before Luna quieted down with a wince. "Oof. Well, at least we know my bow arm still works."

Though Kravek had left, Tina still felt a little pang of sympathy for him as she glanced at the boot lying on its side in front of the door. She looked back down at Luna. "Luna, the wizard who came here is the one I believe created the Dragon Eaters. And I think what we went through in the Maw of Kaelus was a trap set for anyone trying to follow his trail."

Luna sighed. "Somehow, that doesn't surprise me, Tina. The way he treated Leilani and Nana was despicable."

Tina's ears swiveled toward Luna. "Leilani and Nana?"

Luna nodded. "His assistants. Two Kamadene women. They looked like sisters, but one had scales of a different color." The mink wrinkled her muzzle and laid her ears back against her hair. "He treated them like slaves whenever I saw them all together."

Tina lowered her head and looked back down at Luna's hand. She rested her own hand on top of it. "I think it possible the two Kamadene women may still be alive. If they can be saved, I'll do all that I can."

Tina rose from the bed and walked to the counter next to the end table. She looked down at the collection of her robe and accessories with the knowledge she would be returning to her cursed size soon. Looking on the other side of the sheets from which she'd taken her current attire, Tina noted a small glass jar in which was contained the shards that had been removed from Luna's body. She picked up the jar and examined them briefly. "I thought I removed all the shards from your wounds."

Luna turned her head so she could see the jar. "The surgeon said he found a couple more when he reopened the wounds."

Tina ran her short claws over the glass jar. "Luna, would you mind if I kept these?"

Luna shook her head with a small smile. "I don't mind. Though I would like to keep that big one."

Tina noted the largest of the shards in the jar. "What for?"

"Call it proof for my claim of working with Tina van Schtoffen." Luna grinned.

Tina smiled at Luna and pulled the top off the jar. She removed the largest shard carefully and examined it. She set the shard down and then put the lid back on the jar. "Once I'm back to my normal... well, the size I've grown accustomed to, I'll disenchant it for you. I'd bet my glasses these shards still have the shatter spell on them. And I want to keep them because, sometimes, I just need a reminder that I'm not infallible." Tina climbed up onto the counter and seated herself with the jar in her hands. She considered Luna briefly. "Luna... I don't know what stories you've heard about me, but I'm just a wizard who's done the best she could with what she had."

Luna offered an understanding smile. "Isn't that what we all do?" She let the smile fade as she laid her head back down and closed her eyes. "Thank you, Tina."

Tina looked at Luna curiously. "For what?"

"For coming back to check on me. And for making my life more interesting for awhile. I think," Luna sighed softly, "I can rest now."

Chapter 17

After Tina had returned to her cursed size of six inches tall, she disenchanted the shard which she'd be leaving behind for Luna. Then the wizard collected a length of string from the surgeon's supplies, a foot-and-a-half long, and tied it firmly around the neck of the bottle. It was only half her height but too big for her to carry. Using her magic, she shrank the bottle, shards, and string until she could hang them around her neck. She looked down at the bottle and turned it so she could look at the shards which produced the quiet sound of stone scraping against glass.

Walking back to the edge of the counter, Tina climbed down and slipped under the door. On the other side, Kravek was standing with one elbow resting on the mantle of the fireplace. Tina cleared her throat, and the black bull turned his head. She adjusted her glasses. "Where are Vira and the surgeon?"

Kravek walked over to Tina and settled down onto his knees. "They said they needed to get more thread and a new needle from the store."

Tina stepped onto Kravek's hand when he set it onto the floor. "I guess they trust us not to take anything." She looked up at Kravek's face. "How's your forehead?"

Kravek knocked on it with his fist. "I am a bull. But it was enough to get her point across."

Tina giggled. "I wasn't really expecting her to throw a boot at you."

Kravek chuckled. "Neither was I. Speaking of which," Kravek stood up with Tina in his hand, "was I just seeing things, or were you about four feet taller in there?"

174

Tina climbed onto Kravek's shoulder from his hand. "Four-and-a-half, actually. I can adjust my size once in awhile."

"But you can't make it permanent?"

Tina shook her head. "It requires suppressing my own magic in order to suppress the magic of the curse. I can only do it with these little pills I learned how to make." She sighed. "If I wanted to be 'normal' again permanently, I'd have to give up the practice of magic entirely." She shook her head. "After a life spent studying it, I don't think I could manage."

Kravek nodded. "I can understand that." His tail swept around, and the tuft of fur on the end of it slapped against his side. "So, there's a Maldavian on the town's doorstep, and we think we know where the Dragon Eaters came from. What's next?"

Tina wiggled her whiskers. "We just need to wait for Belthazuul's Albatross to return now." She laid her ears back against her hair and lowered her gaze. "Kravek... you far exceeded what I paid you for your service some time ago."

Kravek lifted one floppy ear and held it over Tina. "You may think so. I don't."

Tina looked up at Kravek's ear and swatted at it lightly. "No?"

Kravek nodded as he let his ear back down against the side of his head. "It's easier not to drink when I'm keeping busy." He rubbed one finger against Tina's back. "For now, that's pay enough for me."

The corners of Tina's mouth curled upward slowly. She felt warmth spreading into her cheeks and cleared her throat as she rubbed at them. "Well, in that case, let's go back to the front gate. I think the people will feel less on edge if I'm out there."

Tina took hold of Kravek's ear and climbed up to the top of his head. She shifted his mane around until she'd made herself a softer, more comfortable place to sit.

Tina and Kravek left the surgeon's house and headed for the front gate, but as they passed the town hall, Tina tugged on

Kravek's ear. "Wait a moment, Kravek." She pointed to the familiar rabbit woman who was sitting on a bench in front of the town hall porch with her black-furred son in her lap.

Beth was humming quietly to Aiden who had a smile on his face. She looked up as Tina and Kravek approached, and her long ears straightened up. Tina was a little surprised by the conflicted look on Beth's face.

Kravek crouched down in front of Beth as Tina climbed down onto his shoulder to put herself at eye level with the rabbit. "Beth? Is everything all right?"

Beth lowered her gaze from Tina and looked down at Aiden. "He's napping." She gently nuzzled the top of his head. "Tina... please tell me he's a wizard so he can leave this place."

Tina considered Beth's words. She reached up to tug on one of Kravek's ears and held her hand out toward Beth. Kravek raised his arm toward Beth with his palm flat and his fingers open. Tina walked out onto his hand, and then she leapt to Beth's shoulder. Seating herself next to Beth's head, Tina laid her tail across her lap. "I know you want a better life for him, Beth, and—"

Beth shook her head. "It's... not just that, Tina." She put her arms around Aiden and hugged him. "I couldn't... go after him. I wanted to. I wanted to chase him. I wanted to stop him from going out into that field, but..." Tina watched a tear streak down Beth's cheek, "...I just couldn't... make myself do it. He's my son, and I love him. But I couldn't move."

Tina understood how Beth felt. "Beth, I do want to take Aiden with me when I leave this place." When Beth turned her head to look at Tina, the wizard saw both hope and hesitation in her eyes. "He doesn't have the gift of a wizard. But he does have a gift for magic. I'm not an expert when it comes to shaman, but I know enough of them to recognize their empathic gift and how to proceed in getting Aiden the training which would allow him to use that gift." She gestured toward Aiden. "I had a hint when Aiden felt no fear of Belthazuul in spite of his imposing presence.

It was as if he knew Belthazuul wasn't going to hurt him."

Tina folded her hands in her lap. "Shaman possess the ability to both sense and project emotion. That's how they can influence spirits so effectively."

"You mean," Beth looked down at Aiden, "that's all it took?"

Tina nodded. "Once I had a hint of what to look for, finding it was easy." She adjusted her glasses. Then Tina put her hand on the side of Beth's neck. "If you want to remain in Likonia, Beth, you can be more hopeful you will see Aiden again if you let him go to Kerovnia."

Beth looked back at Tina on her shoulder. "But you said–"

Tina held up a finger. "I was talking about training a wizard. There are other shaman who can train Aiden at the Council of Stars, but as any of them would tell you, training a shaman doesn't take nearly as long as training a wizard." She put her hand back down in her lap.

Though Beth's expression remained solemn, a glimmer of hope could be seen in her eyes. Tina decided to give Beth another reason to be hopeful, though she knew she would also be giving her a decision to make. "Kravek and I need to go to the gates, Beth, but before we go, you should know that if you can find work in Kerovnia, you are welcome to accompany him."

Beth looked at Tina again. "You mean... I could come with him?"

Tina nodded. "Because Aiden has the gift for shamanism, it would be better for him if you were there." She rested her hand on the side of Beth's neck. "Take your time to think about it. This is a decision which will affect both of you a great deal."

When Beth looked back down at Aiden, she closed her eyes and nodded her head. Tina could only imagine what was going through Beth's mind. The mouse woman rose from Beth's shoulder and waved to Kravek. The black bull lowered his hand so Tina could step onto it before he put her back onto his shoulder.

* * *

The tension in the air at the front gate of Likonia seemed to have abated a bit with Belthazuul's inaction and Tina's arrival. The dragon of rock and soil remained motionless as Tina remained seated on the ground in front of him with her legs crossed and her hands folded in her lap. Kravek was sitting ten yards behind her and eating the rest of his payment from Tina.

Tina's gaze was settled on Belthazuul's face, and the two of them were simply staring at each other in a way which to others might have seemed eerie. But Tina knew that a dragon such as Belthazuul could very well be sleeping in his statuesque posture. Even so, she wanted him to know where her attention lay.

It wasn't until Tina could see something moving in the air far behind Belthazuul that she moved her eyes. She blinked a few times and touched the side of her glasses. The runic circle appeared in the right lens, and its layers rotated. Her vision grew sharper, and within the circle, Tina could see off into the distance far beyond her normal scope.

Twisting and flowing through the air with the smooth movements of a snake was a white-scaled Maldavian with a long, slender body that barely possessed a humanoid shape. Though the Maldavian lacked any sort of wings, she moved through the air as if gravity had no claim on her. Her underbelly was covered by golden scales which swept all the way back to her tail but ended shortly after reaching it. Her head resembled that of a wolf, though the only thing even resembling fur on her face was the golden mane which flowed from the top of her head and swept down the back of her neck. A pair of long whiskers trailed out from the sides of her scaly muzzle, and they swept and flowed with the movements of her body. Even the four horns on her head swept back majestically as she flew toward Belthazuul.

Flying beside the serpent-like dragon was a pair of Maldavian Albatrosses. She recognized one of them as Norita, Belthazuul's Albatross. The other Albatross flying beside the white Maldavian had a stronger physique. A male Albatross, his white scales, golden-feathered wings, and even his back-swept horns made him look much more like the new Maldavian who was approaching. Tina smiled to herself. She recognized the dragon and her Albatross.

Landing next to the imposing Belthazuul, the newly arrived Maldavian looked much smaller in comparison even though she was taller than the largest of buildings within the city of Likonia. She looked up at Belthazuul and bowed her head, speaking in the Maldavian native tongue. *"Return to the Ring of Fire, Belthazuul."*

Belthazuul's stone head turned as he fixed his gaze on the other Maldavian. He then bowed, his body moving with the sound of grinding stone. *"Yes, Lady."* Belthazuul turned his attention back on Tina. "We shall have to have another staring match another time, Wizard. It has been enjoyable." Belthazuul then fixed his gaze on Norita. Without a word, he sank into the ground to become nothing more than a massive mound of soil. Norita dived into the soil herself to join him as the two swam through the soil back toward the woods.

Tina smiled at Belthazuul's remark as he departed and rose to her feet. She bowed to the white-scaled Maldavian. *"It has been too long, Methystra."*

The white-scaled Maldavian turned her attention down to Tina. She bowed her head. *"Welcome back, Theorist van Schtoffen. I wish you could have returned in better times."* Methystra looked at the guards standing at the ready on the wall. *"Belthazuul's orders have been rescinded for the time being, Lady van Schtoffen, but the council remains ready to issue them again. I sent him away only because two dragons in one place at this time is tempting bait for these Eaters of Magic."*

Tina adjusted her glasses. *"Methystra, there is no need to be quite so formal. We are long friends. Please, call me Tina."*

Methystra looked down at Tina. The Maldavian parted her jaws and breathed out a thick mist which spiraled around her body rapidly. All that could be seen of her for a few seconds was a column of fog. A shape descended down through the fog as the shadow of Methystra's form disappeared. Stepping out of the mist was a much smaller, far more humanoid form which more closely resembled a Maldavian Albatross than one of the true Maldavians. The new form however lacked the telltale feathery wings specific to the Albatrosses.

The clothing she wore looked like silk and was wrapped around Methystra's wrists with a stretch of cloth leading back up to her neck. Tina could see the cloth hugging the woman's torso where it crisscrossed on her chest. More of that cloth was hanging around the woman's waist with a trail leading down in the back over top of her long, tapered tail with a similar stretch of cloth hanging down in front. Her golden hair was bushy, but swept straight back on her head with her four golden horns framing it.

A smile appeared on Methystra's muzzle. *"It's good to see you, Tina. I take it by your presence here the Council of Stars has become involved in all of this."*

Tina nodded. *"The High Theorist sent me here to learn more about the Dragon Eaters, or as Shalizan and you have called them, the Eaters of Magic."*

Methystra's smile faded at the mention of Shalizan. *"You saw Shalizan before he died?"*

Tina rested her hand on the necklace which contained the lava-colored crystal hanging against the front of her robe. *"I did. He wished me to tell you his last thoughts were of you, Methystra."* She lifted the necklace from her chest to look down at it. *"I think he also must have wanted something between you and Angelica before he died. I hold her in this gem for now. He wished me to cast a Ritual of Preservation on her."*

Methystra lowered her gaze. Tina could see the thoughtful look on the Maldavian's face, but she shook her head. "*There is something I would say to Angelica should I be afforded the opportunity. But for now,*" she looked to Tina again, "*I would ask you to keep Angelica with you. I do not know Shalizan's intent in preserving her, but she may be able to help you before this is over.*"

Tina could see the mixed emotions swirling in Methystra's eyes. She removed the necklace and held it up toward Methystra. "*Methystra, I do not know Shalizan's mind. But Angelica was a faithful and devoted Albatross. I think her last moments should be spent with someone who loved Shalizan as much as she.*"

Water edged Methystra's eyes, but she swept it away with her hand. "*You know not how truly you speak, Tina.*" She gently put her finger on the tiny necklace and ushered it back to Tina's chest. "*But I believe Angelica would rather ensure that her Shalizan was avenged.*"

Tina didn't agree, but she could see how the subject was upsetting Methystra. She pulled the necklace back over her head and let it settle back against her chest. "*Methystra, there are many things I would like to discuss with you, but I am uncertain how well the Likonians will react to you if you were to walk among them.*"

"*Not well.*" Methystra rose to her feet. "*Especially not since one of my kind was sitting on their doorstep ready to destroy their town.*" She turned her head to look back at the Albatross standing a respectful distance behind her. "*Arkus, please return home and tell the council I have arrived safely and sent Belthazuul back to the Ring of Fire. I mean to remain here for the time being.*"

The white-scaled Albatross bowed his head to Methystra, but shot Tina a glance. Tina could see the warning in it and knew well enough the Albatross's meaning. Spreading his golden, feathery wings, he leapt into the air and flew back in the direction from which he'd come.

Methystra looked down at Tina as her long tail swept back and forth behind her. "*If you wish to speak in private, I can surround us in mist.*"

Tina giggled. *"Or we could simply continue to speak in Maldavian. I do not get the impression the Likonians have learned your language in so short a time."*

Methystra shook her head. *"A few have,"* she looked up at the wall where the guards seemed to be more at ease with Belthazuul gone, *"though I do not see any of those whom I know have learned our language."* She then looked at Kravek. *"Will your Albatross be joining us?"*

Tina blinked and looked back at Kravek. *"My... Albatross?"*

Methystra nodded slowly. *"Though I can see you did not create him, I do see the flow of greater magic between the two of you."* Methystra raised one eyebrow. *"He is not your companion?"*

Tina's face reddened as she recalled what kinds of greater, yet subtle magic could form between two people. She cleared her throat and folded her arms across her stomach. *"He has been my traveling companion, but I only met him when I arrived in Likonia."*

Methystra tucked one arm across her stomach while she rested her other hand on the side of her muzzle and smiled. *"I see. I did not think your affections could be so quickly won, Tina."*

Tina's face reddened a little more deeply, and she reached up to adjust her glasses, quickly changing the subject. *"About the Eaters of Magic,"* her ears pressed back against her hair, *"I have come to learn a few things about them. I wonder if you might be able to help me confirm them, Methystra."*

Methystra's knowing smile only made Tina's face all the redder before the Maldavian let the subject shift as Tina guided it. *"What is it you wish to know?"*

"Your people can see the flow of magic in the world. Tell me, are the Eaters of Magic natural beings?"

Methystra shook her head. *"They are not. We have seen them many times before."* She frowned. *"We thought at first the Council of Stars was angry with us when we did."*

"Because they were created by magic?" Tina asked.

Methystra bowed her head. *"Because they were created by*

a wizard." Methystra looked wounded as she continued, *"My people thought at first we had somehow angered your Council of Stars by opposing the Likonians interloping on our lands. The Council of Stars has long been our ally, Tina. To believe your people had turned on us for such a reason was... disheartening.*" Her wounded expression changed to one of relief. *"You do not know the weight it lifted from our hearts when Norita gave our elders your message.*"

Tina sighed with her own sense of relief. *"That explains a little bit.*" She smiled at Methystra. *"I am glad to have been able to help lift that burden, Methystra.*"

Tina sat with her hands folded on her lap while Methystra settled onto her knees in front of the tiny wizard. She pulled her glasses off and used the edge of her robe to clean them. She spoke in the plain trade language with the knowledge Methystra was fluent in it. "There's something which seems very odd about this entire situation, Methystra." She put her glasses back on the bridge of her muzzle. "While I have seen the aftermath of the Dragon Eaters' presence, I have yet to see them for myself. You confirmed my own conclusion about their origin, at least. If I'm to undo them, I need to at least examine them. They apparently roam, but they must have a home of some sort. I've been told they only emerge in the days before, during, and following the full moon."

Methystra nodded. "That is the only time we have seen them, save in one instance."

Tina's ears straightened up and swiveled to face Methystra. "When was this?"

Methystra gestured toward the south. "An Idassian wizard erected a beacon of magic to attract them once. It was much closer to the Likonians' mine in the Maw of Malidath." She set her hand back onto her knees and gave Tina a stern expression. "The Likonians have been disturbing the resting places of the betrayers, Tina. That is one reason we have been opposed to their presence. They placed their colony directly between the Maws of Kaelus and

Malidath."

Tina wiggled her whiskers as her tail lay across her lap. "Why do you suppose that is, Methystra?"

Methystra shook her head. "We did not know at first, but when they started digging into Malidath's grave, we suspected it was because they wished to take Malidath's blood."

Tina wrinkled her muzzle. "Malidath's blood?"

Methystra bowed her head. "When the All-Father imprisoned Kaelus and Malidath, he ensured Malidath would never taste the breath of life again. As a result, Kaelus's blood remains a part of his body, but Malidath's blood seeped through the stone. I am certain it caused Malidath great pain, but once exposed to the air, it fused with the stone and turned to an ore imbued with the power of a Maldavian. I think your people call it aetherium."

Tina's ears stood up. "Methystra, do you think Governor Keldo knew about this?"

Methystra shook her head. "I am uncertain, but it was not very long after the Likonians built their city that they started digging." She put her hand on her chest. "Once we found out about it, Belthazuul caved in the entrance to their mine, and we forbade them from digging any deeper." Her hand settled back into her lap. "Then the Dragon Eaters appeared."

Tina lowered her head to look at the ground as she drifted into thought. "...An ore like that would be invaluable to many magic users. Perhaps that is how Governor Keldo enticed the wizard into working for him." She sighed and rubbed the bridge of her muzzle with her fingers. "But I suspect trying to confront the governor about it will yield nothing useful without some more solid evidence. And I'm certain the High Theorist will want something more substantial as well." Tina finally rose to her feet. "Methystra, could I impose upon you to show me to this mine?"

Methystra bowed her head. "I would be happy to, Tina." She pointed toward Kravek with a grin on her face. "Will your Albatross be coming?"

Tina muttered. "He's not my Albatross." She looked back over her shoulder at Kravek. "But he's been very helpful since I came to Likonia." She looked up at Methystra again. "So I would like to ask him, if you don't mind."

Methystra's knowing smile was all the answer Tina expected from the Maldavian at first, but she spoke as she rose to her feet. "When you are prepared, I will take you." She looked at Kravek with that same smile still on her lips as she gave Kravek and Tina a respectful distance.

Kravek lifted one of his ears and let it flop against his neck as Tina approached. "Why was she smiling at me like that?"

Tina waved her hand dismissively. "She's just trying to pull on my whiskers. Kravek, I need to go to the mines south of here. Methystra's offered to carry us, if you'd like to accompany me."

"Carry?" Kravek looked at Methystra curiously. "As in... fly?" He put his hands out in front of him and wiggled his fingers as if imitating a pair of wings.

Tina tilted her head. "...Kravek, you're not afraid of flying, are you?"

"Not flying." He opened his palm and smacked his fist into it. "Falling is more like. I'm very heavy, Tina. And I hit the ground very hard."

Tina giggled. "Don't worry. You'll never fly more safely than with a dragon like Methystra."

"I would have never supposed I'd be flying." Kravek looked down at the unfolded cloth and picked up the last piece of bread from it. He broke off a little of the crust and popped the rest into his mouth. He offered the piece of crust out to Tina. "Dinner, and I'll come along for all the use I can be."

Tina smiled and took the crust of bread. "It's a deal."

Chapter 18

While the trip south to the Maw of Malidath would have normally taken a few hours on foot, Tina and Kravek had ridden on Methystra's back. The Maldavian had followed the coast for half an hour before the grey stone of the mine could be seen. It was a rock formation as tall as Methystra in her true form, though much larger in its entirety. Rising right on the edge of the water, the rock formation looked unnatural, though they could all see it had sustained some damage. On the northern face could be seen the remnants of the main entrance to the mine. What was left of a shattered wall of wooden pylons lay strewn about the area, and a great fissure was rent through the entire formation with rocks collapsed into it. Tina thought it looked like Belthazuul had done his work well in sealing the entrance of the mine.

As Methystra drifted down from the sky and landed in front of the fissure, she rolled one shoulder down while perched on all fours so Kravek and Tina could dismount her back. The black bull looked thankful to have his hooves on solid ground again. Methystra's form was swiftly surrounded by a spiraling mist once more before her more humanoid shape emerged. A foot-and-a-half shorter than Kravek in that form, she looked up at Tina on Kravek's shoulder and spoke in the common trade tongue. "This is as far as I will go for the time being."

Tina adjusted her glasses. "Not going into the mine with us?"

Methystra shook her head. "A dragon of clouds such as I does not belong beneath the earth and sea, and you will need to pass through the Maw of Malidath in order to enter the mine."

She pointed toward the western side of the rock formation where one side of the large hill of stone disappeared into the water. "True to the story of Malidath, his maw lies beneath the sea. I will grant you both enough breath to enter the maw."

Tina looked at the condition of the mine and tapped the side of her muzzle in thought. "Belthazuul really did make the entrance impassable. I hope he left the air shafts intact."

Methystra turned around to face the mine. Parting her jaws, she breathed out a thick fog which rapidly grew until a large cloud swirled in front of them. With a sweep of her hands, Methystra guided the cloud to drift around the mine. It formed a sheet which cascaded over the mine like a layer of silk. There were several dips in the layer of mist, but two spots in the sheet of cloud entirely disappeared. Methystra looked back at Tina. "There seem to be three shafts still in place, though my clouds seem repelled by them. The air is stale, but breathable." She lowered her hands, and the clouds drifted into the air like pillars of steam and dispersed.

Tina stood up on Kravek's shoulder and rested one hand on the side of his neck. "Whenever you're ready then, Methystra."

Methystra held her hand up for Tina to step onto it. Once the wizard was standing on her hand, the Maldavian turned toward the water and walked. She swept her long, twisting tail at Kravek in a gesture for him to follow. By the water side, Methystra knelt down and lifted Tina to the end of her muzzle. "Breathe. Once you have taken in my breath, do not let it out."

Tina nodded, already familiar with the nature of the magic Methystra was using. Removing her glasses, she held them up for Methystra. "Kravek will be my eyes down there. This is my last set of glasses, so please look after them for me. I don't want to risk losing them in the water."

Methystra moved her other hand up so Tina could set her glasses down onto it. She then lowered the hand and lifted Tina to the end of her muzzle. "Breathe." The Maldavian then pressed her lips to Tina's. Once she felt Tina's mouth was open, she exhaled a faint mist into the mouse woman's lungs.

Tina felt the familiar tingling of a spell of multiplying breath as it flowed into her lungs. It was cool, and she felt as if she'd just inhaled thick air. It took her a moment to adjust to it as she felt the tingling spreading not only through her lungs but flowing into the rest of her body. She nodded to Methystra while keeping her mouth shut, and the Maldavian set Tina down into the water.

One of Kravek's ears twitched. Tina realized it must have looked as though Methystra was kissing her, and she smiled, having to restrain a giggle lest she lose her breath.

Methystra then rose and walked to Kravek. She put her hands on the sides of his muzzle and turned his head down. "Breathe." The Maldavian then pressed her lips to Kravek's, and the black bull looked momentarily startled. But Tina could see his lungs swell as he drew in Methystra's breath. She then realized just how much it looked as though Methystra was kissing Kravek. She wiggled her whiskers and turned away, disappearing into the water.

Extracting a small portion of her gift, Tina summoned a sphere of light between her hands under the water. Though the water was clear enough to see through, she knew it would get darker as they moved into the shadow the mine cast. She expanded the sphere until it was as large as she, and then she heard Kravek's legs splashing the water nearby.

Tina turned around to see his legs leave the water as he dived in and sank to the bottom like a rock. Thankfully, there was a long shelf only ten feet down from the surface, so Kravek didn't sink too far. She kicked her legs and swam down until she was even with Kravek's head while he walked on the shelf. She moved the ball of light to where he could see it, but the black bull seemed to be distracted with his hands resting on his chest. He stood there and blinked while he got used to suppressing the urge to breathe.

Tina had to swim up beside his head and knock on it a few times before she had his attention. She pointed to the ball of light and then to the end of the stone shelf where it terminated at a large formation of stone coming down from the mine.

Once Kravek nodded in understanding, Tina cast the ball toward the rock formation and started swimming. Kravek simply walked along the shelf behind her.

The ball of light came to a stop next to the rock formation. It illuminated the rocks more clearly, and both Tina and Kravek suddenly stopped at what they saw. A Maldavian's head with its jaws spread was turned downward. It looked as if the Maldavian was both in pain and gripped by insane anger. Even though Tina knew they were headed for the jaws of a dragon trapped within stone, she had almost let her breath out when she saw Malidath's ferocious expression.

Tina felt Kravek's hand against her back ushering her forward as he moved toward the edge of the shelf. The dragon's head faced downward and was massive enough that the black bull would have to climb down the side of it just to reach the mouth.

Tina swam ahead of Kravek while he climbed under the water and found grips on the dragon's scales. She waited for him and guided the ball of light along the rocks so he could clearly see good handholds. Once he reached the edge of the dragon's mouth, Kravek gripped it and pulled himself around so he could climb inside.

Having dropped down twenty feet just to reach the edge of Malidath's mouth, Kravek and Tina would have to ascend another thirty feet before they reached the surface. The tunnel they were respectively climbing and swimming through was massive and much larger than the Maw of Kaelus by almost three times, and it wasn't getting any narrower.

As they moved up through the tunnel, Tina felt a strange, crawling sensation in her skin. It was a sensation she'd felt before, and she came to an immediate stop. Turning back around, she tried to wave her hands at Kravek, but he was focused on pulling himself up the near vertical rocks of the submerged tunnel.

Pointing to the ball of light, Tina swept her hand down to cast it in front of Kravek's face. He stopped as the ball floated right in front of him and moved his hand to cover his eyes. When the ball moved away, he looked up at Tina.

She held one hand toward him in a gesture for him to stop climbing. Once it was clear to her that he understood the message, Tina turned back around to look up at the surface of the water. It might take some of Methystra's breath, but she needed to find out if the sensation she'd felt had been what her instincts were telling her. Tina sank back down as she exhaled a small breath. Using her gift, she trapped the escaped air in a bubble and let it drift upward.

Ten feet before it reached the surface, Kravek and Tina were both knocked back by a shock wave as the bubble suddenly expanded a thousand times. The whole chamber rumbled with the explosion as a few rocks tumbled down from the walls. Tina was momentarily dazed by the shockwave and barely managed to keep her mouth shut so the rest of Methystra's breath wouldn't escape. She struggled to keep the air in her lungs, which made it all the more painful after the impact of the blast.

The overwhelming sound of grating stone beneath the water drew Tina's attention toward the mouth of the cave. She didn't need her glasses to see it was slowly closing. Unaware if they could make it to the mouth in time to escape, Tina jerked her head up to look at the surface of the water again. If they could exhale Methystra's breath and make it to the top quickly enough, they might be able to escape.

But what Tina saw at the surface dashed all hopes of that.

A layer of ice had suddenly formed on the surface of the water. She'd led them right into another trap! Tina looked down at Kravek in hopes of signaling him to move to the mouth of the cave, but Kravek wasn't looking up at her anymore. His hands were pressed over his muzzle as he fell down through the water. He landed on his knees and squeezed his eyes shut just as the mouth of the cave closed behind them.

Tina quickly swam down through the water to try to reach Kravek before he let Methystra's breath out, but when she came close enough, she could see his chest wasn't expanded. His lungs weren't full anymore. Kravek wasn't trying to keep air from escaping. He was trying to keep himself from sucking in a lung full of water.

Tina landed on top of Kravek's head and drew on her gift. A sphere, formed of waves which looked like heat rising on a hot day, surrounded Kravek and Tina. Building a sphere of force within her hands, Tina let it expand around her own body, then around Kravek's as it forced the water through the initial, semi-permeable barrier. Kravek tried to draw in breath as the water was forced out, but nothing would come.

Tina let her own breath out, and as she did, Methystra's breath expanded to fill the small space within her barrier. Kravek was finally able to draw a breath, but immediately went into a fit of coughing. Tina knew her own portion of Methystra's breath wouldn't last for long. But it would last long enough.

Tina turned her attention to the layer of ice covering the surface of the water and, with a violent expulsion of her gift, sent a focused beam of force toward it. But to her surprise, the layer of ice seemed unaffected. A second wave of force had the same unyielding result. Without her glasses, Tina couldn't see what was causing the layer to be unaffected by her magic.

She looked down at Kravek and tugged on his mane. "Kravek, I need you to climb!"

Kravek was breathing heavily, his voice raspy with the strain of being without air and coughing. "I-Is this... another trap?"

"Yes, and I can't get us out of it. I need your muscles!" Tina tugged on his hair. "We don't have long before Methystra's breath runs out in this sphere."

Kravek pushed up with great effort and grabbed the wall of the tunnel. Tina could tell he was still struggling as he pulled them up the wall, but there was no other choice. As the bull climbed, Tina felt her skin crawling again. Looking down at her hand, she realized she was growing. She had no idea why, but it wasn't important at that moment as she moved to the back of Kravek's head and climbed down his hair. Her body grew, and she grasped his load-bearing harness to keep from falling.

The black bull didn't seem to notice the change as he climbed with all his effort. Just as they reached the layer of ice, the barrier around them entirely collapsed. Kravek growled under the water and found the highest grips he could. Crouching down against the wall, the black bull pushed up with his legs and pulled with his arms. All of his might slammed his horns into the layer of ice. It cracked under the first impact. Kravek lowered himself again, and with the second impact, his horns punched through.

Kravek threw a hand through the hole and pushed up to drag himself and Tina out of the water. Tina let go of Kravek's shoulders and pulled herself onto the tunnel floor where it leveled out. Kravek and Tina both sprawled out on the ground and gasped for their breath. She still felt a wave of panic, but they had managed to escape the trap. They both sucked in their breath and panted heavily as their bodies were allowed to return to the natural process of breathing. Having been submerged in the water, the air within the tunnel felt significantly warmer in spite of the stale smell of stone.

Kravek panted heavily as he lay on his stomach. "You don't get... paid enough... Tina."

"Every step... of the way... another trap. Someone doesn't... want us following him." She opened her eyes and lifted her hand in front of her face. Though their environment had only partly changed, she could still tell her size had been altered.

Tina looked down at her clothing and wondered for a moment why it all hadn't been torn apart. Her hand came to rest on her head, and she closed her eyes. She hadn't taken one of her pills, and no spell had been directly cast upon her that she could detect. Whatever had altered her size had also affected her clothing. Putting that together with the fact her magic couldn't reach the layer of ice led Tina to only one conclusion. Something in the area was suppressing the effects of magic.

Upon the realization they had entered some kind of magic suppression field, Tina wondered just how she could see the tunnel around them. Her only light source had been one of a magical nature, and Tina didn't see it anywhere. What she could see was a faint yellow light coming from glowing deposits in the walls. The deposits looked like mineral veins.

Sitting up, Tina wrapped her arms around herself and tucked her legs. The water had not been terribly cold, but coming out of it through a layer of ice had quickly changed that. Though the chamber was warmer, she was freezing. "K-Kravek, are you all right?"

Kravek rolled over and pushed himself up to a sitting position. He rubbed the top of his head. "That ice was rough." The black bull lowered his hand from his head as he sat up and noted Tina's size. "Tina, you're big again."

Tina nodded as she shivered. "A-and freezing."

Kravek moved next to Tina and wrapped his arm around her waist. He pulled the mouse woman into his lap and put his thick arms around her. He rubbed her back as he kept her close to his chest. "You'll be all right." The black bull glanced down at her as she shivered in his lap. "How'd your clothes survive the change?"

Tina closed her eyes and rested her head against Kravek's chest. In spite of having gone through the same thing she had, he was incredibly warm. Her tail curled into her lap, and Tina laid her ears back against her hair. "I-I don't know yet, K-Kravek."

Kravek looked down at Tina. After a moment of consideration, he squeezed his arm around her a little more tightly while the other rubbed her back. He then chuckled. "Even big, you're small."

Tina rubbed her incisors against her bottom lip. "The Mateesh aren't a big people, Mister Seven-and-a-half-feet-tall." In spite of the cold, the corners of her mouth curled upward.

Kravek started to let his arms slip from around Tina, but when she reached up and grabbed one of his horns, he stopped.

"Your arms are warm."

Kravek looked down at her again, and one of his eyebrows rose. He put his arms back around her. "What happened down there?"

Tina pulled up Kravek's tail and starting wringing the water out of it. "Something is suppressing magic here." Tina looked at the layer of ice still covering the surface of the water and the hole through which they had come.

"Then," Kravek inclined his head toward the ice, "how did that happen?"

"You thought about that too, hm? If magic is being suppressed here, how could magic trap us in here, especially when one triggered spell occurred inside the field?"

When Kravek nodded his head, Tina finally pushed herself out of his lap and rose to her feet. She walked back to the hole in the ice and knelt down, holding her hand closer to the frozen surface. The air was cold near the ice, but not as frigid as it would usually need to be for ice to form. Rising up, she looked deeper into the cave.

"There is a limited number of possibilities, but I can't come to a conclusion unless we can find the source. But while magic in the area is suppressed, I won't be able to protect us from any more traps." Tina then turned her gaze to Kravek. "You're going to have to protect us both while we're in here."

Kravek crouched on all fours and, with a shake, threw off what water was left on him. Rising again, the black bull gripped one of his horns and turned his head from side to side to crack his neck. "I'll keep you safe, Tina."

Tina didn't know if Kravek would be able to protect them from more traps of magic. But as he offered his arm out to her, she put her arms around it and pulled herself close. If there were anyone in Likonia around whom she could feel safe, Tina believed it was Kravek.

Chapter 19

While the tunnel itself had been large, the chamber beyond could be called massive. Tina could see the deposits of the golden, glowing ore scattered over the walls. The glow provided only faint illumination, but it was enough to light up what would have otherwise been pure darkness. She ran her fingers over the ore. "This must be what Methystra spoke of, Malidath's blood."

Kravek's attention was on the rest of the chamber at the moment. "This place is much bigger than Kaelus's cave. Was Malidath that much larger than Kaelus?"

"I wouldn't doubt it." Tina moved her hand toward her face and had to stop herself from trying to adjust glasses which weren't there. "He was the elder of the two and much older than Kaelus. I suspect we're standing in his stomach." Her attention turned to the ceiling of the chamber. "If I had to guess, he was probably fully grown while Kaelus was somewhere between adolescence and adulthood."

"A teenaged dragon?"

Tina shrugged. "Something like that, though teenaged for the Maldavians would be somewhere in the area of a hundred-and-fifty years old. They're a long-lived race."

"A hundred and fifty years." Kravek rubbed the back of his neck. "I don't think I could imagine living that long."

"It's not all it's cracked up to be." Tina looked around the large cavern. Though the chamber itself was open, there were boulders ahead of them which blocked their view of the floor and much of the lower part of the chamber. "Those must have fallen after the mining of this place started."

"What did you want to come here to see?" Kravek asked Tina.

"Well, at first, I just wanted to see if what Methystra said about the mine was true. If the deposits we're seeing are really formed from dragon's blood, then the aetherium would be valuable to any magic user." Tina wiggled her whiskers. "I wanted to confirm Governor Keldo's motivation. But with the only remaining entrance protected by magic and a magic suppression field sustained within this mine, more questions arise."

"You're wondering if the wizard might have used this cave too, right?" Kravek moved to one of the fallen boulders. He rested his hand on it and pushed firmly.

Tina eyed Kravek. "I know you're strong, Kravek, but I don't think even you could budge one of those things. It's a wall unto itself."

"You never know." Kravek moved his hand off the boulder. "I kind of wanted to see if it would get up like those boulders did in the other cave. Walking around and all that." His tail swept around to slap the tuft of fur on the end against his side.

"You mean the ones who tried to kill us?" Tina walked to Kravek's side and looked up at the boulder. "Remember that I can't use my magic right now, Kravek."

He nodded. "I do. Speaking of which," he looked down at Tina next to him, "why did your clothing and all that grow with you?"

Tina grinned at him. "No free peeks, Kravek." She let her grin slip to a simple smile. "It is extremely difficult to craft items and clothing of a size suited for me. I'm no seamstress. With the exception of my glasses, everything I wear was crafted at a normal size, then shrunk down for my figure." She touched her necklace. "So when magic is suppressed around me, everything grows. When I was my proper size with Luna, I had just taken a pill which serves the same function. But the pill only affected me, not my clothing. That's why I was wrapped up in a sheet."

197

Kravek flicked one of his large ears. "I can understand that. Will you be all right staying in this place for long?"

Tina looked up at the boulders lying in front of them. "I'll be all right. With my gift suppressed, I do admit to some discomfort. But otherwise, all it does is make me a mundane Mateesh female." She stepped up to the boulder and tried to find some hand grips. "I wonder if this magic suppression field is a result of the ore, though." Once she had a firm grip, Tina pulled herself up and found a foothold.

"Do you want a hand?" Kravek stepped up behind Tina.

"I'll be all right. I've had a lot of practice climbing." Tina pulled herself up to the top of the boulder and peered over it. "There isn't much ore in the middle of the chamber. There are some large boulders down there, but I can't see much." She looked down at Kravek. "Will you be able to make your way over?"

Kravek nodded. "I'll manage." He rounded the boulder and found where it rested against the one next to it. Wedging himself between them, Kravek pulled himself up until he could sit on the boulder next to Tina. "Why would Malidath's blood suppress magic?"

"We've always believed the Maldavians are magic incarnate." Tina slid down on the other side of the boulder and dropped to her feet. "Magic from one as powerful as Malidath could suppress the magic of another being who isn't either attuned to him or allowed by him to use magic."

"Is your magic really that much... well, weaker than his?" Kravek slid down the boulder and landed on his metal shoes.

"I may be a wizard, Kravek, but an adult Maldavian, even a dead one, is on an entirely different level." Tina seated herself on the edge of the large, bowl-shaped dip in the floor. "Come on. It'll be easier to cross right through." She scooted herself off the edge so she could slide down the side.

Kravek looked down at the pile of boulders in the middle of the bowl-shaped floor. He scratched the side of his neck in thought, then seated himself and slid down next to her. Reaching the pile of boulders, Kravek put his feet against one to stop himself, then stood up. "Tina, it's pretty dark down here. Are you sure we can find our way around?"

"They're just in the middle, Kravek." She reached back and touched his arm. "Put your hand on my shoulder, if you like."

Kravek rested his hand on Tina's shoulder as she led them around. He looked up at the ceiling. "I don't see any tunnels leading into this chamber, but I can't see that far right now. They must not have dug this deep before Belthazuul collapsed the mine."

Tina nodded. "You're probably right." She stopped in front of a protrusion from the pile of boulders and climbed on top of it. "I doubt they had very lo-Eek!"

Tina felt the protrusion suddenly shift under her and rise up a few feet. She felt it shake back and forth under her, and the shaking sent her tumbling to the floor. The mouse woman landed flat on her back with a loud thud, and pain shot through her head as it struck the stone. She curled up tightly and put her hands on the back of her head. The pain, so sudden and surprising, forced her tears out in an instant. "Ahhahhaoww."

Before Tina realized it, Kravek was suddenly scooping her up in his arms and holding her protectively. "Tina," he spoke quietly, "those aren't rocks."

As Tina lifted her head and looked up, she could see a massive shadow slowly coming into the light of the glowing ore in the higher part of the chamber. The yellow light cast by the ore shone onto scales which matched it in color. The figure illuminated was easily as tall as Methystra's true Maldavian form and even appeared feminine. Her body looked similar in build, and the long claws on her hands were each as long as a curved sword. With her jaws open wide, they were lined by teeth as large and as sharp as spearheads. Form-fitting plates covered her hips, shoulders, and the top edges of her muzzle. The same, stone-like plates protected her forearms and thighs. Horns like those of a Maldavian protruded from above her forehead and swept back to frame a thick, flowing mane. As she breathed, holes in the sides of her chest opened and closed in a slow and steady rhythm.

"Dragon... Eater." Kravek carefully started walking back up the side of the bowl.

Tina felt her limbs trembling as she looked up at the looming beast so close to them. When the Dragon Eater's eyes opened and revealed a pair of green, glowing orbs, Tina felt the blood drain from her face. She put her shaking hand on Kravek's arm. "K-Kravek... get us out of here."

Kravek didn't need to be told again as he turned and ran up the side of the bowl-shaped floor. He almost reached the lip of the bowl when one of his metal shoes slid on the incline, and he turned to put his shoulder against the ground as he fell. When he and Tina came to a stop, he remained crouched over her as he looked over his shoulder at the Dragon Eater. "Tina..."

"Kravek... I..." Tina watched as the Dragon Eater's head came down at them, and she closed her eyes. With all certainty, she didn't wish to see what was about to happen.

To her surprise, the Dragon Eater's muzzle pressed to the floor behind Kravek and swept upward. The monster pushed Kravek up the side of the bowl and dropped the two of them onto the lip. The Dragon Eater perched over Kravek and Tina. She nudged them both with her muzzle, and Tina swore she heard some kind of whimper coming from the beast.

Climbing out from under Kravek, Tina stood up to look at the Dragon Eater. To her surprise, the monster's eyes looked both sad and pleading as she nudged Tina with her muzzle toward the wall of boulders behind them. Tina put her hands on the Dragon Eaters muzzle to stop her, and the Dragon Eater lowered her head. "What... is she doing?"

Kravek looked at the creature's eyes and suddenly looked shocked. "Tina, I've seen those eyes before." He stepped toward the creature and put his hand on top of her muzzle. "You're Leilani, aren't you?"

The creature turned her head to look at Kravek and suddenly seemed surprised. But she quickly nodded in reply to his question. She then pushed her muzzle insistently against both of them to urge them toward the wall of boulders. The sound of shifting rocks made Leilani turn her head to look back over her shoulder. Another whimper came from her, and she turned around and spread her jaws.

Tina squealed as Leilani took both of them into her mouth and practically lunged over the wall. Perching with her hands on top of them, she dropped Kravek and Tina down on the other side. She shoved them back toward the water and then disappeared into the bowl-shaped floor.

Kravek looked down at himself covered in saliva and shook his hands. "She wants us out of here, Tina."

Tina was confused by the Dragon Eater's behavior, but she shook her head. "How are we supposed to get out? Malidath's Maw closed when we triggered the trap."

The sound of stone rumbling rose through the water and drew their attention. A loud snap could be heard before the ice shattered upward, and Methystra's head appeared. She looked down at Tina, but immediately seemed unsettled. "Tina, what—"

Before she could get another word out, an ear splitting roar shook the chamber.

"We have to leave right now!" Tina shouted.

Hearing the roar from within the chamber, Methystra immediately scooped up Kravek and Tina. "Deep breath." She gave them only a moment to get their breath before she dived back into the tunnel.

Kicking with her legs, lashing with her tail, and using her free hand to pull herself along the wall, Methystra was able to carry them through the tunnel and make it to Malidath's Maw before they heard heavy splashes in the water behind them. Grabbing the top edge of the tunnel, Methystra pulled herself up on top of it and climbed her way out of the water. She then leapt off the northern side of the tunnel and scooped up a handful of earth. She tilted it to drop Kravek's backpack and Tina's glasses into her other hand and cast the earth away as she ran.

The sound of the Dragon Eaters bursting from the water like a trio of stalking striders reached Tina's ears, and she looked up at Methystra. Still not back to her own proper size, she could feel the magic suppression field moving with them. She shot her attention to Kravek. "It's the Dragon Eaters! They're suppressing magic around themselves!" She looked up at Methystra. "Can you outrun them?"

Methystra shook her head, and Tina could see she was already panting. "I cannot."

Tina felt a sudden chill of fear for Methystra. If she couldn't use her magic, she wouldn't be able to fly away, and the strain of not being able to draw in her magical manner of breath was going to wear her out. Even dragons with their greatest span of wings couldn't fly without the aid of their own magic. They were simply too large. Her mind raced for a possible solution, but without the ability to use her own magic, there was little Tina could do. Even if she had her magic, the Dragon Eaters were protected.

The sound of the monsters' pounding feet drew closer and closer as Methystra ran for their lives. When she heard them drawing closer, she planted one foot and let all her momentum turn her about. Her tail swept around, and the end of it slammed hard into the head of one of the Dragon Eaters. She had managed to catch it off-guard, and it jerked to one side which slammed it into another. The two of them tumbled to the ground.

But the third one, whom Tina recognized as Leilani, leapt at Methystra! The Maldavian let the momentum of her turn carry her as she ducked low and cast her hand to the ground to let Kravek and Tina roll out of it. But she hadn't ducked low enough. Leilani caught Methystra's shoulder in her sharp claws and tackled her to the ground.

Methystra struck the ground hard, and Tina could hear her roar in panic. Her tail swept up from the ground and slapped the sun-colored Dragon Eater in the back, but she couldn't put any real force behind it. Though the Dragon Eater had a firm grip on her, Methystra managed to get her hands around the Dragon Eater's muzzle to keep it clamped shut.

Tina felt helpless to stop what was happening as she watched the other Dragon Eaters untangling themselves and rising to their feet. "Kravek! We have to help her!"

"How?!" Kravek grunted as he looked about for something, anything he could use as a club, even if it would be futile against such monstrous beasts.

Tina's jaw tightened. She returned her attention to the Dragon Eaters and clutched her hands together. She suddenly felt so helpless. Having to watch Shalizan die was nothing in comparison to being forced to stand there and watch as the Dragon Eaters prepared to tear her friend apart. Leilani, for all the concern she had shown for Tina, was violently raking her claws over Methystra's forearms. Tina realized the monster's green eyes had turned red.

A shadow passed over Tina and Kravek, and Tina looked up to see a boulder the size of the Thorn's Side suddenly crash into the pair of Dragon Eaters who had just managed to untangle themselves. Her eyes went wide in surprise, and Tina whipped around to see from where the boulder had come. Like a colossus at the edge of the woods, Belthazuul was raising another massive boulder from the soil. Lifting it over his head, the titanic, stone dragon cast the second boulder with all his strength.

It sailed out toward Methystra and, with a shattering impact, slammed into Leilani. The force of the impact sent the Dragon Eater tumbling off of Methystra. Deep cuts had savaged the sky dragon's arms, but at least her limbs were still attached. She rolled up from the ground and started running again right away. With the Dragon Eaters dazed by Belthazuul's boulders, Methystra would have a chance to escape. The ground in front of her rose up in a slope, and as Methystra ran up it, she quickly took to the air. The ramp collapsed back to the soil once Methystra had the distance to fly again.

Tina felt a sense of relief wash over her as she let out the breath she realized she'd been holding. She looked up at Kravek. "Methystra's safe. But if we don't get out of here, we'll be far from it."

Kravek scooped Tina up and carried her in his arms as he ran straight away from the Dragon Eaters and headed for the edge of the woods. By the time he had reached them, Tina was sitting in the palm of his hand with her glasses back on the bridge of her muzzle. The Dragon Eaters were still chasing Methystra, but in the air, she was far out of their reach and out of range of the magic suppression around them. Tina put her hand on the side of her muzzle and closed her eyes. Methystra had come dangerously close to death, and Tina felt tears of relief trickling into her fur. "She made it."

"Thank Shahdazhan." Belthazuul's voice came from above Kravek and Tina, and they both looked up to see the massive, stone dragon towering over them. "We must not linger. I will carry you away from here." He set his stone hand onto the ground. Kravek stepped onto the hand, and Belthazuul raised it. He turned, and his body pressed to the ground. Everything but his head and hand submerged into the soil, and all the speed Methystra had in the air Belthazuul displayed moving through the soil.

Tina slumped back in Kravek's hand and put her own hand on her forehead. Her eyes closed, and she let out a heavy sigh. She moved her hand under her glasses, felt the warmth flooding her face, and wiped away the water on her cheeks. Her gift was coming back to her, and Methystra's life had been spared. She wondered why Belthazuul had returned so quickly, but it didn't matter. Tina would not have to witness the dismemberment of a dear friend. For that, she was truly thankful.

Chapter 20

"Where are we going?"

Kravek's voice caught Tina's attention more sharply than she had expected. She hadn't realized she'd fallen asleep or at least slipped into that space between sleep and awake. Being disconnected from her gift for magic for even a little while had made her aware of a sensation of disconnection with the rest of the world as well. But fortunately, the sensation had faded. She sat up in Kravek's hand and adjusted her glasses. Having been her actual size for awhile, it felt somehow reassuring to fit into the palm of Kravek's hand again.

"Isn't Belthazuul taking us home?" Tina looked up at the dragon's head which was still above Kravek.

"That's what he said. But we're sure taking the long way around if he meant Likonia."

"That is correct." Belthazuul's eye swiveled down to look at the pair of them in his hand. "Unless you have reason for me to lead the Eaters of Magic back to Likonia."

"Absolutely not." Tina crossed her legs. "Belthazuul, you are possibly one of the greatest weapons the Maldavians have against the Dragon Eaters. Have you not been able to overcome them until now?"

"I did not overcome them. As with any Maldavian close to them, I lose my power as well along with most of my form." While Belthazuul was moving through the woods, his disturbance of the soil pushed the trees aside. But when he passed, the soil came back together as if he had never been there. "But even the Dragon Eaters have their limitations."

Tina knew that Belthazuul was saying even if the Dragon Eaters were powerful, they could not be invincible. But for all she knew of them and her own abilities, without the use of her magic, she didn't know how she could stop them. She touched her fingers to her forehead and closed her eyes. "Belthazuul, not that I'm at all ungrateful for it, but why did you return after Methystra sent you back to the Ring of Fire?"

Belthazuul's giant eye fixed on Tina. "Methystra may be my superior, but our council decreed I watch over any elder of our people who leaves the Ring of Fire. I did not wish to upset Methystra, so I have been watching from a distance."

Tina sighed in relief. "I cannot express how grateful I am that you did."

* * *

Tina's projection stood within the High Theorist's chamber with its arms folded. Having given High Theorist Sythus her report, she waited for him to digest it all as he sat at his desk. His wings were folded down against his shoulders, and his fingertips tapped together in front of his muzzle.

"This is quite vexing, Lady van Schtoffen." He lowered his hands into his lap. "To stop magic without the power of magic when it is most often magic which must defeat magic. You are certain there is no way you can unravel the protection which shields the Dragon Eaters from harm?"

Tina shook her head. "Magic cannot be used anywhere near them. The only solution I can devise is to find the resonance of their magical protection and try to attune to it. But no power of magic can function around them. Even from a distance, my glasses will not let me peer into the equations affecting the Dragon Eaters. I have tried to follow the prophet's advice to seek out knowledge from the wizard who created them, but it would appear the wizard did not wish his knowledge exposed. Every corner I turn is another trap he has laid beneath my feet. Even dead, the wizard's magic endures."

"The prophet's words." Sythus ticked one eyebrow up. "Recite them to me again, if you would."

Tina laid her ears back against her hair. Relying on the words of a prophet never suited her very well because they could only ever see part of what they were predicting, and many prophets tended to be manipulative. So even what they did reveal could be considered subjective. "Master, I do not think relying on the prophet will lead me to an answer at this juncture. I cannot find any trace of real evidence left behind by the wizard who was killed."

"You told me he was eaten," the High Theorist leaned forward against his desk with his hands folded on top of it, "but are you certain he was killed? From what you tell me, the one who informed you of what happened to him is no scholar of magic. Please, the prophet's words, Lady van Schtoffen."

Tina lifted her hand to rub her forehead, but doing so only made her fingers press through the projection's intangible skin. "His words were 'Discover the truth upon which light is shed in the knowledge granted by those who are dead.'"

The High Theorist's eyebrow ticked upward again. "Those who are dead. You must learn to listen more carefully to the words of a prophet if you wish to find any benefit in them, Lady van Schtoffen. If the prophet had said 'he who is dead,' I would have believed it was the wizard whose knowledge you must seek. But the prophet said 'those who are dead,' meaning more than one."

Tina let her hand drift away from her head and fall back to her side. "Those who are dead? My lord," she sighed, "that only confuses me further. How is it simpler to find many who are dead when I cannot even follow the trail of the one?"

"Because you know the one is covering his trail. Perhaps the many are not." The High Theorist rose from his desk. "I have done some of my own investigating on this end, Tina. And I think it is possible I may have come across something which could be useful to you. I did not think it of importance to your investigation before because I did not yet know exactly with what you were dealing."

The High Theorist walked to one of the bookshelves and removed a red, leather-bound book from the end of one shelf. He thumbed through several book marks before coming to the second to last one. He opened the book and turned it toward Tina to show her the marked page. "Do you recognize this artifact?"

Tina looked at the page. Drawn on it was a head from a beast unknown to Tina. It looked decayed and old but not entirely ridden of its flesh. The top was rounded, and the expression around its empty eyes was one of gloom. Its flat face looked aged, and the only thing resembling a mouth Tina could make out was a vertical slit which extended down for almost a foot between a pair of elongated mandibles. If it had any discernible ears, Tina couldn't see them. In the center of its face was a depiction of an arachnid resembling a spider but with the upper body of a humanoid.

When Sythus turned to the next page, Tina could see the same head but with its mandibles raised and spread wide open. There were sharp hooks lining the interior of the mandibles and a single hole in the middle of them. With the mandibles open, Tina could see the artist had depicted some sort of glow coming from the eyes.

Tina shook her head. "That is a horrid looking thing, master, but I do not recognize it."

"I cannot say I am surprised." He turned the book around to look down at the picture. "Aracheah relics are rare, and those which we do have in Kerovnia are contained by powerful wards. In the Aracheah language, this one is called Exil'idya, he who exiles souls."

"He?" Tina leaned her head back with a look of revulsion. "Is this artifact living?"

The High Theorist shook his head. "Living is a question of debate, but it's not unusual in the complex language of the Aracheah for them to assign even objects a gender."

"I think I understand, master, but why do you bring it up?"

"As I said before, we keep Aracheah relics under powerful containing wards, but we also keep them under powerful protective wards as well so they can't be stolen or misused." He walked back to the shelf and put the book back into its spot. "Exil'idya was contained within our vaults until recently."

Tina's ears stood up. She suddenly had at least a small notion of where the conversation was going. "How recently?"

The High Theorist seated himself back behind his desk. "Of that, I cannot be certain. It seems the caretaker of Exil'idya decided not to report its theft and replaced it with a false one while he conducted his own search." Sythus leaned back in his seat with his hands on his stomach. "While I commend him for trying to rectify the problem on his own, I cannot forgive that he would let such a relic slip from our care without so much as informing, at the very least, me."

"Wouldn't it take an exceptionally powerful wizard to break into the city of Kerovnia and steal such a relic from our very home?"

Sythus wrinkled his muzzle. "Wouldn't it take an exceptionally powerful wizard to create such monsters as the Dragon Eaters?" He leaned forward and once more folded his hands together in front of his muzzle. "Tina... the creation of animate creatures such as the Dragon Eaters would require the summoning of spiritual energy, even souls. Do you have any reason to believe that such a relic could be anywhere in Likonia?"

Tina's mind turned back to one detail which she had regarded as minor at the time it had been mentioned. "...Yes, I do."

The High Theorist sighed in anxiety. "Tina, if the wizard possessed such a relic, it is highly possible he used it to transfer the soul of someone who hated the Maldavians into his creations in order to drive the monsters to destroying them."

Tina shook her head. "I do not think it was a success, my lord."

"I agree. If what you told me about the Dragon Eater who tried to get you to flee from the cavern is correct, then I think the wizard must have used the two Kamadene women to create the Dragon Eaters. Wizards of the *Purita Combus* have been known to bind the souls of their servants to themselves in the event they should have a need for spiritual magic, which, considering they toy with the magic surrounding life and death, is quite often." Sythus leaned back in his seat. "Why he used his servants' souls rather than the souls of more malicious folk, I do not know."

"My lord," Tina's ears swiveled to face the High Theorist, "I believe the wizard must have intended to use the souls of Kaelus and Malidath to drive the Dragon Eaters."

Sythus bowed his head in agreement. "I believe you are right. From your description of what happened in the caverns, I believe he was successful in taking the souls of Kaelus and Malidath from their separate resting places. But if that is true, he must have had the souls contained within Exil'idya already. The only explanation I can come up with as to why he would not have used them was if Exil'idya was stolen before he could deliver the souls to the Dragon Eaters."

Tina looked perplexed. "Why stolen, master?"

The High Theorist tapped his fingers together, then his wings fanned as he rose. "A suspicion. This may be nothing, Tina, but have you confirmed the identity of this 'Captain Cephalin' yet?"

Tina nodded. "Yes, my lord. He is the same Idori Cephalin who it is believed was responsible for the massacre at Empusa."

Sythus rubbed his chin in thought. "Seek him out. After our talk about him, I had your student, Denna, searching through records and documents recovered from Empusa after it was captured from the Idassians in the last war. It would seem that Empusa was second only to the city of Zancrose as a major gathering site for the *Purita Combus*. And, if what Denna has uncovered is true, Idori may be the one who stole Exil'idya from this unknown wizard. And, if that is true, he may truly be innocent of the Massacre of Empusa."

Tina's eyes grew a little wider as she stepped closer to the High Theorist's desk. "How?"

The High Theorist folded his hands behind his back. "The cultists in Empusa were playing with more than just the magic of life and death. In one of their journals, as your very thorough student Denna uncovered, a note was made that a powerful demon was being contained by the cult within Empusa." He lifted his hand and extended one finger. "Such a demon as they made note of would cause Idori to be nigh impervious to magic when the demon has its strongest grasp on his soul. I would have no other evidence to support this if one of our prophets had not tried to look into Idori's memories and ended up nearly dead for her trouble."

"But why would the demon compel him to steal the Exil'idya?"

"Because demons feed on the souls of living beings. If Idori's soul is being fed upon, and the demon believed it had a way to continue to feed on the souls of others without having to destroy its host, then it would most certainly do so."

Tina lowered her eyes to the ground. There was a lot to process, but the High Theorist's advice and knowledge had given her a direction. It would need to be the object of her focus. "If all of our suppositions are true, I will need to confirm them. And if they are true, I must find a way to compel Idori to hand over Exil'idya."

The High Theorist looked at Tina solemnly. "This is a dangerous undertaking, Tina. If the demon suspects you are trying to take Exil'idya from Idori, it will do everything not only to prevent you from finding it, but to prevent Idori from giving it away."

Tina didn't have to search her thoughts for long. "...I think I may know who can persuade him, master. I just hope she has the strength."

* * *

Tina blinked as the magic of her paper doll faded. She looked down to see the shredded paper which remained of it and rested her hand on top of the pieces. Her gaze returned to the window through which she could once again see the starry night cast against a crescent moon. She knew well enough it was just an illusion, but it was still a peaceful scene which was the entirety of its purpose.

Rising from her seat, Tina carried the pieces of the shredded doll to the fireplace and leaned down next to the bottle of dancing flames resting in it. The fires were looking a little dim and lethargic as they drifted about. With the spell placed on the bottle, she knew they wouldn't go out, but it saddened her to see them growing tired. With the investigation going on, she hadn't been paying enough attention to the flames.

Tina knelt down and pulled the cork out of the bottle. Standing it up, she rested the hand filled with shredded paper on top of it and let the paper spill down into the bottle. The flames, excited to be fed, darted around in a flowing spiral as they consumed the paper. Tina smiled as she watched them dance. It seemed like a very simple existence. But after all, the fires weren't really anything more than everglow flames animated by a firefly spell.

Putting the cork back in, Tina set the bottle onto its side. She needed to return to the inn so she could find Exil'idya, but watching the everglow flames dancing around inside the bottle, she found herself wishing for a little more peace.

While she watched the flames drifting about, her thoughts turned to Kravek. After returning to the Stumble Drum, Kravek had told Tina he wanted to check with the foreman at the docks to see if there was any work to be done. She had to admit she admired Kravek's commitment to his duties. The thought of Kravek having lost his people made Tina frown. Through all the work she had been doing over the last few years, she hadn't been keeping up so much with the world as with her job. Out of the last ten years, she had spent only two teaching in Kerovnia. Being away so often had started to wear on her.

The sound of a heavy thud against the door to her room snapped Tina out of her thoughts. Pushing up to her feet, the wizard walked to the doorway and put her hand on the arch. She'd heard a distinct thud against the door, but not much else. Something must have hit the door in the Stumble Drum.

Tina sighed. Even if the sound had been an accident, she needed to stop letting her mind wander and get back to work. If she could find Exil'idya and release the souls of Kaelus and Malidath, the Dragon Eaters would eventually starve as the aetherium in the mine lost its potency. Tina didn't like the idea that Leilani and Nana would pay the price for their master's choice. But with their souls invested in the Dragon Eaters' bodies, she was afraid there was nothing she could do.

Tina picked up the torch from its bracket on the wall, and it ignited on its own. She made her way down the familiar, cobble-stone hall leading to her door and, once at the other end, put the torch into its bracket next to the door. With a twist of the handle, she stepped outside into the Stumble Drum.

Tina hadn't expected to see Kravek and wasn't disappointed in her expectation. She could see the shutters on the front windows of the Stumble Drum had been pulled, but even so, she knew nightfall to be coming on. The chairs had already been stacked on top of the tables, though she couldn't see Willa or Beth in the tavern area. Even Mr. Kilba was absent as Tina turned to look behind the bar.

The sudden, sharp impact of metal against Tina's shoulders slammed her down against the counter. She saw stars and felt a tingling pain shoot from the base of her neck all the way down her spine and jump into her fingertips. In her dazed state, she heard metal scraping against the bar counter as fingers wrapped around her, and she was lifted. Her glasses had fallen from her face when she was struck which made the world that much more blurry while she was still reeling from the blow.

As Tina was lifted up in front of someone's face, she heard a familiar voice. It was little more than an angry growl with barely intelligible words coming out.

"I. Owe. You. Much."

It was Captain Cephalin's voice. Tina gasped as he squeezed her tightly in his bladed gauntlet. He growled at her, and Tina felt his hot breath wash over her as he raised her to the end of his muzzle. She didn't have time to conjure a spell as he spread his jaws.

They snapped closed suddenly with a sickening crunch.

Chapter 21

Captain Cephalin's hand slammed against the bar counter and fell open which tossed Tina across the countertop. She rolled to a stop and pushed up onto her knees. She didn't feel any pain, and as she patted her own body with her hands, she was relieved to find herself intact. Looking up, she saw Willa Hodgis standing over Idori's crumpled form and holding a cast iron cooking pan. The badger woman kicked the captain of the guard in the side to shove him off the bar counter and onto his back.

"That'll teach you to manhandle a lady, ya brute." She kicked the unconscious wolverine in the leg for good measure.

Tina put her hand on her chest and let out a sigh of relief. "Willa... am I ever glad to see you."

Willa put the cast iron pan on her shoulder, cocked her hips, and shifted the pipe in her mouth to one side so she could grin at Tina. "Wouldja look at that. Ol' Willa Hodgis saved a wizard. My grand kids are going to love this story."

Tina, in spite of the panic which had just overtaken her, couldn't help but laugh appreciatively. She moved to the edge of the countertop to look down at Captain Cephalin. "Is he alive?"

"I may be a clonker, but I'm not a killer, Wizard." Willa dropped the cast iron pan onto the counter top with a thud. "Probably won't thank me when he wakes up."

"Willa... how did you know what was happening?"

The badger woman shrugged her shoulders and pointed back over her shoulder. "I heard Idori growling from the kitchen. Came out here and saw him about to take the lion's bite outa you. I don't care whatcha done, ain't no one deserves to be eaten like that." She folded her arms across her chest. "You want to tell me what's going on?"

"Well, I can tell you why he was trying to eat me, at least. But I need to see the governor right away. Is there anyone you can send to the docks to tell Kravek what happened and bring him here?"

"Beth's still awake. I'll send her off." Willa pulled the pipe from her mouth. "Your dragon is waiting for you in the town square. Caused quite a fuss to have a Maldavian sitting in the middle of town, you know."

Tina sighed. "I know. Thank you, Willa. I owe you my life."

Willa pointed at Tina with the mouthpiece of her pipe. "You don't owe me nuthin', Wizard. I'd do the same for Beth or any other woman in trouble in this town. You just make sure ya give them monsters one for Ol' Willa Hodgis." She nodded in self-satisfaction.

* * *

Having collected the governor, Kravek, and Methystra, along with a few of the guards and the injured Luna, Tina stood on Kravek's shoulder as the governor unlocked and opened Captain Cephalin's quarters. He stepped out of the way as Kravek ducked under the door and headed into the captain of the guard's quarters. The captain's room looked as simple as any other guard's room. There was a pair of bunks in the room with a fireplace settled against the far wall. Both of the bunks looked as though they had been made up, but only one of them had anything around it. There was a couple of boxes under the bunk to the right of the door. One of them was a long, wooden crate.

Kravek pointed to it. "That's the crate I carried to Dragon's Mouth."

Tina climbed off Kravek's shoulder and leapt onto the

bunk over the wooden crate. She perched on the side and looked down at it as the runic circle appeared in her right lens. "Take it out and open it, Kravek. I can see the magic around it, but I detect no protective spells."

Kravek scooted the box out and pulled the loose top off it. Inside was a lot of packing straw to cushion what the crate had carried. In the middle of the straw was a shape which Tina noted looked as if it could have held Exil'idya. Kravek settled on his knees over the crate. "What was in this?"

"An item of powerful magic, stolen, I believe, from the wizard who created the Dragon Eaters."

"Why would he have stolen it?" The governor moved into the room and stood where he could look down into the empty box.

"There's a lot to explain, but the item is missing." Tina looked back over her shoulder at Luna. "Do you know of anywhere Idori might have hidden something he didn't want anyone to find?"

Luna walked to the fireplace and knelt down in front of it. She lifted the grate and rested her hand on the ash covered bottom. "Down here." The mink curled her claws under the edge of the fireplace's false bottom and started to lift it up, though she immediately dropped it and grunted as she put her hand on her shoulder. "It's iron. I can't shift it with this arm."

Kravek moved to the fireplace and, after Luna lifted it enough for him to fit his thick fingers underneath, pushed the iron panel up. He leaned his head away immediately. "That is ugly."

Such a statement was encouraging given the context. "Pull it out please, Kravek."

Kravek reached into the space under the fireplace and pulled the object out. It was the monstrous head Tina had seen depicted in the High Theorist's book.

Tina sighed in relief. "This is exactly what I needed to

find. Take it outside and put it on the ground. And everyone, please stand back from it." She climbed back to Kravek's shoulder as everyone vacated the room.

Outside, Methystra stood with her arms at her sides as she looked at the wretched thing Kravek was carrying. "That..." she took a step back, "Tina, I sense the souls of Maldavians bound within that monstrosity."

Tina climbed down from Kravek's shoulders and moved to the ground. She ran out a few feet in front of Kravek and spread her arms in a gesture for everyone to move back. "Kravek, put the head down on the ground and step away."

Kravek stepped forward and rested the creature's skull down on the ground. He then stepped back to join the group of guards. Methystra stood behind and well back from Tina as the wizard folded her hands together and quietly chanted an incantation. The shawl hanging in the crooks of her elbows floated upward and formed a semi-circle with arms drifting down to Tina's sides.

Tina adjusted her glasses and quietly spoke a single word in the Arachean tongue. *"Awaken."*

A glow rose in the eyes of the creature's skull as it lifted from the ground on its own and floated upright in the air. Its mandibles spread to reveal the many hooks on the inside of its mouth and the single hole Tina had seen in the High Theorist's book. A grey mist drifted out of the creature's mouth, and Tina held her hands up as her shawl floated in front of her with its length creating an 'X'. The grey mist drifted backward from her and disappeared into its mouth, though the glow remained in the creature's eyes.

Tina spoke again in the Arachean tongue. *"That which has been bound within, return to Cerra so it may breathe again."*

Exil'idya shuddered back and forth several times before it flipped over, and its mandibles stretched upward. A column of light shot into the sky with a deafening boom. Emerging with the column of light, the ghostly shapes of two monstrous Maldavians rose up to tower over the town. The two dragons let out loud roars which could be heard for many miles in every direction. Both of the Maldavians had two pairs of wings each which stretched out and spanned the entire city in all four directions, though one dragon was significantly larger than the other. The Maldavian spirits folded their wings and looked down at the group gathered around Exil'idya.

Methystra, her eyes wide, spoke quietly. "Kaelus and Malidath..."

The two Maldavians looked at Methystra. Then, the smaller of the two, Kaelus, looked up at Malidath. Malidath bowed his head to his brother, then turned his head toward the sky and closed his eyes. He breathed in deeply and released his breath slowly as Kaelus lowered himself down onto his knees.

He bowed his head as he looked at Tina and spoke in the Maldavian tongue. His voice was deep and resonant, yet soft and subdued. *"Thank you, Wizard, for releasing us from that dark place."*

Tina's shawl drifted down and came to rest in the crook of her elbows once more. She bowed her head to Kaelus. *"The one who imprisoned you there wished to use you and your brother to destroy your brethren, Kaelus of Maldav."*

"We know," Kaelus replied, *"but he was mistaken in choosing us."*

Tina's ears stood up and swiveled to face Kaelus. *"What do you mean?"*

Kaelus bowed his head. *"As much as Malidath and I wished to overthrow our father, it was not out of malice for our people we chose to do so. We believed our great father, Shahdazhan, was leading our people down a path which would eventually bring about their destruction. Even now, it may still be so. But that is a tale which has yet to be written. And though we stand before you now, we have not long in this world. Freed from Exil'idya, life will take*

219

its course and deliver us to our great father in the afterlife."

Kaelus closed his eyes. *"I can only hope that being reunited with our mother, Alysryzara, has calmed his anger. We have both accepted responsibility for the atrocity which was committed upon that day. Such is why Narash could not use us to fuel his... monstrosities."*

Tina's face paled. *"Narash...?"*

"The Idassian wizard, Narash Advonar, Mage Lord of Kylith." Kaelus spoke the name with notable distaste. *"It is he who tried to summon us and twist our souls to his will to drive these Eaters of Magic."*

Tina's whiskers twitched. *"Narash Advonar."* She turned her head to glare at the governor, though she didn't catch his eye as he stared up at the two Maldavian spirits. She sighed and looked up at Kaelus. *"Kaelus, do you know why he created the Eaters of Magic?"*

Kaelus nodded. *"We do. But it was not out of a wish to produce a threat to negotiate with our people. Narash sought the destruction of the monolith wherein lies the soul of Maldav, our progenitor, and Shahdazhan, our great father. In his musings near Exil'idya, Malidath and I overheard him speak of it twice. Once in those occurrences, he spoke in the presence of one who resides in this city. We can feel his familiar spirit nearby."*

"Who, Kaelus?" Methystra spoke up as she finally stepped forward.

Kaelus turned his gaze to Methystra. *"One who Narash called by name; Idori."*

Luna looked stricken by the statement and closed her eyes. She put her face into her hands and whimpered.

Kaelus looked down at Luna. *"We have heard your voice before in many heated discussions with this Idori."* The towering Maldavian's expression softened. "Your beloved is afflicted by the presence of a demon of magic, Luna Copaire. We know of the place from whence it came, and if you wish, we can spare him its

220

endless hunger."

"You have long suffered its presence within him, though you did not know of its existence." Kaelus lowered his hand and a mist flowed around the edge of his finger as it became tangible enough to lift Luna's chin. *"You should know now, though he possessed not the will to tell you, he stole Exil'idya from Narash in order to protect your people from the Eaters of Magic. Narash wished to destroy Likonia as well to bar further interference from its people. Furthermore, Idori prevented the demon which dwelt within him from using Exil'idya to steal the souls of the people in Likonia to feed its hunger."*

Luna lifted her head, and though tears streamed from her eyes, the corners of her mouth quivered as a frown fought with a smile. To Tina's surprise, Luna spoke back to Kaelus in Maldavian. *"Thank you. I knew... something was wrong."*

Kaelus bowed his head. *"We Maldavians value loyalty and strength. The two of you have shown both. Such devotion deserves a chance uncorrupted."*

Tina drew in a deep breath and let it out slowly. She had not been a friend of Captain Cephalin since their arrival, but knowing his actions had been to protect the people of Likonia and to resist the will of a demon cast his character into a whole new light for her. But there was still a task to be done.

Tina stepped forward. *"Kaelus, Malidath, do you know how the Eaters of Magic may be undone?"*

Kaelus rose as Malidath lowered himself down to meet Tina's gaze. Malidath's voice was much deeper than Kaelus's, and he spoke more slowly as his tones rumbled throughout the area. *"They will undo themselves. Narash was foolish to go forward with his plan once he learned we would not aid him. He bound the souls of his servants, Leilani and Nana, into the Eaters of Magic. He first bound them to see if it was possible. When he discovered it was, he released them for a brief time to make preparations. Now, they are bound within the Eaters of Magic permanently."*

"*But the need for power of the Eaters of Magic is too great without our magic. Narash uses my blood now to sustain them, and only when Cerra's Grace is at its fullest glow is their magic strong enough to venture from my body. And when I pass from this place, even that will no longer sustain them.*" Malidath wrinkled his snout.

"*Leilani and Nana are to be mourned. As long as Narash remains bound within the first of the Eaters of Magic, so too shall they be bound into the second and the third, and all will perish with the passing of Cerra's Grace on this night.*"

Tina had mixed feelings about the passing of the Dragon Eaters. Though she wanted them undone, she wished that Leilani and Nana could escape the fate to which their master had condemned them. "*Is there no way the women may be saved?*"

Malidath rose and shook his head. "*Narash may well escape his death if he chooses to unbind himself from the Eaters of Magic. In doing so, his servants will die. Their only salvation could have been in Narash's death, but as he possesses the greatest portion of magic invested in the Eaters of Magic, it cannot come to pass.*"

"Then," Tina adjusted her glasses, "*Narash was not killed.*"

Malidath shook his head. "*He lives within the first of the Eaters of Magic. And while it sustains him, no magic may touch him but his own.*"

Kaelus rested his hand on his brother's wing, and Malidath folded all four of them. "*Our time has come, Wizard of the Council of Stars.*" He then turned his head to look down at Luna. "*We know you have tried to find peace between our people and your own. For that, we, in passing, wish to grant you the chance to be with your beloved again.*"

Malidath looked down at Tina once more. "*We can do no more to aid you but in moving on, ally of Maldav.*" He bowed his head. "*And so, we grant you our only boon.*"

Tina bowed in return to Malidath. "*May your great father forgive and welcome you, Kaelus and Malidath.*"

Kaelus and Malidath bowed their heads to Tina before turning them toward the sky. With a final, trumpeting roar, the ground shook, and the column of light coming from Exil'idya brightened. The whole city was flooded with light for a few seconds before it faded from view and plunged the city back into darkness.

Exil'idya fell to the ground. The light had left the relic's eyes, and its mandibles folded closed. Tina walked up to it and wrinkled her muzzle as she rested her hand on the side of it. A problem created by magic had to be defeated by magic, and so it had. But the Arachean relic was far too dangerous an object to leave lying about even within the vaults of Kerovnia. "I do not possess the power to destroy this." She looked up at Kravek. "But I will see it destroyed by those who do."

Chapter 22

"What now, Lady van Schtoffen?" Governor Keldo looked down at the wizard. Tina was standing on the bunk in Idori's quarters. Next to her was the unconscious captain of the guard.

Tina looked up as she drew her hands away from Idori's head. She gave Luna an even smile and nodded at the mink, then turned her head and looked up at Harkon Keldo. "Governor, do you realize what your reckless decision has cost you and your people?"

Keldo lowered his head and closed his eyes. "I do. But you must understand, Lady van Schtoffen, I was trying to protect my people." He turned with his hands folded against his stomach. "I am not ashamed of going to the lengths I did in hiring a wizard." The fox's ears lay back against his head as he spoke quietly. "The Council of Stars would not help us, and because of the High Theorist's decision, the king could not help us either. My people have been struggling to survive."

"Much of which was caused by your town being placed so close to the Maldavian Monolith, Governor." Tina adjusted her glasses, and then folded her arms. "I have discovered many things since coming here, Keldo. I know about the aetherium mine, I know that you refused to move this colony from between the graves of Kaelus and Malidath, and I know that you are the one who 'hired' Narash Advonar to summon the Dragon Eaters as leverage against the Maldavians so you could force them to allow you to keep the colony here. But what I don't understand is how you could have not known the person you were hiring was one of the most powerful wizards in all of Idassia."

Tina let her tail sweep behind her in agitation. "Even you must have known who he was and that the Mage Lord of Kylith would have an ulterior motive. How could you possibly have met with a 'rogue' wizard who was an Idassian, especially one of such high renown as Narash, and not have known something was amiss?"

Governor Keldo considered Tina for a few moments, but she could see his tongue was failing him. She finally sighed. "Governor, if you can offer me no answer, I will have no choice but to bring you back to Kerovnia to face a tribunal. Please do not make that necessary. I admit we have not been on the best of terms since I came here, but I truly believe you were working for the benefit of your people."

Governor Keldo finally sighed. "I did not find him. He approached me. I do not know how he knew of what was troubling my people in Likonia, but he did. And as hard as it may be to believe, Lady van Schtoffen, I had never before met Narash Advonar. As the Mage Lord of Kylith, he is spoken for by the ambassador to the Idassian War Council, Elbus Keledore. I knew him only under the name he gave me – Ashnar Ravodan. I realize now it's an anagram. But I had no reason to suspect he was not who he said."

Tina sighed. "And because he was an Idassian, you thought he wouldn't be tied to the Council of Stars either, didn't you?"

Keldo nodded. "Yes."

Tina turned to one side with her arms folded and looked down at Idori. She took long moments to consider. There was much to weigh in one direction or the other, but when it came down to it, the Council of Stars was not entirely blameless. As the investigating wizard, Tina would be the one to recommend the next course of action involving Likonia and Governor Keldo.

"I'm not going to chastise you like a child, Governor," Tina finally looked up at Keldo, "and as far as I am concerned, I do not believe there is a reason to hold you responsible for the decisions the wizard made. But," she pushed her glasses up on the bridge of her muzzle, "I also cannot in good conscience withhold from Methystra who is responsible for bringing Narash to this place. His monsters killed her mate and are responsible for the death of Shalizan's Albatross, Angelica. Because of your actions, should the Maldavians decide to act on that, the Council of Stars will not intercede on your behalf."

Governor Keldo started to speak, but a groan from Idori brought their attention to the wolverine. Luna put her hand on Idori's brow and looked down into his eyes as they opened. The wolverine jerked in surprise at first, but when he tried to sit up, he groaned again and lay back down with one hand on his head. "Nrg. Who tried to break my head?"

"Me." Tina climbed onto Idori's chest so she could look at his face. "But to be fair, you were trying to eat me."

Idori grunted, but simply laid his head back. He brought his hand up and put it on his forehead. But when he opened his eyes again, Tina could see something was different. The wolverine moved his hand away, and wrinkled his forehead. Tina climbed off his chest as he slowly moved up to a sitting position. His ears were swiveling for a few seconds before he looked down at Tina. "They're... they're gone."

Tina adjusted her glasses. "What's gone?"

"Those voices..." Idori put his hands on the sides of his head and pushed his claws through the fur. "Those... endless voices." He looked down at Tina again. "What happened to me?"

"You were afflicted with the presence of a demon of magic, Idori. But the demon is gone now, sent back to wherever it came from by a pair of Maldavian brothers to whom you should be thankful."

Idori had turned his head to look at Tina a little too quickly and put his hand on the back of it. He lay back down. "Wizard, I'd owe you for nearly cracking my skull," he put his hand down, "but I can't imagine Maldavians would have raised a hand to help me unless you had something to do with it."

Tina pushed her glasses up on the bridge of her nose. "The only part I played in it was releasing them from imprisonment. In truth, Idori, the only person you owe anything to is Luna. You earned the respect of Kaelus and Malidath on your own, and Luna's devotion to you earned you both their compassion."

Idori looked up at Luna with his ears swiveled forward. He closed his eyes, and while he did sigh in a small measure of exasperation, Tina saw something on Idori's face she hadn't witnessed since she came to Likonia. He was smiling. "Secret's out, huh?"

Luna returned the smile, and as if it were a matter of dire urgency, she pressed her lips to Idori's and gave him an affectionate kiss.

Tina blushed at the sight and turned away to clear her throat. "Governor, I think we should leave these two alone. I imagine they've been missing each other for a long time now."

* * *

Keldo held his hand up for Tina to step off onto Kravek's shoulder, and all three of them headed down the street for the Stumble Drum. "With the souls of Kaelus and Malidath having moved on, I imagine you will be returning to Kerovnia to make your report as soon as the Thorn's Side departs."

"I would hope to be able to leave on the Thorn's Side, yes. But I mean to remain here for a few days to make sure the Dragon Eaters are truly passing." Tina folded her hands in her lap while seated on Kravek's shoulder. "I just wish there were something I could do to save Leilani and Nana." She shook her head. "But I have no idea how I may achieve it when the Dragon Eaters are such formidable foes. And then there's the business of Narash Advonar. Even with the Dragon Eaters power deteriorating, I do not imagine he will simply let himself die in order to sustain their existence when he no longer has a sustainable source of magic to keep them going." She gave a sigh. "It is rare that the truest of villains ever really pays for his choices."

Governor Keldo sighed as well. "I fear you are correct." He lifted his head and looked at his house sitting on the northern side of town just inside the raised portion of the wall. "I will ask that Methystra and Belthazuul take me with them when they are ready to depart. As much as I fear the judgment of the Maldavians for my part in causing the death of Shalizan, I hope that my going with them willingly will show that there is a hope for peace still between our peoples." He chuckled. "With Malidath and Kaelus moving on and the aetherium gone from the Maw of Malidath, perhaps we can come to a more amiable agreement which won't involve my people having to move the colony to start over again."

"Why were you so desperate to have that mine, Keldo?" Kravek spoke up finally.

Keldo looked up at the black bull as they continued to walk. "Trading aetherium would help to keep this town on its feet, Kravek. As young as Likonia is, most of the other goods we could have offered needed to remain in the town. But we've no wizards or magic users here, so I thought the aetherium's value as a trade good would augment the town's sustainability and make us vital so growth would be encouraged." He sighed. "But I see now it was a foolish decision. I tried to take too much from the Maldavians."

"There is no crime in wanting to be able to help the people you govern, Keldo," Tina laid her tail across her lap, "but there might have been a better means to achieve it."

"You are probably right, but I didn't have the wisdom to see it."

"Something confuses me." Kravek flicked one of his floppy ears. "If the Dragon Eaters really wanted the monolith, why didn't they just go after it instead of constantly coming back to the town and turning back?"

"I suspect," Tina spoke up then, "it had something to do

with Leilani and Nana as well as the amount of magic it took for Narash to maintain his control over them. You remember when we were in the Maw of Malidath and Leilani tried to push us out of the cave? I think their compassionate nature must have been something Narash had to fight against in order to control them.

"If you remember, Leilani's eyes were green within the cave, but red outside when they were chasing Methystra. I believe it was an indicator of either Narash asserting direct control or the presence of a dragon nearby. He might have instilled a natural hunger in the Dragon Eaters for magic, but if that were enough, Leilani would have eaten me as soon as she saw me."

Tina pulled her glasses off and folded them up to hang them from the front of her robe. "But in truth, this is all just speculation." She turned her gaze back to Governor Keldo. "I need to speak with Methystra before she departs. I have something which should be given to her." Her hand moved to the necklace containing the lava-colored crystal. "Then we just have to wait out the night."

Governor Keldo lifted his head to look up at the night sky. "It is still several hours before the night passes." His expression turned solemn. "I am not one given to whimsy, but I see a shooting star. Perhaps we should use it to wish Leilani and Nana the best of fortune. They may have been our greatest protectors."

Tina turned her gaze to the sky. She saw the silver line of light passing across the sky. She closed her eyes and took a moment to offer up her own wishes of fortune for the two Kamadene women. But when she opened them again, she saw another shooting star cross the sky. "That's strange."

As they watched the sky, more silver lines of light passed across it and headed west. Tina narrowed her gaze. She'd seen star showers before, but for one to be occurring on this night of all nights sparked a hint of suspicion. She removed her glasses from the front of her robe and put them on the bridge of her muzzle. The runic circle appeared in the right lens, and Tina immediately recognized exactly what was occurring.

Before she could say another word, a trumpeting roar came from the west. Kravek and Keldo immediately turned to see the source of the sound. With the gates open, they could see the light of the falling stars pouring down from the sky in droves. As they approached the ground, the lights collided with the bodies of the three Dragon Eaters and illuminated them brightly. All three of the towering monsters were glaring at the city, and their eyes glowed bright red.

Chapter 23

Kravek rushed to the western wall as the gates to the city were slammed shut. The governor was swiftly behind the black bull as Kravek carried Tina up to the walkway. The three of them looked out to see the Dragon Eaters at the center of a cluster of spiraling lights which looked like a vortex of fireflies. Tina adjusted her glasses as she surveyed the scene. "No…"

Kravek looked at Tina on his shoulder. "What's going on?"

Tina shook her head. "Narash is committing everything to this. He's summoning star metal from beyond the sky to empower the Dragon Eaters. With so much of his power invested in that spell, he will die once the effects of it wear off."

Kravek grunted. "Serves him right, but when is that?"

"Too long." Tina snapped her attention to Governor Keldo. "Get your guards and evacuate the city right now. Wake up Captain Morgan and tell her the Thorn's Side needs to carry as many people as it can out of the city."

Keldo pointed to the Dragon Eaters at the edge of the forest. "They're already upon us!"

"Don't argue! Just do it!" Tina looked up at Kravek. "Do what you can to help them." She ran down Kravek's arm and leapt onto the wall. Kravek snorted, but nodded as he and the governor rushed back down the stairs.

Tina touched the tattoo on the side of her neck. Her voice was suddenly amplified a hundred times. "Belthazuul! Methystra!"

The ground on the western side of the city rose with the rumbling of stone as Belthazuul's towering form emerged.

231

Methystra drifted down from the sky and floated just above the city wall as she looked down at Tina. "We see them, Tina."

"I can't ask you two to remain here to protect the city, but if there's anything you can do to slow them, I would be very grateful."

Methystra and Belthazuul exchanged a glance before Belthazuul spoke. "Wizard, even my patience has its limits. If you believe there is any chance Methystra and I can help to destroy these creatures once and for all, we shall do it."

"If anyone can do it, I believe it to be you, Tina." Methystra rested her hands on the wall. "Let us show these beasts why you earned the name *Kedish Kerasta.*"

Tina smiled in spite of the situation. "Thank you, Methystra."

The cloud dragon turned her head to smile wickedly at Belthazuul. "Let us turn earth and sky against these monsters!" Methystra rose from the wall and flew up into the sky, breathing out a dense mist. It gathered around her in a spiral as she rose.

Belthazuul watched Methystra climb into the sky. Looking down at Tina, he raised his hand with the sound of grating stone. "May the stars guide you."

Tina grinned, thinking the true reply to the Council of Stars salutation hardly appropriate to be spoken to Belthazuul. "And the soil sustain you."

The reply curled the corners of Belthazuul's stone mouth. Raising his head toward the sky, he let out a quaking roar before diving back against the ground. His body shattered into shards of stone which melted into the ground.

Tina looked up at the sky and spotted Methystra. The cloud dragon was spiraling around madly as she cast off sparks and mist. The growing fog expanded rapidly and flashes of light filled the forming cloud. It was a truly rare sight to see the birth of a storm as rolling thunder announced the approaching gale. The clouds spread, and Tina saw the stars falling from the sky dissipate rapidly. The grey clouds blotted out the light of the moon, Cerra's Grace.

The sound of stone and soil erupting near the wall drew Tina's attention to the ground. A row of iron spikes each the size of a jouster's lance burst through the topsoil. With each passing moment, row after row of the iron spikes erupted from the soil as they extended toward the edge of the woods. The field of spikes would make the path to the city all but impassable as it grew on all sides.

The sound of thunder rumbled as lightning rained from the sky and struck the spikes. Though Methystra and Belthazuul could not assert their power directly against the Dragon Eaters or around them, they had created an environment through which even the titanic beasts would have a perilous journey as the magnetized iron spikes drew bolts of lightning.

Tina turned as she heard footsteps running up the stairs leading to the walkway. "Luna! You should be helping Idori."

Luna, with her bow clasped in hand, drew an arrow from her back and nocked it against her bowstring. "The best way for me to help Idori now is to protect this city."

"Your arrows will not harm the Dragon Eaters." Tina pointed to the trebuchets behind the wall. "Get some of the guards ready to heave rocks over the wall to slow the Dragon Eaters down, and have the rest evacuate the people from the city. If we're to face the Dragon Eaters, it will be without the threat of the people in the city being killed."

Luna grunted but put her arrow back into its quiver. She barked orders out to the guards on the wall. Tina could tell Luna's injuries were slowing her down, but the mink was determined to carry out her duty.

Tina leapt down from the wall as guards rushed from it and into the town. Touching her golden armlet, a cluster of runes appeared on Tina's legs, arms, shoulders, and around her torso. Once at the edge of the stairs, she leapt twenty feet to the roof of the nearest building and landed on her feet. Running across the rooftops to avoid being trampled, she headed for the Thorn's Side.

As she reached the eastern wall of the city, Tina could already see many inhabitants of the town being rushed out through the gates. Some were heading for the Thorn's Side while others were moving to smaller, personal boats which would be able to hold five or six at the most. The fishing vessels would at least be enough to get them away from the city.

Tina looked for Captain Morgan among the people being led out of the city, but she suspected the captain was already aboard and guiding them to quarters and cargo areas. With another gigantic leap, she landed on the bowsprit of the Thorn's Side and ran down it. Sailors were hurrying about on the deck already and preparing the ship to launch from the pier.

Tina's suspicion was confirmed as she saw Captain Morgan shouting orders and directing evacuees below decks. She leapt to the mast and took hold of it with her short, sharp claws to put herself at head level with the captain. "Jessica!"

Captain Jessica Morgan snapped her head up at hearing Tina's voice and looked to the mast. "Tina, the Thorn's Side can't hold everyone in the city."

"I know, but take as many as you can and at least get them away from the shore. We can't stop the Dragon Eaters from reaching Likonia, but Belthazuul and Methystra are delaying them. Listen, Jessica." Tina removed the golden, rune-covered plate from her left ear. "If I don't survive this, I want you to take this to Kerovnia and deliver it to the High Theorist. He needs to know what happened, and that will tell him of everything I've heard since I came here."

Tina tossed the rune-covered plate at Jessica, and it expanded in the air on its way to the Kylathian. The captain caught the plate and grasped it firmly. "I'll be giving this back to you soon, Tina."

Tina half-smiled at Captain Morgan. "And I'll be listening

to those drawn-chords of yours again soon enough. Good luck, Captain."

Captain Morgan returned the half smile. "I'll do whatever I can to help. Live to fight another day, Tina." She cut one of her rare salutes and returned to giving orders.

Tina leapt off the mast and landed at the base of the bowsprit. After running to the tip, she made another gigantic leap and landed on the wall of the city. There wasn't much she would be able to do without her magic to stop the Dragon Eaters. But she would at least see to the safety of the people and delay the monsters as long as possible.

As Tina leapt from rooftop to rooftop, she could see the Dragon Eaters moving into the field of spikes and lightning. The red monster parted his jaws, and gouts of flame poured from them onto the spikes. The intense heat melted entire areas of metal and scorched the soil. The blasts of lightning around the Dragon Eaters were a continuous, cacophonous symphony, and though they battered the monsters, they were only slowing the creatures' approach.

Upon reaching the town hall, Tina saw the flaming boulders being hurled from the trebuchets fly out over the field. Few actually found their targets, but those that did shattered upon impact. Turning his attention away from the spikes, the red Dragon Eater caught one of the flying stones and hurled it back with immense strength. It crashed straight through the western wall of the city and, with deadly accuracy, smashed one of the trebuchets which turned it into a pile of burning lumber. The two accompanying Dragon Eaters caught stones of their own and hurled them into the city. One of them slammed into a building and collapsed half of it, setting fire to the rest.

Tina saw one of the boulders flying back aimed straight at the town hall. She ran to one side of the building and leapt off just as the flaming boulder plowed through the second story and left a gaping hole. With a rough landing on a nearby building, Tina lost her footing and tumbled down the slanted roof. She managed to catch the edge of it to keep from falling to the ground below. After pulling herself up, she saw another boulder fly over the town hall and graze the front of the Stumble Drum before slamming into the building next to it. Even from the town hall, she could see the roof of the front porch had been damaged.

Tina set her feet on the side of the building where she'd landed and leapt back to the damaged roof of the town hall. Most of the people were already past the middle of the city, but there were a few stragglers still running through the street.

As another boulder flew toward the buildings, the runes faded from Tina's body, and she called upon her gift. She swept her hand to one side as she kept her gaze on the boulder, and it bounced in mid air. The boulder spun wildly, and she thrust her other hand out with her fingers curled. The boulder stopped in mid-air, though it continued to spin.

Tina swept one hand repeatedly under the other. The fiery ball of stone spun more and more wildly with each sweep of her hand. Turning her eyes to the Dragon Eaters, Tina focused on the male and sent the boulder flying back at him with much greater force than that of the trebuchets. The male had apparently not been expecting it as the fiery boulder slammed into his shoulder. He twisted to one side and pitched backward, crashing to the ground.

Her magic may not have been able to affect the monsters themselves, but the boulders were good ammunition accelerated by her gift. As another volley swept into the air from the remaining trebuchets, Tina clasped her hands in front of her stomach and gathered her gift. With a shout and a thrust of her hands, she amplified the force of the boulders as they flew. Two found good purchase on the taller of the two females, both of them slamming into one leg and taking the beast to the ground. Another struck the yellow Dragon Eater's head. Leilani pitched backward and collapsed onto a set of the iron spikes behind her which hadn't been melted. She let out a cry of agony, and Tina felt a momentary pang of guilt for having caused the worst of the injuries to the one who had tried to protect her.

When the yellow female rose from the spikes and glared at her with glowing red eyes, Tina reminded herself that even if Leilani had been protecting them, she was not in control of herself now. Tina's attention focused on the red male as all three Dragon Eaters got back up on their feet.

Tina prepared to accelerate the next volley, but the red male held his hands up in front of himself with his fingers curled. She hesitated as he blew waves of heat into his hands. The waves built in intensity as they formed into a sphere of pure force. She realized suddenly what he was doing. She touched the rune on the side of her neck and yelled. "Everyone get down!"

Tina leapt down from the town hall rooftop to the ground as the red male raised the ball of force into the air. With an over-head sweep of his fist, he smashed the gigantic ball of force. A wave exploded outward and warped the field of iron spikes before it slammed into the wooden wall of the town. The wall shattered like ice smashed by a sledge hammer, and an entire row of build-ings was ripped apart.

The guards hit were scattered by the wave of force as their trebuchets became nothing more than splinters of wood. The town hall buckled, and it collapsed into the building next to it as Tina was sent flying by the dissipated spell. The sapphire in her armlet flashed as she hit the ground, absorbing the force of the impact. But that didn't stop the world from spinning wildly as she bounced past several buildings.

Tina tried to rise. Though she had come to a stop, the world was still spinning, and she ended up slamming face first into the ground. She hadn't expected Narash to expend so much of his remaining magic in a single attack.

Tina heard a voice which she recognized calling to her, but, dizzy as she was, she couldn't make any sense of it. She saw a spinning image of Kravek bouncing in her field of vision even though he seemed to be standing still. His voice was reaching her, but nothing he said made any sense in her state of disorientation.

Tina managed to shake off some of the dazed state. She realized Kravek was holding one side of the porch to the Stumble Drum on his shoulders. He was calling out to her, but even though the world had slowed in its spinning, everything was blurry, and Kravek's words were running together in a dull rumble of sound.

Luna slid to a stop next to Kravek as Tina stumbled toward them. The mink reached under the edge of the porch and dragged out an unconscious Beth. Kravek let out a snarl as he tried to push the porch roof up from his shoulders, but it was still clinging to the side of the Stumble Drum.

Tina's hearing finally cleared in time for her to hear Kravek yell out. "Aiden!" The black bull suddenly thrust his arm out to sweep Luna out of the way. With a loud crack, the porch roof tore away from the Stumble Drum, and Kravek managed to divert it from falling on top of Luna. But as it came down, he couldn't move out from under it in time. He let out a roar as it collapsed on top of him.

Tina screamed.

Chapter 24

Tina felt the surge of adrenaline bringing her senses into focus again. The world was still blurry as she realized her glasses had been thrown off when she'd been tossed halfway across the city. Though she felt battered, she managed to call out her gift and apply magical force to the roof. Throwing it off Kravek, she rushed to him and skidded onto her knees in front of his muzzle. Luna grabbed Aiden's unconscious body from the porch of the Stumble Drum.

"Kravek! Kravek, wake up!" Tina smacked Kravek on the front of his muzzle.

Kravek groaned, and his eyes slowly opened. He struggled to push himself up, but could only get up onto his hands before he collapsed again. "Nngh. Tina... my legs won't move."

Tina bit her lip and looked toward the Dragon Eaters. They had just reached the fallen wall. She knew once they drew closer, her magic would be suppressed. Her mind raced for a way to move Kravek.

Luna knelt down next to Tina and held her glasses out for her. "You might want these."

Tina took her glasses from Luna and put them on her face. "Luna, Kravek can't walk."

Luna nodded and turned her head. Guards from the wall were just reaching them with others either on their shoulders or being dragged. She looked down at Tina and shook her head. "I don't think there are enough guards still standing who can carry him."

Tina looked at Kravek with worry in her eyes. If she tried

moving him, it could worsen his injuries. But the alternative was unacceptable, and standing there doing nothing would not help Kravek. She didn't have time to use the spell to summon Shasta.

But then it hit her. She'd already used the spell to bring Shasta into the area. Tina needed only call out for her construct for it to appear from the soil. And Belthazuul had easily poured enough magic into the ground recently for her to call on it before the Dragon Eaters arrived.

Rising to her feet, Tina ran back from Kravek to make some room. Drawing a rune into the dirt, she called on Belthazuul's magic. In seconds, Shasta pushed her way out of the soil.

Tina turned her attention to Luna. "Shasta will carry all of you out of here, but I need something from you first, Luna. Are you still able to draw your bow?"

Luna nodded. "My bow arm is still strong."

Tina climbed Luna's side all the way up to her shoulder. "Then I need you to fire me at the Dragon Eaters."

Luna's ears shot straight up. "You have a death wish!?"

Tina clapped her hands together. "We don't have time for this! The Dragon Eaters breathe through those holes in the sides of their chests. I'm going to hold tight to one of your arrows, and I want you to fire me into one of those holes. These monsters are too powerful for anything to assail them from the outside. But if I can get inside the lungs, I might be able to tear up something vital with my claws."

"You can't think you're going to live through that." Luna suddenly looked worried.

Tina sighed in resignation. "But the rest of you will. Please, Luna. I don't have time to come up with another solution." She could tell Luna didn't like the idea of being the one to send Tina to her death.

But the mink pulled one of her arrows from her quiver and yanked the head off. "I need a vantage point and a clean shot."

Tina nodded and slid her golden armlet off. She dropped

it into Luna's hand. With a quick incantation, she removed her shrinking spell from the armlet, and it expanded to its original size. "Put that on your arm. I'll activate it, then you should have enough strength to leap to the top of a building. Once my magic is suppressed, there's a chance the armlet won't work any more, so you'll have to climb down yourself."

Luna glanced at the armlet, and then slid it onto her good arm. With a few words from Tina, runes appeared around Luna's ankles, wrists, shoulders, and waist. She stood up and looked at the second story of the Stumble Drum. "I haven't done this before, so help me if you can."

As Luna leapt, Tina called on Methystra's magic in the air to use the wind to guide her to a soft landing. The mink turned to face the approaching Dragon Eaters and nocked her headless arrow. "This isn't going to be an easy shot."

From atop Luna's shoulder, Tina focused on the nocked arrow, and the runic circle appeared in her right lens. She had to match the equation for her personal momentum with that of the arrow's momentum. A series of silver-blue runes appeared on her arms and legs, then a matching series appeared along the shaft of the arrow.

Tina set the spell, then climbed out onto the shaft and moved to the tip of the arrow. Wrapping her arms, legs, and tail around it, she looked up at Luna. "I have faith in you, Luna."

Luna bowed her head. "In case we never see each other again, Tina… thank you for bringing Idori back to me."

Tina wiggled her whiskers. "Whether we see each other again, Luna, I wish you and Idori a long life together."

Luna drew in her breath and raised her bow. Taking aim for one of the lung holes in the side of the Dragon Eater's body, she let her breath out. At the bottom of her breath, she let the bowstring snap forward and cast Tina into the wind.

* * *

Tina slowly pushed herself up. Looking at her hands, she realized she had returned to her five-foot size. She tried to reach for her gift, but her magic was being suppressed as she had expected.

She rose to her feet and looked down over herself. It wasn't just her own gift which was being suppressed, but the magic which altered the size of her clothing and accessories as well. She could feel the metal plate on the back of one of her ears, but it wasn't amplifying sound.

It didn't need to for Tina to hear the sound of slick flesh, muscles, and organs working around her. Looking around the chamber in which she found herself, she realized she was standing on a flesh floor within the Dragon Eater between his chest cavity and his belly. Within the Dragon Eater's chest, she could see his lungs above her working, and with her eyes, she followed a series of tubes of flesh leading back to the sides of the creature's chest. One of the tubes had a tear in it from where she had grown rapidly to her natural size and ruptured the flesh.

Looking up between the creature's lungs, Tina saw his heart beating. It was about ten feet out of her reach, and she thought it was oddly shaped. There was a strange protrusion of muscle on the front of the heart which looked as though it were opening up.

Before Tina could get a look at what was coming out, she felt herself sink up to her knees into the flesh. It held her tightly, and she panicked as she was caught. She tried to grab her legs to pull them free.

Tendrils rose out of the flesh and grabbed her arms restricting them painfully. They yanked her down as more wrapped around her thighs and locked her in place. Tina struggled, but to no avail. She was trapped.

A voice from above caught Tina's attention. "This is certainly a surprise." The source of the voice moved closer before deposits of aetherium inside the Dragon Eater's body glowed brightly and illuminated the upper torso of an Idassian male. "I did not think the Council of Stars would send someone so lofty as yourself to Likonia, Lady Tina van Schtoffen." The Idassian male spoke with genuine interest and surprise. "I suppose with Harkon Keldo's negotiation skills, I should have expected no less."

The Idassian male moved in close to Tina. She could see how the lower half of his body was surrounded by the same kind of flesh which held her down. But in his case, the flesh was extending from the muscle around the Dragon Eater's heart, and he seemed to be in control of it. The flesh moved about like a snake as it brought him closer to her.

Tina could see the bright orange fur interspersed with sharply-defined black stripes, and the characteristic, squared muzzle of the tiger-like Idassian. His green eyes were fixed on her as he spoke.

"So this is Tina van Schtoffen. *Kedish Kerasta*. The Tiny Tempest." He folded his hands across his chest. "I suppose I should not be surprised you made it past the traps I left behind. Even in Idassia, you have gained a reputation for resourcefulness and resilience."

The Idassian straightened up and curled his fingers at Tina. The flesh in which she was bound rose, pushing her up so she was even with him. "Your magic will not work in here, Lady van Schtoffen, but I am completely attuned to these creatures." He held his hand out toward Tina and balled it into a fist.

Tina felt the sudden pain of her limbs bending in places where she didn't have joints. She gasped, but couldn't even find the breath to scream as she felt the bones in her arms and legs being flexed outward. She bit her lip, and her incisors cut into the flesh as the Idassian's magic held Tina's bones right at the edge of breaking.

When the Idassian relaxed his fist, Tina felt the pressure relieved and gasped for air. It was a kind of pain which she had never before experienced in her life. The Idassian lowered his hand. "But for all of your resourcefulness, without your magic, what are you? Just another mortal, as are we all. I would wager you don't even have any fighting skills."

Tina panted for her breath but managed to turn her eyes up to look at the Idassian. She forced her words between pants. "You... aren't exactly... unknown... either... Narash."

The Idassian moved back in close to Tina and cupped her chin to lift her head. "Good. Then you know who you are up against. I am Narash Advonar, Mage Lord of Kylith, just as you have supposed. But you may think of me as 'Death.'" He gripped both sides of her jaw with one hand. "Tell me, did that simpleton Lazur live long enough to hand my book over to you? Or did curiosity get the better of him and fry the fool?"

Tina glared at Narash but didn't answer. Though she put on the mantle of defiance, her mind raced for a way to escape his grasp. But without her magic, she could do nothing more than struggle against the grasping flesh.

"Why do all of this, Narash? Why create these creatures when you could have just negotiated with the Maldavians?" Tina tugged at her arms. She knew the answer already, but she needed to buy time. "As a mage lord, you should know they hold wizards in high regard."

Narash folded his arms across his chest and nodded. "Indeed, I do. And it was that regard which bought me the time to create these masterpieces of magic." He gestured to the chamber around them with one hand. "These monsters are contradictions simply by virtue of their existence. They were created by magic to destroy magic. True masterpieces, don't you think?"

"Why even create them?" Tina struggled with one of her hands as she felt it beginning to slip free, but the flesh suddenly tightened. Muscular contractions drew her hand back into the flesh and locked it in place again.

Narash ticked his finger in the air in front of Tina. "Do not think me so foolish, Lady van Schtoffen. This is a trap you cannot escape. There is nothing left which you can do to stop me." He ticked his finger toward the lava-colored crystal in Tina's necklace, the colors in it having grown dim. "Even the Albatross you carry with you cannot protect you."

The long, snaking body of flesh to which Narash was attached drew him back. "You have very successfully limited my options. I had intended to use the souls of Kaelus and Malidath to fuel these beasts, but they were not as compliant as I had hoped. Now that their souls have been released, you have forced me to bind myself entirely to this creature to accomplish the destruction of the monolith."

Tina wrinkled her muzzle. "Narash, you must know that destroying one of the monoliths would have a dire outcome. You know what happened to the Medishina when their monolith was destroyed."

"An overwhelming force is magic when it is unleashed." Narash loomed over Tina. "The ground will shift and crumble and swirl like the clouds of a storm. Spires of stone will rise from deep within the earth, erupt through the soil, and shatter, destroying everything around them."

"Even your Dragon Eaters can't survive an earth storm, Narash."

"You speak a truth." Narash gestured toward the deposits of aetherium lodged in the Dragon Eater's organs. "But I was doomed myself when Kaelus and Malidath were released. Having to use my own magic to sustain these creatures is too great a feat even for me, and the star metal's power will not last."

Tina stopped struggling. After the stress Narash had put on her bones, trying to escape was causing her more pain. She would have to think of another way. "Why, Narash? Why destroy the monolith?"

Narash's snaking lower body carried him in front of Tina. "It has always been the aim of *Purita Combus* to carry out the Red Phoenix's will. Destroying the Maldavian Monolith is simply another step in bringing about the end so the world can be reborn from the ashes."

"Destroying the monolith is insane, Narash. Do you really think that the Red Phoenix, the spirit of death, needs the help of mortals to carry out its purpose?"

Narash bowed his head and shrugged his shoulders. "Life ends, wizard. Whether it is by the hand of a mortal, magic, or malady, all life ends. At least my own end will serve a proper purpose." He smirked as he moved in close to Tina and cupped her jaw. "I would think to let you witness it, to be there when the end comes. But I doubt you would appreciate it as much as it should so be. So I will say goodbye to you, Lady van Schtoffen, and carry out my work. Know that what magic you have left will serve the noble purpose of the Red Phoenix."

Tina watched as Narash unsheathed his claws and raised one of his hands. He moved his head in close, and Tina was surprised when it appeared he was going to kiss her. But, familiar with several of the *Purita Combus's* spells of death, she realized what he was about to do to her. He was going to draw the soul from her body and steal her gift for magic to allow the Dragon Eaters to sustain themselves for awhile longer.

But then one of Tina's ears flicked. She heard a series of deep, resonant booms coming from far away. The Dragon Eater suddenly rocked back as something slammed into his chest. Tina recognized the sound of the booms. It was the cannons on board the Thorn's Side!

A second impact made the Dragon Eater stagger. The third knocked him from his feet. As he slammed down onto his back, Narash was thrown against the back of the fleshy chamber, and Tina felt the grip of flesh on her slacken as she too was thrown. She rolled end over end before she landed flat on her back on the back wall. Something thumped against her chest, and she heard the jingling of rock against glass. Looking down, she saw the small jar that held the stone shards which had been pulled from Luna's wounds.

Narash rose and growled. "That ship has had too long a lifespan." He looked toward Tina, and the flesh around her threw her over onto her back. It wrapped around her arms and raised her up again. Narash drew in close and clutched Tina's jaw once more. "But first, your own extended lifespan is long overdue for its end. Goodbye, Tina van Schtoffen." Narash raised his hand and hurriedly pressed his lips to Tina's.

Tina opened her mouth to meet Narash's kiss this time. When she did, she blew as hard as she could. Narash let out a choking sound as the jar of shards lodged into the back of his throat. He clawed at his neck and tried to cough up the small glass jar.

Tina raised her leg. She stabbed her heel as hard as she could into Narash's throat. The glass jar of brittle shards shattered. There was a dull thump, and Tina felt the sting when the shards within the jar exploded and ripped their way through Narash's flesh. She jerked her foot away with a wince, then glared at him. "Our lives are not yours to dictate."

Narash's empty gaze was more than enough comfort as his arms fell to his sides, and he collapsed next to her. She felt the flesh trapping her arms slacken suddenly, and Tina pulled herself free.

Rolling onto her stomach, Tina realized how quickly the magic suppression had faded as she looked at her tiny hands. Without Narash's spirit to control the magic flowing from the aetherium, it would answer to anyone. Rising to her feet, Tina looked up at the glowing deposits of aetherium. If she could assert her power, the Dragon Eater she dwelt in might even be brought under her control.

Before Tina could even attempt her idea, she fell to her knees and screamed as the creature she was inside of suddenly let out a deafening roar! Outside, it could have been heard for miles. Inside, it made Tina feel as though her head would explode. Collapsing onto her back, she was dazed by the deafening sound. She had expected killing Narash to cause the creature to destabilize and fall apart. But instead, she could practically feel it going into a blind rage. The creature rising from the ground suddenly tossed Tina onto her stomach. The jolt was enough to get her head back together, but the creature's sudden turn threw her against the side of his chest.

She wasn't going to be able to do anything if the creature's movements kept throwing her around. Looking at the hole she had created when she entered the Dragon Eater's chest, Tina gripped with her short claws and ran on all fours for the opening. With another sharp jolt, the creature slammed down onto his back, and Tina could see the ground.

Throwing herself at it, she hit the dirt outside and took off to get away from the Dragon Eater before he might have rolled on top of her. She hadn't heard another volley from the Thorn's Side, but she wasn't hearing much of anything at the moment.

Stopping at a relatively safe distance, Tina turned about to see why Narash's Dragon Eater had fallen. To her surprise, she realized the other two Dragon Eaters had suddenly turned on the large male! Leilani and Nana were both clawing at him savagely, but even their combined strength didn't hold him down.

Nana, perched atop the red monster, let out a cry of pain as she was grabbed from behind by the red Dragon Eater's tail and slammed onto her back. Leilani tried to grab for Nana, but was swept up by the red Dragon Eater's arm and tossed bodily into the town hall. The building was obliterated, and as the male Dragon Eater rose to his feet, he twisted and slung Nana back toward the fallen western wall where she hit the ground hard.

Looking up toward the clouds, Tina realized the storm was still swirling overhead. Fueled by Methystra's magic, it was just what Tina needed. She wasn't fond of excessive force, but with the red Dragon Eater no longer protected by Narash's magic, it was time for Tina to live up to the name her people had given her.

Calling upon her gift, Tina multiplied her organic variable again and again. She looked to the storm and raised one hand toward the rumbling clouds. Draining the power from the area surrounding her, she intended to draw the lightning from the clouds and to act as the conduit to guide it into Narash's Dragon Eater. She held her other hand toward the raging monster. The clouds overhead flashed. Tina drew on every ounce of magic she had within herself as she prepared herself.

When she heard the rumbling overhead and saw the constant flashes within the clouds, Tina realized Methystra must have sensed her intent. The lightning was being held back and grew in intensity as the whole town was illuminated by the flashes of light.

As Tina felt the force of the storm reaching its peak, she screamed out! "NOW!"

With all her magical might, Tina latched onto the power around the Dragon Eaters and instantly sapped it. She knew she could only do so with so much power for an instant. But that would be enough. In that instant, Methystra released the lightning within the storm. Bolts of lightning exploded from the clouds as Tina took control of what power she had taken. Forks of lightning from the mouse wizard and the storm overhead intersected instantaneously. They struck the Dragon Eater, and plowed into the monster's body unhindered. The explosion of electricity shattered the Dragon Eater's body in a blinding flash. It let out a sudden roar of pain which was drowned out by the wave of resulting thunder.

Tina fell onto her hands and knees as she felt her heart pounding. She gasped desperately for breath, but with her eyes fixed on the Dragon Eater, she watched as the pieces of its body crumbled under the force of thunderous fury.

As her field of vision grew dark, Tina thought she had probably exerted herself beyond her capacity to recover. After all the injuries she'd received and the stress put on her bones, the added weight of expending her gift made it hard to breathe.

But it didn't matter. Narash had been utterly destroyed. That was satisfaction enough for Tina to carry with her into the darkness as it enveloped her.

Chapter 25

Tina felt a familiar moment of vertigo and disorientation. It had come quickly. It was as if she had just awakened from a long sleep in a pitch black room. She felt unsure if she was actually awake. She felt as though her mind was hesitating to acknowledge it as the weight of lethargy made her feel sluggish. She heard a groan, but in her hazy state, it took her several seconds to realize it had come from her.

"You're not dead. I imagine you feel like you are. But you're not."

Tina opened her eyes and wondered if she might find herself in a realm of clouds and wandering wisps of light with some divine oracle meaning to give her sage advice before she returned to the world. But the wizard found herself staring up at a wooden ceiling. The only light she saw was the flickering of flame cast from a fireplace nearby. She also felt its warmth which was a welcome sensation.

Tina tried to sit up, but shifting her head made it hurt. Her eyes closed again, and she put her hand on her temple. "Who's there?"

"Who else?" Kravek chuckled.

Tina opened her eyes again and turned her head slowly to look across the room. Lying flat on his back, she saw the black bull who had quickly befriended her when she arrived in Likonia. A smile spread across her lips. "Kravek..."

He lifted his hand to make a gesture for her to stop. "Leilani said you very nearly died. Just rest."

"Leilani?" Tina's eyes turned toward the ceiling as she

thought. She had destroyed Narash's Dragon Eater. "How did she survive?"

Kravek shook his head. "Don't know. But after you destroyed that big red brute, Leilani and Nana both just... fell apart. It looked like they were made of dirt or something." He gestured toward the door. "But Leilani and Nana both came out of the dirt like they were rising from their graves."

"You talked to them?"

Kravek nodded. "Neither one of them speaks Madrian or Levansian. But I speak Kamadene." He then gestured toward Tina. "From the way Leilani described it, she and Nana were both controlled by Narash most of the time." He shook his head. "I'll let her tell you about it. But Leilani is the one who found you lying in the road. She recognized you," the black bull closed his eyes and laid his head back, "from the Maw of Malidath."

Tina put her hand over her face and rubbed her forehead. "Kravek, that's all good to hear, but... why am I still alive?"

Kravek chuckled. "You can ask Nana about that. After Leilani found you, Nana healed you." He rubbed the end of his muzzle. "She's a shaman."

Tina let out a single, weak laugh. "A shaman. What a wonder." She then sighed quietly and let her body relax. "How long have I been here? How long have I been unconscious?"

"Two weeks. Long as I've been here." His expression turned sad briefly. "I was starting to worry. I'm relieved you finally woke up. Nana's been in here every day 'mending your spirit', as she put it. I could tell she was worried as well."

Tina turned her head to the side again and opened her eyes. For some reason, that made her feel good. "Were you really worried about me, Kravek?"

The black bull turned to look at Tina. She could see he was considering his answer carefully, though she wondered why. He finally replied. "Yes. Tina, I wasn't there when you killed Narash's monster, but when Luna shot that arrow... I was afraid it was the last time I was going to see you." Kravek had a pained look on his face. "We've only known each other for a few days. But that thought made me hurt." He lowered his gaze to the floor. "It made me hurt in a way I haven't felt in six months. Maybe it's because I've been drowning myself in booze and the days we've been together, I stopped. Maybe I'm lonely, maybe... I miss my home and my people."

He looked at Tina again. "But the days I was with you, I wasn't drinking, and... the pain wasn't there."

Tina felt her cheeks flush.

Kravek turned his head to look up at the ceiling again. "I don't know how much longer you mean to stay Tina, but I'm glad you're still here. Both alive and in Likonia."

Tina didn't have to wonder what Kravek meant. She closed her eyes. Though she was awake again, her body felt exhausted. There was even a deeper inner ache with which she was familiar. She'd stressed her gift to the point of nearly destroying herself. That well of magic within her felt as though it was still putting itself back together again. It hurt.

"Kravek," Tina spoke quietly, "when I do leave here, I mean for Leilani and Nana to come with me. Great magic has been cast upon them both. I'm going to ask them to come back to Levansia with me. If Beth decides, I want her and Aiden to come as well. I imagine Captain Morgan has left already, so I will have to wait for the next ship, but—"

"She's still here."

"What?" Tina opened her eyes and glanced at Kravek.

"Captain Morgan and her crew are still in port, as is the Thorn's Side." Kravek drew in a deep breath and slowly let it out. "She and her sailors have been helping repair the damage to the town. Methystra and Belthazuul have even been helping as well. From what Captain Morgan told me—"

"Jessica's been here?"

Kravek nodded. "She came to visit you. She'd talk to me a

little as well."

"Visit." Tina looked around the room. "Kravek, where are we?"

The room they were lying in was simple. The walls were made of wood as was the ceiling. A door stood on the wall facing the feet of their two beds. The door was closed for the moment, but Tina didn't see any light coming through the cracks. Opposite the door was a lit fireplace.

"The Stumble Drum. The front porch was destroyed, but the inn survived. Less could be said of the town hall."

Tina turned her gaze on Kravek. "Is this your room? Is that why you're here?"

Kravek snorted quietly. Wrinkling his nose, he shook his head. "This is my room, but that's not why I'm here. Governor Keldo wanted to put you up in his house, but... I wouldn't let him."

Tina smiled. "So, you wanted me all to yourself, hm?"

Kravek turned his head to look at Tina. His soft brown eyes met hers. "I wanted to look out for you. I may not be able to move my legs, but I wanted to know every day you were still all right."

Tina slowly pushed herself up. It hurt her head to rise, and her body ached. But she wanted to look at Kravek as she leaned forward on her hands. "Your legs?"

"Nana told me when the porch landed on my back, it must have broken my spine." Kravek closed his eyes. "Now... I can really be as useless as I've felt."

Tina snapped her fingers to get Kravek's attention. "Kravek, you aren't useless." He turned his head to look at her as she spoke. She realized her tone had come out more harshly than she'd meant. She cleared her throat and turned her head to look away. "You've been very helpful to me since I've come here, Kravek. You straightened me out when I let fear take away my confidence. You saved my life at least twice since I've been here. You are not useless."

Kravek half smiled.

Tina turned her head to look at Kravek again. "Methystra couldn't heal your back?"

Kravek shook his head. "Healing isn't her gift. Nana did what she could for me. But I guess shaman do better with spirits than spines. I still can't move my legs."

Tina lowered her gaze. She hesitated to say what came to mind, but Kravek deserved at least a chance to be able to walk again. "We... Kravek, the Council of Stars possesses many talented healers." She took a moment to clear her throat. "If you would like to come with me back to Kerovnia... perhaps they can mend your spine. With time, you might be able to walk again."

Kravek glanced toward Tina, and then laid his head back down against the pillow on his bed. "I think I'd like that."

Tina nodded, though she felt a faint blush coming to her face. "Once you've recovered, you can always come back to Likonia. I'm sure they will still be able to use you at the docks."

Kravek tucked his arms behind his head. "Maybe."

"If you're looking for other work though or maybe to get out of this place, you could always seek employment in Kerovnia."

He glanced toward Tina. The black bull was silent for a few moments as the corners of his mouth curled into a small smile. He let it slip away as he cleared his throat. "Oh, perhaps. If I find the right employer."

Tina slowly smiled herself. Closing her eyes, she breathed out a quiet sigh. "I'm sure I can make a recommendation and provide a reference for you."

Kravek put one hand down on his stomach and closed his eyes. "I think that will do just fine. Thank you, Tina."

* * *

It had been five days since Tina had awakened from the comatose state into which she'd fallen. Kravek's condition hadn't improved, but it was enough for Tina that he'd survived. Having accepted Tina's proposal for him to come to Kerovnia so he could be healed, the black bull was already on board the Thorn's Side. Tina looked over those who stood in front of her on the pier as the ship was preparing to set sail.

Idori Cephalin and Luna Copaire were both there. Tina was glad to see Idori looking better, and the seemingly permanent scowl he'd been wearing since her arrival was gone. He still wore his bladed gauntlets, but Tina figured the captain of the guard had to have some weapon on hand. Luna was out of her bandages and was leaning against Idori with his arm around her waist.

Governor Keldo, in his robes of office, was leaning on a walking stick and standing next to them. Though he often smiled in a way which made Tina suspicious of him, he'd at least accepted responsibility for the events which had happened as a result of his decision. Tina expected he hadn't seen the last of the repercussions from those choices, but she would not inflict on him anything more than what he'd already brought on himself.

Methystra stood in her reduced, humanoid form next to the governor. With one hand on her hip and the other on the shoulder of the shrunken Belthazuul, who stood next to her, she looked quite pleased that her magic had been involved in the downfall of the Dragon Eaters. Belthazuul, even reduced in size as he was, still stood head and shoulders over the others present. The black scales covering his body and the rigid cut of the scales along his jaws and eyebrows made him look like a proper villain. But Tina knew much better.

Standing on the deck of the Thorn's Side with her arms around the black bunny child in front of her, Tina could see Beth waiting for her to come on board. Tina had to admit she'd been glad Beth had decided both to let Aiden be trained and to come to Kerovnia with him.

"Well," Tina adjusted her glasses as she looked up at the group gathered in front of her, "this has been an interesting chapter in the story of my life. I will have to make sure I record all of it in detail in my journal once we've set sail."

Methystra grinned at Tina. "I'll like to read that someday, especially the parts about your interactions with your Albatross."

Tina blushed. "Methystra!"

The cloud dragon snickered.

But the mention of an Albatross reminded Tina of something. She pulled off her necklace and clasped the lava-colored gem in both hands. "Methystra, I know we talked about this before. Angelica probably did want revenge on the Dragon Eaters... but they're gone now, and I think it's time Angelica was returned to Shalizan's side." She focused on her necklace and extended her gift into the metal. It reshaped slowly and let the lava-colored crystal fall into Tina's hand. She hadn't used her magic since her recovery, and she felt strained to use it again so soon. But this was important.

After she put her necklace on again, she held the crystal up toward Methystra. "You loved Shalizan most in life."

Methystra's smile slowly fell. She stepped forward and moved to her knees as she held her hand out. Tina deposited the tiny crystal into the palm of Methystra's hand. Looking at it, Methystra appeared conflicted.

Tina put her hand on one of Methystra's fingers. "I don't know what your relationship with Angelica was during her lifetime. But both of you loved Shalizan best."

Methystra covered the crystal with her other hand and looked down at Tina. "...I loved Shalizan as much as I was able." She looked down at the crystal. "...But she loved him most."

Tina smiled. "The word she chose for the Ritual of Preservation was 'who'. I think she wanted me to point out who killed her master." She stepped back to make room for Methystra and gestured toward the crystal. "Instead... tell her what you just told me."

Methystra looked down at the crystal again. Rising to her

feet, she cupped both hands together and blew a white mist into her hands. It flowed between her fingers as she whispered the incantation which would prepare the crystal to release Angelica. Drawing her hands away, the mist held the crystal in the air as it began turning and casting off lava-colored lights all around them.

The mist spiraled down from the crystal as it took on the colors within the gem. The faces of the crystal peeled off and dispersed into the mist, growing in size. Each one reflected in its surface a piece of Angelica's body. When they all came together, Angelica stood in front of Methystra with her halberd grasped in hand, and the shards of the crystal disappeared. She stood still, unmoving, not even breathing as the mists dissipated. Tina could see the look of anger on her face, but she knew it would not last.

Methystra stepped forward and touched the end of her snout to Angelica's nose. She spoke quietly the words which would unleash the effect of the ritual. *"Breathe deep. Think true. Speak readily. What was granted is due."*

Angelica suddenly drew in a deep breath and the look of anger melted from her face as if she'd heard from whom the words had come. Looking at Methystra, Angelica suddenly looked sad. But the one breath would not allow her to say more than she was granted.

Methystra hugged Angelica and touched her cheek to the Albatross's. She spoke in native Maldavian. *"Tina told me what you wished to say and why. But those who wronged my love and your master have paid for their crimes, Angelica, Dragon Daughter."* She released Angelica from the hug and rested one hand on the side of her face while looking into the Albatross's eyes. *"But... ask. And I will tell you of the two of us who truly loved your master most."*

The question deepened the sad expression on Angelica's face and her lips quivered as she let the one word she'd been granted slip from them. *"...Who?"*

Methystra lovingly smiled. *"None could love Shalizan*

more than you, beautiful Angelica. Return to him." She put her arms around the Albatross again. *"Be with your beloved now for the rest of time."*

The halberd which Angelica held fell to the deck. She put her arms around Methystra and pressed her face against the side of the white-scaled Maldavian's neck. Tina didn't know what the Albatross wanted to say, but she didn't think it mattered. The tears running down her cheeks held all the semblance of joy which water could offer.

As the two Maldavians, one Albatross and one true, shared the brief hug, Tina watched as Angelica's body slowly faded away. Closing her eyes, Tina thought to herself. Even though Angelica had wished for revenge, she would find more peace in death with her last moments being those of love. And the false satisfaction of revenge would have been meaningless in comparison.

* * *

Tina sat on the banister of the Thorn's Side in front of the ship's navigation wheel. The salty air ruffled her hair and filled her nose. With Leilani and Nana, Beth and Aiden, and Kravek all in their quarters, Tina thought how many lives the events in Likonia had changed. She ran her fingers over the small socket on her necklace in which was set the tiny doorknob which led to her tower. She'd have to remember to set it into a safe place on board the ship again.

Captain Morgan cleared her throat. "So, you've defeated monsters even Maldavians couldn't overcome and a powerful mage lord, saving both the Maldavians and even magic in this part of the world." The Kylathian offered a satisfied grin. "What are your plans now?"

Tina's fingers rubbed on the doorknob set into her necklace. A smile spread across her lips. "What else? Save the world."

Tina and Captain Morgan shared a brief laugh over the

small, personal joke. Then Tina rose from the banister. "There is one last thing I have to do now that we've set sail. Excuse me."

"Before you go." Captain Morgan reached into the breast pocket of her doublet and pulled out a narrow, golden plate with runes lining one side of it. She held the plate out toward Tina. "I told you I'd be returning this to you soon."

Tina wiggled her whiskers. She reached out and touched the plate, and it shrank in size until it was small enough to fit on the back of her ear.

After putting it back into place, she smiled at Captain Morgan. "One of these days, Jessica, I'll prove you wrong. But I'm glad it wasn't this time."

The grey feline swept her captain's hat from her head and flashed a toothy grin. "I await the day." She plopped her hat back onto her head and adjusted her eye patch.

Tina ran down the banister and dropped onto the deck. Climbing under the door leading into the hallway where the personal quarters stood, she glanced at the small split in the wood where her doorknob had been placed before. Passing it by, she went to Kravek's quarters. Once more squeezing under the doorway, she adjusted her glasses to see if Kravek was still awake.

But his eyes were closed, and it looked to Tina as though the black bull had fallen asleep. It was getting into the evening anyway.

Glancing around, Tina spotted Kravek's hide backpack resting on the floor under his bunk. She walked over to it and settled down on her knees as she looked at the side pocket of the backpack. Touching the small button which held the pocket closed, Tina whispered quietly. The threads holding it in place unraveled. The button fell off, and she caught it. Setting it into one of the pockets on the back of the pack, she removed the doorknob from her necklace. It grew in size to fit the palm of her hand.

Pushing it against the hide of the pocket, she whispered one more brief incantation. The metal of the knob punctured through the hide of the pocket flap, then spread just enough to hold the knob in place securely. After pulling the knob back through the button hole, she closed the flap. Rising back to her feet, Tina brushed her robe off and turned around to head back to the door. After all, saving the world isn't a one person job.

~ The End ~

Author's Note

I'd like to take this opportunity to thank you for taking the time to delve into this world of my creation. I hope you enjoyed the book. It wasn't until the later years in high school that I took much interest in writing. To me, it seemed as though all my writing and English classes were about reading sentences out of a book and putting them down on paper with whatever corrections a particular lesson required me to apply. It wasn't until my junior year in high school when another student shared some of his writing with my class that I understood what could be done with a little imagination and hard work. I had read books before then, but I never really thought that someone like me could write a book. Seeing another student create an interesting story opened up a new world to me, and it made me want to share new worlds with others. I have spent years developing my own writing skills since then, and through many hardships and trials, devoted myself to the pursuit of becoming an author. I hope you enjoyed *The Dragon Eaters* and look forward to future publications. This is only the beginning.

Follow me on Facebook
https://www.facebook.com/duke.kittle

CPSIA information can be obtained at www.ICGtesting.com
Printed in the USA
LVOW13s0917010514

384019LV00001B/1/P